SNOWBOUND *Colorado* CHRISTMAS

LOVE SNOWBALLS IN FOUR COUPLES' LIVES
DURING THE BLIZZARD OF 1913

SUSAN PAGE DAVIS
DARLENE FRANKLIN
TAMELA HANCOCK MURRAY
LENA NELSON DOOLEY

BARBOUR
PUBLISHING

ISBN 978-1-60260-116-1

All scripture quotations are taken from the King James Version of the Bible.

This book is a work of fiction. Names, characters, places, and incidents are either products of the author's imagination or used fictitiously. Any similarity to actual people, organizations, and/or events is purely coincidental.

Published by Barbour Publishing, Inc., P.O. Box 719, Uhrichsville, OH 44683, www.barbourbooks.com

Our mission is to publish and distribute inspirational products offering exceptional value and biblical encouragement to the masses.

 Member of the
Evangelical Christian
Publishers Association

Printed in the United States of America

Introduction

Fires of Love by Tamela Hancock Murray
Thalia Bloom looks forward to her party, except for seeing heartbreaker Maximilian Newbolt. Sparks fly between them. Maximilian is waylaid by an allergy to a strawberry and rhubarb tart, and illness means he must linger. Aunt Dorcas is even unhappier than Maximilian, discouraging any newfound love between the couple. Has God used a fruit tart to free this couple from the bondage of fears and insecurities so they can find true happiness in love?

The Best Medicine by Lena Nelson Dooley
When Thomas Stanton shows up at the holiday party of Rose Fletcher's best friend, his appearance reminds Rose of the infatuation she felt for him when he worked on her father's ranch. Although her heart wants to continue those long ago feelings, her mind remembers her that he doesn't share her faith in God. Thomas can't understand why Rose seems so standoffish. Will it take God's intervention to show these two people just what He has planned all along?

Almost Home by Susan Page Davis
Patricia Logan leaves Thalia's party and heads for home at her uncle's ranch. Her ride is sidelined by the blizzard. A chance meeting with Jared Booker, an old friend, prompts Patricia to beg for a lift. They set out on horseback and become snowbound in a shack for two days with an outspoken midwife and their past. Can they rekindle their old camaraderie and see it transform into lasting love?

Dressed in Scarlet by Darlene Franklin
Natalie Daire, a rich young heiress, has a car accident on the way home from a friend's holiday party and finds herself snowed in with the other guests at the Brown Palace Hotel in Denver. Fabrizio Ricci, the mechanic who fixes her car, is also snowbound at the hotel. Can these two people from opposite ends of the social spectrum find true love?

Fires of Love

by Tamela Hancock Murray

Dedication

To John, my hero who braves all the elements.

For thou, Lord, art good, and ready to forgive; and plenteous in mercy unto all them that call upon thee.

PSALM 86:5

Chapter 1

Denver
Early December 1913

Thalia Bloom watched white flakes drift to the hard ground in front of the Denver home she shared with her aunt. Feeling a chill seep through the drawing room window framed by heavy green draperies, she rubbed her hands together. "The snow is so pretty. I wonder if there will be enough to build a snowman."

Viewing the precipitation for herself, Dorcas Bloom shook her head, although too gently for her graying hair to fall out of place. "Not at the rate it's falling. I don't imagine we'll have more than an inch or two. Besides, snowmen are the least of your worries. Tonight's party should be your main concern."

Thalia turned to her aunt. "I'll admit I'm a bit nervous to be hosting the first Christmas party of the season."

"I wouldn't worry if I were you. Everybody on the guest list is congenial."

As long as Maximilian Newbolt stays away.

"Do you have everything set for music and parlor games?" Aunt Dorcas asked.

"Yes, I believe so. But the entertainment doesn't hold a candle to the food." Sugary smells of Cook's pastries mingled with robust aromas of spiced beef and country ham. If Thalia hadn't just eaten a light meal, the scents would have influenced her appetite. "Cook will be getting a good Christmas bonus from us this year."

"I agree. And Eliza, too."

"That's for sure." Their maid had been instrumental in the party preparations.

"But you can take all the credit for the decorations," Aunt Dorcas pointed out.

Thalia gave a contented sigh and noticed with renewed satisfaction the fresh scent and soothing look of the pine tree decorated with dried wildflowers. On the mantle and tables, cream-colored beeswax candles flickered in silver candlesticks adorned with red ribbons, adding mellow light sure to flatter everyone's complexion.

"You can credit others, but I couldn't have done any of this without you." Wistful, she drew closer and took hold of her aunt's hands. "In my whole adult life, I couldn't have done much without you. I remember all the times you wrote to me in boarding school. I wanted to quit sometimes, but you kept me going. And since I've been home, you have been so kind. If

I ever lost your affections, my heart would break."

"Now, child, don't go getting sentimental on me." Dorcas released Thalia's hands. "Let's think of the party. I can't wait to see our guests."

"Assuming the snow doesn't deter them." Thalia's gaze went toward the window.

Aunt Dorcas's gaze followed. "Oh, pshaw! A little snow will only make the scene more picturesque. I daresay every guest will be talking about this event for months. Even Maximilian Newbolt." Her pale lips curled into a wry line. "Especially Maximilian Newbolt."

Maximilian. The man who broke her heart. "I sent invitations in plenty of time, but I didn't see a response from him." Her voice sounded more hopeful than she meant.

"He wrote that he plans to be here. The letter must have gotten misplaced before you had a chance to see it."

Thalia tensed. "Maybe I shouldn't be so blunt, but I wish you hadn't invited him."

"But, my dear, he's a widower now. He hasn't been out and about in months. Not since our dear little Norma died so tragically. She was such a sweet angel." Aunt Dorcas looked heavenward. "The world is a bit colder without her." As though ice touched her shoulders, she shuddered and turned back to Thalia. "But now that she's gone, surely you wouldn't deny your cousin's widower the joy of our Christmas party, would you? After all, for Norma's sake, we need to tend to him. My regret is that we can't be more attentive since he lives in Aurora."

Thalia didn't answer. Let him stay in Aurora for all she

cared. At least since he lived fifteen miles away, they didn't see him in church or feel obligated to invite him to their home except on special occasions.

Undeterred—or perhaps encouraged—by Thalia's silence, Aunt Dorcas continued. "Of course, no one could ever live up to Norma. He'll never find another love."

Thalia swallowed. Aunt Dorcas didn't present a threat to Norma, so she never had reason to be anything but sweetness and light to the older woman. Putting such an unkind thought out of her mind, she posed a question. "Do you want Maximilian to find a new love?" Why did she ask such a thing? Maximilian's romantic affairs were none of her concern.

Dorcas paused for only the slightest bit of a second. "No, I don't want him to find someone new. I don't think a remarriage for him is in anyone's best interest. He may think he'll be happy with someone else, but he never will. I feel sorry for the delusional woman who thinks she could ever take Norma's place in his heart. Now you, on the other hand—well, it's high time you married."

Searching for an excuse not to face her aunt, Thalia swiveled around. "Does the bow in the back of my dress seem straight to you?"

Aunt Dorcas paused. "Yes, I believe it does. I must say, I like the new style."

Thalia turned back around. "You mean, old style? This high waist makes me feel as though I'm a member of Napoleon's court instead of plain old Thalia Bloom."

"You are neither plain nor old. I might speculate that you'll have heads turning tonight. And as I said before, it's about time, too."

"Oh, Aunt Dorcas, please don't start up again. You know I have no intention of marrying."

"Why ever not?"

Thalia tried not to display her impatience. Her aunt had asked many times. How could she tell her that once Maximilian had broken her heart, she couldn't risk making it vulnerable again. No, better to be a spinster, to serve the Lord through church work and charitable deeds, than to be trapped in a loveless marriage.

Rather than waiting for Thalia to answer, Aunt Dorcas flitted her hand. "What a waste that would be if you didn't. Josiah Billings has been looking your way. He can hardly keep his eyes off you in church."

Josiah looked attractive enough, but they had nothing in common. "Oh, please. All he thinks about is baseball."

"I'm sure as pretty as you look tonight, you can set his mind on other things."

Thalia decided to turn the tables. "What about you? I'm sure you'll have Mr. Snead and Mr. Carmichael coming to fisticuffs over you before the night is through."

"They can come to fisticuffs, but I'm not ready to mother a brood of ten Snead children nor watch every penny Mr. Carmichael earns. In my youth I was the belle of the ball, but I never felt led by love—or the Lord—to marry any of my suitors."

"Are you sorry about that?"

She answered without missing a beat. "Not at all. I was perfectly happy tending to my brother during his last days, God rest his soul."

Thalia remembered Uncle Tyler. A strange old bird, he proved a handful for his much younger sister. Truly Aunt Dorcas was a saint.

"Enjoy this time, Thalia," her aunt advised. "This is your night."

Thalia laughed and looked at the banquet table. Their maid, Eliza, was in the process of setting out food. "Do you think this platter of sandwiches looks good here in the center, Miss Thalia?"

Thalia surveyed the table with a discerning eye. "I think I prefer to keep that spot for the soup tureen. Why don't you place the sandwiches beside it? Then everything will be perfect." She smiled. Pleasing scents drifted to her nostrils. Certainly with a table so fully stocked with beef, ham, chicken, and different types of rolls for sandwiches, along with preserved fruits and vegetables, relishes, pickles, pies, pastries, and cakes, no one would go hungry. For the hundredth time, Thalia wondered if hosting a full dinner would have been easier than setting out a buffet.

As the grandfather clock in the front hall chimed the hour, Thalia looked toward the polished curved staircase just visible from the dining room door. "Rose should be joining us any minute."

"I admit, I thought she would have appeared by now. But the poor thing was so tired from her train ride. And I didn't think you would ever let her break away from your conversation over tea long enough for both of you to prepare for the party."

Thalia's chuckle displayed more chagrin than humor. "I know. It's just so exciting to have a chance to see her after a whole year."

Just then Rose entered.

"Oh, there you are, Rose. You must have heard us talking about you." Thalia smiled. "You look refreshed after your nap."

"I feel much better, thank you. I don't usually fret over my appearance, but I hope I look all right for the party. I haven't seen so many people for so long that I want to look my best."

"You look splendid." Thalia compared their outfits. "And the color of your dress looks quite nice with your hair. A little part of me wishes my hair were the same shade of auburn."

"Oh, no. You look quite striking with those black curls framing your face, Thalia," Rose argued. "And you chose wisely in your dress, too. That shade of pink brings out the warmth in your complexion. If I weren't your best friend, I'd think your skin had never seen a drop of sunlight or winter's blast. Lucky you."

Aunt Dorcas clucked and shook her head as a guest knocked on the door.

Soon the maid announced the arrival of the new doctor in town. When they entered the drawing room, the three women wore their best smiles.

Aunt Dorcas was the first to speak. "Dr. Stanton. My, but how handsome you look tonight." She shot a look toward Thalia.

Thalia tried not to send her gaze skyward and back in response to her aunt's broad hint. Denver's new doctor was indeed handsome, but he didn't ignite sparks for her. Not the way Maximilian once did. She shook her head in small, swift motions to shoo the image from her mind.

"Is anything the matter, my dear?" Aunt Dorcas asked.

"Oh no, ma'am. I'm fine." Without further prompting, Thalia greeted the doctor and introduced him to Rose.

"Am I the first to arrive?" Dr. Stanton asked.

"Yes, but I think I hear Patricia Logan's voice in the foyer. Dr. Stanton, I must introduce you to Miss Logan. She's an old school chum of mine." Thalia ignored Aunt Dorcas's cautioning look.

A beeping horn got everyone's attention.

Aunt Dorcas put her hands to her ears. "Oh, those wretched automobiles! They will be the death of everything that's good in this world."

Thalia laughed. "You can't stop progress, especially now with mass production."

"Maybe, but who in the world would drive an automobile in this weather?" Aunt Dorcas wondered. "Whoever it is must be freezing."

"I'd venture a guess it's Natalie," Thalia said. "She loves to show off her new Cadillac Model 30."

"If I owned such a fine machine, I might put up with a little cold weather to show it off," Dr. Stanton said. "You make her out to be quite a character."

Thalia smiled. "That she is."

Soon the guests had gathered by the food and fire. Introductions were few since most were acquainted, and as more partygoers arrived, laughter and conversation filled the house. Comments about the snow sounded as brisk as the whirling wind outdoors, and occasionally a guest or two would peek out the window to see its progress, but sparse flakes concerned no one.

Everyone who promised to attend arrived. Everyone except Maximilian. Thalia felt relieved yet somehow disappointed. Fighting conflicting emotions, she told herself she didn't want to see him again. Not now. Not ever. Why, she was even glad he didn't have the nerve to show up at her party.

Thalia was surprised to hear a knock almost a quarter hour after the person she considered to be the last guest had arrived.

"Ah, a latecomer," Aunt Dorcas noted.

In her mind, Thalia ran down the guest list and came up with only one missing name.

No, it couldn't be. Maximilian couldn't have decided to appear after all.

Chapter 2

S cat, cat!" Almost dropping the package he held, Maximilian Newbolt shooed a solid black stray so it wouldn't cross the flagstone pathway, sugared with snow, in front of him. He felt relieved when the animal meowed in his direction but went on its way. The last thing he needed was even more bad luck, especially in front of Thalia's house. Prideful about his new Studebaker, he'd driven it in spite of snow-dusted roads and threatening clouds. He'd already gotten a flat tire on the way to the party and had escaped muddying his new overcoat only by inordinate care. Now snow fell with vigor. How many more pitfalls must he sidestep?

He rubbed the white rabbit's foot he carried in his pocket for luck. Tonight would determine his future. He would keep looking for signs until it became clear whether he should stay in Aurora or seek his fortune in California. His cousin Jake's offer to buy an orange grove together tempted him. Working outdoors with his hands would prove quite a contrast to managing the mining company, wasting away with paperwork in his drafty office, never seeing the light of day during winter's deep freeze, only to return after a long day to a house that was empty except for his loyal servants. But even the most dedicated staff, paid to wait on him hand and foot, couldn't—and shouldn't—replace true love or family.

His life had become cold and empty. As cold and empty as his heart. He remembered the day he discovered Thalia didn't love him. Could he change her mind? Or would God send a sign—a sign he was destined for California?

He scratched his itching nose. Surely that was a sign of impending company. Wonder who would soon be visiting him? Not that he had many visitors. The flurry of caring friends ceased a couple of months after Norma's untimely death. Not that they weren't sympathetic. His unwelcoming attitude had discouraged kind overtures. He couldn't put up a front of the truly grieving widower after such an unhappy union. The fact filled him with guilt.

Even now, with his official period of mourning over, he still felt reluctant to get back into the social scene. When he first received Thalia's invitation, he had almost responded with regrets. But his valet, Addison, had encouraged him to go. Sad how he talked to his closest servant more than anyone else these days. Indeed it was high time for him to renew his old acquaintances, whether he wanted to or not.

Which acquaintances would be at the party? The Blooms' Victorian-style house, with fussy white gables prominent against bright pink, boasted quite a few carriages and even a couple of automobiles parked in front. He recognized most of the conveyances and could gauge who appeared on Thalia's guest list based on the fact. He wondered if he could pick back up with the old crowd now that Norma was no longer at his side.

He knocked on Thalia's front door. Muffled voices coming from indoors sounded animated. As he awaited an answer, he regarded the falling snow. "I hope we don't get a blizzard," he muttered, and knocked on the first wood available, which happened to be the front entrance, in hopes of warding off such a plight.

The Blooms' maid opened the door, a look of irritation on her young face, probably because he had seemed impatient with his knocking.

He hoped a pleasant smile would put her in a better mood. "Good evening, Eliza." Shaking snow from his wool coat and stomping on the woven mat, he stepped inside and was greeted by warmth. "I see the party's in full swing. I hope I'm not too late. I had a flat tire on the way."

"I'm sorry to hear that, Mr. Newbolt. You aren't too late. Miss Dorcas has been expecting you." She took his coat and hat.

Miss Dorcas? What about Miss Thalia? He let out an "oh" without worrying if his disappointment showed. Darting his gaze to Eliza, he anticipated a comforting look but received none.

In keeping with Eliza's prediction, it was not Thalia but Dorcas, in a dress of filmy white, who greeted him first. "Oh, Maximilian, I am so glad you decided to join us." She motioned for him to enter the parlor.

"Yes, thank you for the invitation." Excitement and cheer

gladdened his spirit. Maybe accepting the invitation had been the right thing to do after all.

A survey of the room, filled with men and women dressed in their best, rewarded him with a glimpse of Thalia. The instant he recognized the figure in pink, his senses tingled with anticipation. Shiny hair the color of a deep, cloudless night crowned a face fairer than any statue of Venus. He'd anticipated that seeing her again now that he was a free man would be difficult, but he hadn't realized how much of an effect she still had on him. Why did she have to be such a marvel, a marvel with an unyielding heart? His mouth dropped with awe and yearning before he gained enough awareness to compose himself.

"What's the matter?" Dorcas prodded.

He shook his head and regarded the elder Miss Bloom. "Nothing. Nothing at all." Desperate to deflect questions, he handed his hostess the package containing a small but dense fruitcake. Its sweet aroma penetrated its wrapping of cheesecloth tied with a green ribbon. "I had my cook bake this fruitcake just for you. It's her Christmas specialty. I hope you enjoy it."

"Oh, I remember Ginny's fruitcake. So dark and moist, just the way I like it. Norma always served it at Christmas." Her eyes grew misty, but she kept her voice cheerful.

"I know. That is a fond memory for me, too." One of the few, although he decided not to reveal that to Norma's aunt. "Do enjoy the cake. Ginny retired as of yesterday."

"Really? Is she ill?"

"No, thankfully. Her son's wife just gave birth to their ninth child, and he invited her to live with his family. I can't believe she took him up on it."

"My, I'm sure with all those children, they could use two extra hands."

"I'm sure." He sent Dorcas a half smile. "I even offered her a raise in salary to stay, but she respectfully declined."

"So you're eating cold sandwiches until you find another cook?"

"Oh, I have another cook." He grimaced at the memory of burned toast and undercooked potatoes. "She's quite in-experienced. Breakfast and lunch weren't especially good today. But she's young and her family needs the money, so I don't have the heart to fire her."

"She'll improve."

"I hope so. Although I must say, I look forward to sampling some good food tonight."

Dorcas gave the cake she held a little squeeze. "Maybe you should have kept this for yourself. Really, Maximilian, you didn't have to bring a thing. It's gift enough for me knowing that you have finally gotten out of that lonely house of yours. Norma would want you to enjoy life now that your time of mourning is well over."

"That's comforting, especially coming from you." He smiled and darted his glance to Thalia long enough for his treacherous feelings to return. He felt compelled to move toward her. "If you'll excuse me, I'll take a moment to speak to Thalia."

"Oh, but you shouldn't have to chase your hostess. She'll make her way over to you soon enough." Dorcas surveyed the party guests as if desperate to find someone. Soon she smiled and tapped his forearm. "Now who do I spy but Bryant Emmet? He's someone you need to meet. He just moved here, and he's very interested in the mining business."

Discussing business at a lively party didn't appeal to Maximilian, but he knew from experience that there was no arguing with strong-willed Dorcas Bloom.

Thalia looked across the room and caught her aunt chattering with the latecomer. A guest whose silhouette she would have recognized in the darkest alley.

Maximilian.

Almost spilling her punch, she recovered her composure. Maximilian's form was unmistakable. Tall and slender but not skinny. Dark hair gleamed under the light. Despite the ins and outs of fashion, he remained clean shaven—a wise choice considering his fine yet manly features. She took in a breath then swallowed. She wanted to greet him, but again, she didn't.

"Who's that you're looking at so hard, Thalia?" Josiah wanted to know. With curious eyes, he peered in Maximilian's direction. "Oh, Newbolt came, did he? It's been a long time since he's been out and about. Can't say I missed him much." He chuckled and shook his carrot-topped head. "Look at him talking to your aunt, standing there as though he's king of the world. And look at how he's dressed. He's quite the dandy, isn't he?"

"Don't make fun of him," Thalia snapped. Then, regretting her force of emotion, she softened her stance. "His official period of mourning the loss of his wife is over, and so what if he wears dashing clothes now? I do believe this is his first party since her death."

"That's right. I'm sorry. I remember now. She was your cousin Norma, right?"

Thalia nodded and tried not to stare at Maximilian too long. She could see him excusing himself from Aunt Dorcas. Since he looked in her direction, she guessed he planned to make his way toward her. But just as quickly, her aunt took him by the elbow and guided him toward Bryant Emmet. She felt grateful for the reprieve.

"Thalia?" Josiah asked. "Are you listening to a word I'm saying?"

"Something about baseball?" she guessed.

He grinned. "What else? You know, seeing Newbolt brings me a thought. I wonder if his church has a team. Maybe our church team could play a few games against them for fun."

"I doubt if he's given it any thought. Spring's a long time away," Thalia pointed out.

"You're right about that. Much too long, if you ask me."

In her head, Thalia didn't want to talk to Maximilian, but her heart insisted that she seek him. "Excuse me, Josiah, but I must greet Maximilian since he just arrived."

"Sure. I'll come along with you and ask about the teams."

If only Josiah would be lured to the table for refreshments—anything to keep him from following her. In the same instant, she realized his insistence on accompanying her would save her from speaking with Maximilian alone.

Aunt Dorcas gave Thalia a warning look when she and

Josiah interrupted their conversation with Bryant. Ignoring her, Thalia smiled and hoped her face didn't reveal her excitement upon seeing him once more. Just being near him, taking in a whiff of the spicy shaving lotion he wore, being near his confident essence, sent old feelings rushing anew. "Maximilian. How nice of you to join us in our celebration. It wouldn't have been Christmas without you."

The expression in his eyes told her that he was just as conflicted about seeing her as she was him. But he locked his gaze with hers, and for her, everyone else in the room melted into oblivion.

"Thalia."

The way he caressed her name with his voice filled her with a craving to be closer to him. She felt wobbly. In spite of her desire not to look away from intense brown eyes flecked with gold, she searched for a nearby chair. Too bad Mrs. Hansen already occupied the only one in reach. Far be it from Thalia to take a seat from a frail dowager. At least now she could look back into Maximilian's eyes. Judging from his stare, he would be content to gaze at her all night.

Why did she have to react this way? She couldn't. Not after what had happened.

If Josiah noticed her reaction to Maximilian, he didn't let on. "Remember me, Newbolt?" He extended his right hand.

Maximilian returned the gesture, and the men exchanged a hearty shake. "Of course. Josiah Billings. Still a big baseball fan?"

Josiah swung an imaginary bat, almost coming into contact with a burning candle in the process. "If I keep practicing, I'll be a regular Ty Cobb."

Dorcas laughed louder than she should have. "Thalia, let us leave the men to their sports talk."

"Oh, but you have always encouraged me to take an interest in baseball." Thalia couldn't help but chide. "And look, there's Mr. Carmichael. Have you had a chance to speak with him yet?" She waved toward the balding man.

He smiled and started toward them.

Dorcas threw Thalia daggers with her stare, but Thalia smiled when he approached. "Mr. Carmichael, have you had a chance to see Mr. Newbolt?"

"Evening, Newbolt." The older man extended his hand, and Maximilian accepted.

Though they exchanged pleasantries, as Thalia expected, Mr. Carmichael didn't dwell on Maximilian too long. Instead, he focused on Aunt Dorcas.

"The food you got here tonight is mighty good, Dorcas. If you don't mind me for asking, where did you buy your beef?"

Obviously not expecting such a question, Aunt Dorcas dropped open her mouth and paused. "Uh, Swanson's."

"Swanson's?" He let out a whistle. "They're the most expensive place in town." He lifted his right index finger. "Now let me recommend a place that'll save you lots of money, especially if you tell them I sent you. . ."

Taking his victim by the arm, he led her toward the refreshment table. Thalia imagined they would go over each plate and discuss the price of every foodstuff available. She tried not to giggle—or think about the tongue-lashing she would receive later.

With her aunt at bay, Thalia had a suggestion for Josiah. "Wouldn't it be fun if we played a few records on the Victrola?"

His eyes brightened. "Sure it would."

"Maybe you could go through our collection and pick a few songs."

"Sure. That would be swell." He headed for the Victor Talking Machine, a small wooden box with a large horn. Such machines had become popular for anyone wishing to listen to recorded music.

Maximilian shook his head. "Josiah hasn't changed since the day he turned ten."

Realizing his observation wasn't far from the truth, Thalia decided not to comment.

Maximilian glanced toward the window. "If it weren't snowing outside, I'd ask you to take a walk with me in the moonlight."

"But alas, it snows. I hope this weather won't be too much of an inconvenience for my guests." She sighed at the falling flakes. "It is quite pretty, though."

"Not nearly as pretty as you," he proclaimed. "You look even lovelier than I remember." He captured her gaze with his once more.

Taken aback and yet delighted by his compliment, she forced an answer. "It—it appears the snow is falling harder."

"How do you know? You're not looking out the window."

"Oh, you are incorrigible." She broke the lock on his stare.

"I know where a window is—a window where no one else is looking. And if I were a betting man, I'd say it's right near a fire so we can stay warm as we watch the snow."

"If you mean the window in the study, you would have lost the bet. Aunt Dorcas told Eliza to keep the fire lit to accommodate the overflow. Judging from how sparse the main room has become, I would venture it's already been discovered. If it's privacy you want, I doubt you'll get it there."

"Too bad. Wonder how we can get away from Josiah?"

A giggle escaped Thalia's lips in spite of her best efforts to contain it.

"Certainly your aunt doesn't think you should yoke yourself to such a juvenile."

She felt mirth leave her expression. "She said that, did she?"

"She spoke quite approvingly of a possible match. You—you're not engaged to him, are you?"

The thought sent a shudder down her back.

His eyebrows rose just a tad. "Does that mean you can't stand the thought?"

She felt her cheeks flush. "Was I that obvious?"

He chuckled.

"I've told Aunt Dorcas time and time again that I have no desire to marry, but she won't listen. She seems to think Josiah is the perfect match for me. Probably because he has more than enough money to offer me a lifetime of security."

"So do many other men."

Discerning that he referred to himself, Thalia tried to hide her surprise and made sure not to encourage him. "There are things far more important than money."

"Watch it. People may think you're a woman who has always

had more than enough."

"Do they?" Her voice snapped no less than if it had been a blow to his cheek.

He flinched. "I'm sorry. I didn't mean to sound harsh. I have no right to chastise anyone about poverty, since I've never gone to bed hungry. Forgive me. And you are right; there are other important things."

"And you are right. I shouldn't be so defensive." Ashamed, she glimpsed at the Oriental rug on the floor and back up again. "God has blessed me with enough, and because I don't have to worry about where my next meal is coming from, I can focus on ethereal things. Not everyone has that luxury."

She saw Maximilian grimace and thought he wasn't sure about what she said—until she heard Josiah.

Excited, he held a waxy red disc for their inspection. "Look, you've got 'Take Me Out to the Ball Game.' I didn't even know they'd recorded that."

"Then your night is made." Thalia's voice betrayed more sarcasm than she meant.

Josiah didn't seem to notice. "Come on in and listen. Every-body's asking for you. They want you to play the piano for a sing-along."

"That does sound fun," Thalia said with feigned enthusiasm. Sitting by the fire with Maximilian—even among other guests—seemed much more appealing. She tried not to look too vexed as she set her gaze on Maximilian. "Looks as though we'll have to delay your plan to watch falling snow."

Though she had dreaded the thought of seeing him again,

her feelings for him took her by surprise. She needed to sort them out. She would definitely try to see him again in relative privacy before the party ended if it was the last thing she did.

Chapter 3

Maximilian wanted to accompany Thalia and Josiah to the music room, but he held back. Thalia proclaimed she never wanted to marry, but then again, he'd seen many women say the same and go on to wed and bear a brood of children. But with Thalia, things were even more complicated. Obviously he had stepped into Josiah's territory—at least as far as Josiah and Dorcas were concerned—and he wasn't about to interfere and offend Dorcas. Not when he still hadn't seen a clear sign about when—and if—to tell Thalia his thoughts about going to California.

Too busy catching up with friends to eat earlier, he decided to swing by the banquet table one last time before entering the music room. Besides, there was no doubt Josiah would be hanging all over Thalia. He wasn't sure he wanted to witness that.

"A penny for your thoughts, Maximilian."

Snatched from his dream world, he looked in the direction of the voice and discovered a friend of Thalia's, Edith. "You came in out of the blue. How long were you standing there?"

"Long enough to see you pondering the mysteries of the universe. I thought perhaps my penny would be well spent to learn your thoughts."

"That's where you're wrong, I'm afraid. My thoughts are hardly worth a penny."

Edith laughed. "I doubt you would find many in agreement with you." She took a small bit of an especially appealing tart. "Mmmmm. Delightful. You must try one."

"You and I are the only ones hovering around the banquet table. What does that say about us?"

"Oh, it might say that we are among the hardy souls who aren't afraid of a little snow. A lot of people left already, you know."

"Yes, I thought it seemed as though the crowd had dwindled."

"Poor Thalia." Edith brushed crumbs off her blue dress. "She worked so hard on this party. It's a shame it had to be cut short due to the weather."

"I would dispute that it's been cut short. Seems to me lots of people are still having a good time."

"I know I am with so much food. After this I won't need to eat for three days." She gestured toward him, holding the last bit of tart. "I recommend trying one before they're all gone."

"I don't know if I should indulge. I already had a piece of mince pie." The remaining two slices of pie, with rich fruit filling and flaky crust, tempted him.

Edith regarded the pie with less enthusiasm, judging from

the way she wrinkled her nose. "I don't care much for mince pie myself."

"Oh, but you might put aside your distaste for it and try it around this time of year."

"Why?"

"You've never heard the old saying?" Since she obviously hadn't, he continued. "For each piece of mince pie you eat at every Christmas party you go to, you'll have a month of happiness the following year."

Edith laughed. "What a silly superstition. Are you saying I need to go to twelve parties this month and eat mince pie?"

"If you want a year of happiness, I suppose so." He smiled. "A year before I married, I managed to eat four pieces over the season, and I had the best spring of my life."

"Goodness, Maximilian, I can't believe here in the twentieth century that an educated man such as yourself—a graduate of William and Mary College in Virginia, no less—would believe in such nonsense. I would credit your happy spring to coincidence."

"Promise me you won't tell my old professors," he joked before turning serious. "I know I might sound silly, but I do have my reasons for thinking the way I do."

"Does Thalia know your reasons?"

He thought for a moment. "No, I suppose not."

"Then no wonder you and Thalia never wed. She'd never put up with such foolishness. At least not without a very good reason."

Maximilian winced. Thalia was full of vigor and fun but

much too serious about religion. Sure, he went to church and had no doubt about the existence of God. He even prayed to Him when he needed something. But trusting the rabbit's foot in his pocket seemed the better bet. The rabbit's foot he could see, but not God.

"Did I say something wrong?" Edith asked. "I'm so sorry. I suppose that was insensitive of me, especially since Norma—"

"I think I'll take you up on your suggestion about that tart." Looking away from Edith, he reached for a delectable-looking puff pastry too quickly and knocked over a pepper shaker meant for a nearby platter of roast beef. Black particles of the spice scattered on the tablecloth. "Oh, no."

Edith shrugged. With a well-tended hand, she righted the shaker and swished the offending pepper onto the floor. "See? No harm done."

He shuddered at her cavalier attitude. "Don't you know a spilled pepper shaker is bad luck?"

"Not those old tales again. Honestly!" She grinned. "I have to say, coming from you, I find them quite amusing."

He wasn't sure—or perhaps he was too sure—about Edith's flirtation. Though charming, she wasn't interesting enough for him to consider complicating matters with thoughts of her other than as a food critic. He decided to taste the tart Edith recommended. He nodded his approval as sweet fruit and buttery pastry pleased his taste buds.

"Is it good?" Approaching from another direction, the female's voice was teasing.

Maximilian nodded to Mabel, an acquaintance of Thalia's

since girlhood. "Edith suggested I try one. Clearly, Edith, you know your way around a buffet table."

"Thanks. I think."

A horn squawked four times. "Oh, bother," said Edith, "It's Papa. He must have come early because of the snow."

"At least you won't be stranded," Maximilian pointed out.

Edith sent him a look. "I could think of worse fates." She waved and headed for the door. "Toodles."

As soon as Edith was out of sight, Mabel shook her head. "That Edith. She's so bold. Nothing like Norma. You never could guess what she was thinking."

The observation brought back a few too many memories. "True."

"You can always tell what Edith is thinking. She wears her heart on her sleeve," Mabel noted. "I, on the other hand, believe that a woman should shroud herself in mystery."

Maximilian fought back a grin. Clearly Mabel was unaware of her own transparency.

She bit into a sandwich. "We'd better eat hearty since we'll be fighting a lot of snow and wind on the way home. In fact, I'm thinking of abandoning ship as soon as I finish my punch. Who knows? This could turn out to be a blizzard."

"Blizzard? I think this is hardly what one would call a blizzard." He took another bite of pastry and looked outside. His mouth dropped. "Oh, you're right. The snow has accumulated quite a bit. Much more than any of us imagined."

She nodded toward the entrance. "I see most of the other guests are giving us the old twenty-three skiddoo."

Though several could still be heard singing in the music room, along with the piano and a banjo, their numbers did in fact seem to be dwindling by the minute. Even then, he looked toward the front door and noticed a couple of the guests leaving. "So it seems."

"How about you? Do you plan to stay?"

He thought about the long journey back to Aurora. While not arduous in fair weather, the falling snow would increase its difficulty by automobile. With the amount on the ground, he wondered if even a horse would improve his journey's success. "I suppose I should be leaving, much to my regret. I was rather late in arriving as it was. I had a flat tire on the way."

"You don't look the worse for wear." Then, seeming to be embarrassed by her bold observation, she continued. "At least you won't be the first to leave."

"True." The word sounded strange, as though someone else had uttered it.

"Is something the matter, Maximilian?"

"I—I had some news for Thalia, but I don't know if I can tell her now." Indeed, talking proved difficult. Was this the sign he wanted?

"News?" Mabel licked her lips. "Is there something I can tell Thalia for you?"

"No." Maximilian swooshed his tongue around his mouth. Why did the inside of his mouth feel as though he'd been attacked with itching powder? His arms felt the same. He didn't want to scratch, especially not in front of Mabel, or anyone else. But he had to do something. "I'm so sorry. I have some pressing business I must tend to."

She looked doubtful, but he had no recourse except to ignore her. With as much dignity as he could muster, he walked as quickly as he could without running, down the hall to the library, certain no one else would be there. He opened the door and felt a draft in spite of the lit fire on the opposite end of the room. Undeterred, he ignored the cold and shut the door behind him, noticing the musty, leathery odor of aging books. The room was dark except for the fire and the glow from the blanket of white snow streaming through the window.

Wanting to assess his condition and stay warm at the same time, he went to the fireplace and rolled up his shirtsleeve. "Oh no! Hives!" Unable to control the urge, he scratched.

"Hives!" A female gasped.

Maximilian startled and swirled in the direction of the voice.

Her companion interrupted. "I beg your pardon, sir. Can't you see we want privacy here?"

Maximilian saw none other than Whit, a known rake and cad. Hovering behind him was a girl he had known since she was a baby—Nanette. Such a young woman had no business to be involved with a scoundrel. Though he couldn't see her expression in the dim light, he could feel her embarrassment.

Whit's eyes didn't meet his. Without a doubt, he had caught them in a stolen kiss. Maximilian squashed the urge to warn the girl about Whit. Judging from her blushing cheeks and unwillingness to look him in the eye, admonitions would only be greeted with deaf ears.

"What's that?" Whit's pointing motion brought with it a whiff of a liberal application of bay rum.

Taken aback even though he knew Whit saw the condition of his arm, Maximilian blurted, "What's what?"

Whit moved toward him and pointed to red bumps. "Look, you've got them on your face, too."

Maximilian touched his face and discovered welts.

"You don't have the measles, do you?" He cringed and stepped back. "I couldn't abide catching the measles."

"Measles? No, no. It's nothing like that, why, it's. . ." He searched for an explanation until he recalled the only cause for such symptoms. "Do I look flushed?"

They nodded.

A feeling of impending doom visited him. "Then it could only be one thing. I must have somehow eaten rhubarb. And that means trouble." His stomach tightened.

"We've got to get a doctor right away," Whit said. "That new doctor in town is here, isn't he? What's his name—Stanton?"

Maximilian tried to think, but his brain was getting too foggy to remember. "Uh, I. . . why, I think so. Yes, I was introduced to a doctor named Stanton. A charming fellow, as I recall. Forgive me. I'm not usually this muddleheaded."

"Of course not. You're sick," Nanette said.

Whit agreed. "Don't try to say anything else. Nanette, go get the doctor."

She nodded and exited the library.

"Sit on the couch," Whit advised, pointing to a short sofa upholstered in a paisley print near the fire. "I won't hear an argument." Without further ado, Whit took an unlit candle from a silver stick, lit it with the fire, and proceeded to light a lamp.

Even in his weakened and somewhat frightened state, Maximilian felt he had to argue, though on a different point. "Come here, Whit."

"I'm not sure I want to."

"Fine. Stay there by the light."

"What's so important?"

"I decided to spare you by not saying this in front of Nanette, but if you want to play games, save them for women sophisticated enough to know the score. Don't sully an innocent girl."

"I don't know what you're talking about."

Maximilian knew well that Whit knew exactly what he meant. "Nanette's children will be going to Sunday school in this town some day. Unless you mean to be the gentleman with her, find someone who doesn't expect marriage. And that goes for the other young girls around here, too."

His pleasant features darkened into a sinister scowl. "See here, sport, this is the twentieth century, not the Dark Ages. I never have and never will force my attentions on a woman. Nanette knows the score."

"It was too dim to see a lot in here, but I could feel her excitement and hear the rapture in her voice. She isn't skilled in the games you play. And you know it."

"Who do you think you are, her father?"

"No, but I know her father, and if he were here, that's what he'd say, and then some. Don't let me see you with her again unless your intentions are honorable."

"Or what?" Whit snarled.

"I know my voice is hoarse and I sound strange when I speak now, but you can take my word that you don't want to cross me when I'm at full strength." Breathing had become difficult, but Maximilian tried not to show it for fear of appearing weak.

"I won't stand here and be insulted. I'll let it slide this time since you're ill. But don't expect me to play nursemaid." He left without another word.

As soon as Whit departed, Maximilian heard footfalls of several people rushing in. No doubt they wanted to view him as though he were a sideshow exhibit. He wished he didn't have the presence of mind to be chagrined, but he did.

Thalia rushed to his side to sit beside him on the couch. "Maximilian, what's wrong?"

Though he had managed to ward off Whit from making more advances toward Nanette—or at least he hoped, at this point his tongue felt too thick for him to respond. All he could do was shake his head. He wished Thalia didn't look so alarmed.

"The doctor will be here any minute. He went to his buggy to retrieve his bag. You're in good hands," Thalia assured him.

Maximilian heard an authoritative voice. "Move aside, every-one, please. I need to see the patient."

Obeying, the partygoers vacated the room, leaving him alone with the doctor.

His consoling voice matched his concerned countenance. "How are you feeling?"

Having spent his voice protecting Nanette against Whit, at this point he could only shake his head.

"Can you breathe okay?" Even as he asked, Dr. Stanton took out his stethoscope and warmed the shiny metal tip against his palm.

Maximilian shook his head. "Throat's sore and a little tight."

"We can take care of that. Has this happened before?"

He nodded.

"How many times? Do you recall? You don't have to speak, just hold up your fingers to indicate the number."

Sensing the question's importance, he tried his best to recall every incident. The time at his aunt's had taught him a lesson but good. He hadn't gone near the fruit since. He held up one finger. Maximilian thought, trying to recall when he had felt so miserable. He couldn't remember. Except. . .except the time he encountered rhubarb at his aunt May's. But surely he hadn't eaten any rhubarb tonight.

Maximilian sighed. "Fruit. Rhubarb."

His brow wrinkled. "Have you eaten rhubarb today? I don't remember seeing any on the table."

Maximilian shook his head, feeling foolish. He always took care not to eat the cursed fruit. How he managed to encounter it now, he had no idea.

Dorcas peeked her head in the door. "Is there anything I can do?"

The doctor looked at her. "Not right now, but you could wait a minute while I question Mr. Newbolt." After Dorcas exited, he turned back to his patient. "Maximilian, when did you first notice your symptoms?"

He tried to recall. "About. . .fifteen. . .or twenty minutes ago. . .itch in my throat. . .nose started running." He reached in his pocket, pulled out a rumpled handkerchief, and blew his nose.

The doctor placed the stethoscope against Maximilian's chest. "When did you notice the rash?"

"A few minutes later." He tried not to cough but couldn't help himself. The hacking resounded throughout the library, embarrassing him with its vigor.

"Does your throat feel full?"

He tried to swallow then nodded.

"We need to figure out if you had any rhubarb." The doctor put the stethoscope into his jacket pocket. "If not, we have to find out what else you're allergic to."

He called in Dorcas, who appeared with Thalia.

"Ladies, was there any rhubarb in anything you served tonight?"

Thalia blanched. "Yes. Why?"

"From the best I can tell, Mr. Newbolt is allergic to rhubarb, and he has had a reaction."

"Oh, no!" Their hostess gasped. "Maximilian, did you eat one of the tarts with red filling?"

"Yes. . .strawberry, Edith said. Delicious. I had. . .another."

"It's all my fault." This time she wailed. "That was a new recipe that called for strawberry and rhubarb preserves. Oh, what have I done?"

The doctor stood and turned to Thalia. "We need to get him into bed. Could we move him to a guest room?"

"Of course. We have several bedrooms. Actually, one is on the first floor. It would be easier to put him there. I'll have Eliza start the fire." Dorcas moved toward the door.

"After he's in bed, we need to make a tent out of a sheet and fill it with steam. You do have a teakettle on the stove, don't you?" As he spoke, Dr. Stanton held out his hand to Maximilian. Grateful for the assistance, he accepted it and balanced himself on his feet.

"Yes, I can get whatever you want." Dorcas clasped her hands as if trying to keep them still. "Perhaps you could help take Maximilian down the hall and help him get into bed. There's an old nightshirt of my brother's in the top drawer of the bureau."

"I'll do that, and Miss Bloom, please bring a glass of water and a spoon when you return."

A glass of water sounded good to Maximilian, as did any help he could get. A few moments later, feeling woozy, he offered no resistance as the doctor helped him dress for bed and tucked him underneath the covers.

As soon as he was in bed, the doctor asked for his wrist and checked his pulse rate. Though Dr. Stanton kept his expression neutral, Maximilian didn't take comfort in his lack of consoling words. But at the moment he was too tired to ask questions.

Thalia waited as long as her patience allowed before returning to the first-floor guest room.

Lord, please heal Maximilian!

She knocked on the door. "May I come in?"

"Yes," the doctor answered.

As she entered, Thalia noted with satisfaction that being sure the spare room sparkled had paid off. Even though earlier that evening, neither she nor Aunt Dorcas had any idea they'd have overnight guests, both women liked to keep every place in the house presentable whether they planned for it to be seen by visitors or not. Maximilian was sure to rest in comfort—or, at least in as much comfort as possible for someone ill—in a room as well appointed yet homey as he would find in Denver.

The doctor stood over his patient. Maximilian looked helpless lying alone in the four-poster bed with several woolen blankets and the sheets pulled up to his neck, his head nestled in fluffy down pillows. If only she hadn't served rhubarb.

For fear of disturbing them, she didn't want to make her approach too close. "Is he going to be all right?" Her worry expressed itself in her voice at the sight of the hives on his forehead.

The doctor turned a kind expression toward her. "Oh, it's you, Miss Thalia. I thought you were your aunt returning with the things I requested. Yes, I believe he'll be all right."

She hoped the doctor felt as confident as he appeared. "Is there any way I can help?"

"I've been thinking about the best way to tent him for the steam. I asked your aunt for supplies. Maybe you could get us an extra sheet. And bring a couple of towels and a bowl. Miss Bloom is bringing the teakettle and a glass of water."

"I think there's an extra sheet right here." Thalia made haste to open the bottom drawer of the cherrywood bureau. A faint yet sharp smell of mothballs greeted her as she reached for seldom-used linens. At least they were clean and would do the job.

Turning around, she saw the doctor checking Maximilian's pulse. "How is it, Doctor?"

"No change." He studied his patient. "At least he's asleep now."

"I wonder if he'll sleep through the night."

"I wouldn't count on it, although I'll make him as comfortable as I can." The doctor took a seat in the blue brocade Chippendale chair beside the fireplace and pulled it up next to the bed.

A knock indicated that Aunt Dorcas was back. Thalia opened the door and let her aunt in.

The doctor took the tray from Aunt Dorcas, set it on the bedside table, and took the sheet Thalia had draped across her arm. "Probably the best way to do this is to tuck this behind the headboard and drape it across Mr. Newbolt." He leaned toward his patient and gently shook him awake. "I really hate to disturb you, but we need to get you to sit up in the bed."

Thalia watched as Aunt Dorcas and the doctor arranged Maximilian in bed.

"Before we finish making the tent, I want to give him some bicarbonate of soda." The doctor prepared the medicine and handed the glass to Maximilian. "Drink this right up."

Maximilian took the glass without hesitation and drank a swallow, then grimaced.

The doctor seemed amused but consoling. "I know it doesn't taste good, but it should help you. If you drink it fast, you won't taste it very long."

Thalia felt sorry for Maximilian as he obeyed then let out a burp.

The doctor smiled. "See, it's already helping some."

He glanced toward the two women. "Pardon my faux pas."

Thalia smiled at him. "Think nothing of it."

She watched as the doctor and her aunt made a tent for Maximilian out of the sheets, using boiling water poured in the bowl for steam.

"Breathe in as much steam as you can," the doctor advised while taking his pulse. "Try to relax but don't fall asleep. And if you get too hot inside there, let us know. We can raise one corner of the sheet so you can have some fresh air."

Thalia hadn't expected such an elaborate remedy. Seeing the patient covered in such a way increased her anxiety. Once Maximilian was settled, she couldn't wait to ask the doctor his opinion. Seeking more reassurances, she motioned to him to step outside the door with her so the patient wouldn't overhear what was said. "Will—will he be okay?"

"I hope so."

Her stomach lurched. "You—you hope so? You mean, you don't know?"

"Most allergic reactions cause more discomfort and inconvenience than any real harm, but there is the possibility that the allergy could develop into something more serious, especially since he had such a severe reaction so quickly."

"You—you don't think he could. . ." She didn't want to say the word, but she had to. "Die?"

"I'm hoping for the best."

His noncommittal answer left her with more anxiety. No matter how much he had hurt her, Maximilian couldn't die. He just couldn't.

Thalia's gaze went to the window at the end of the hall. The night sky was almost white with falling snow.

Chapter 4

Alone in bed with only sounds of the crackling fire and his labored breathing to break the silence, Maximilian tried to take in as much air as possible. The feeling of suffocation left him fearful. He had to summon the will to keep going. Though oppressive, the steam did open his throat.

Thank you, Lord, that Dr. Stanton was here.

Contemplating his predicament, he didn't know whether to feel foolish or angry. All those years ago, Norma had told him Thalia didn't love him, but even now, she wouldn't play a mean trick on him by slipping rhubarb into strawberry preserve tarts. He could see by her unmitigated shock at his sudden illness that she didn't know he was allergic to the fruit. Then again, rhubarb wasn't a common ingredient in foods he ate, so even Norma never witnessed what effect the fruit could have on him.

There was no one to blame but himself. He should have asked before he ate any red-colored confection. He thought he had tasted something a bit different in the tart, delicious though it had been. If only he had possessed the foresight to stop eating when he had a chance. Maybe one bite wouldn't have been as devastating as two entire tarts. Then again, he had let Edith distract him with her prattle.

He could play the blame game, but it wouldn't change a thing. Without thinking, he had eaten the tarts, and now he was paying. Paying dearly. He could only pray he wouldn't pay with his life.

Three soft raps at the door got his attention.

"Maximilian?" Thalia's voice sounded sweet, concerned. He wished he hadn't ruined her party by becoming ill and disrupting the fun. "May I come in?"

He considered how he must look and what she must think of him, lying limp underneath sheets, breathing in and out laboriously like some kind of fiend. He hated for Thalia to see him in such a state. Surely every sign pointed to California—first the flat tire, the near miss with the black cat crossing his path, the spilled pepper, and now this horrid illness. But now that the signs seemed so clear, he wished he could stay in Colorado. Maybe then he could change her mind.

Unwilling to let pride stand in the way of seeing Thalia, he uttered a response. "Yes. You may come in."

The soft swishing of a skirt marked each of her steps. Recalling how she looked earlier that evening, he pictured her in a pink party dress, resembling a bouquet of delicate spring roses in defiance of the snow outside.

"How's the patient by now?" The expression in her voice sounded blithe. He wondered if she was putting on an act for him.

"Do I seem to be all right? No, don't answer that." He took in another breath and tried to swallow in spite of his tightening throat.

"Don't try to say anything. We can talk later. Just relax," she instructed.

New footfalls announced someone else's arrival.

"Thalia, let me take care of this," he heard Dorcas say. "You don't need to be in here playing nursemaid while you have other guests to attend to."

"Thank you, but it's all my fault this happened, and I'll take care of him. Anyway, everyone else is pretty tired. It's late, and I think they'd like to go to bed."

"No doubt. Thankfully we have enough guest rooms to accommodate everyone, although I do believe you should bunk with Rose tonight."

"She won't have a roommate. I'll be here. I can sleep on the chaise lounge."

In between breaths, he objected. "No...don't..."

"That seems highly improper to me." Dorcas's voice sounded sharp.

"Please Aunt Dorcas. Under the circumstances, I believe my honor will remain intact. You can check on us anytime you like."

She sighed with clear exasperation. "Oh, all right. Call me if you need anything."

Hearing Dorcas exit left Maximilian feeling relieved. He would have to thank Thalia later. Whether he could credit feeling better to the steam or just knowing Thalia remained nearby, he didn't know. Or care.

The next morning he awoke, his throat feeling less constricted. Steam poured into the tent. Obviously Thalia had kept the mist going throughout the night. How could he express his gratitude?

He lifted the sheet enough to see. Still in her party dress, Thalia had fallen asleep in the chaise lounge by the fire, which had died down overnight but still held some warmth. He tried not to awaken her, but as soon as he stirred, she moved. Her eyes opened.

"I didn't mean to wake you." Maximilian folded the sheet away from his face. He realized talking didn't take the monumental effort it had the previous night.

"That's okay." She jumped from her seat and rushed to his side. "My prayers are answered. You made it. You made it through the night. I hardly slept a wink, wanting to be sure you were okay. You seemed to be able to breathe better in the wee hours. I was so relieved!"

Her relief scared him. Had he been closer to death than he imagined?

"Do you feel better? You look better." Her body sagged, releasing emotional strain.

He nodded and caught the faintest whiff of tuberose perfume that still clung to her from the previous night. The sweet aroma made him think of his garden in spring. He could get used to the scent forever as long as Thalia wore it.

Not noticing the effect she had on him, she regarded his face. "The hives have gone down considerably, but you appear a bit flushed. Your cheeks are red—like a cherub's picture on a Christmas card." Her eyes widened and she seemed fully awake.

"That doesn't sound so flattering since I'm not a cherub." He sneezed.

Placing the back of her right hand on his cheek, she looked at him with less concern. "You're not terribly hot. I think it's probably just the steam."

Facing away from Thalia, he sneezed again.

"Or maybe you have a cold."

Groaning, he remembered changing the flat tire in the freezing weather. "Don't tell me that, even though you're probably right. I must be the worst party guest on record. Maybe I can go ahead and try to go home. I can be my valet's problem there and not yours." He tried to rise but realized he felt too weak to move.

She shook her head. "You're exhausted from the stress of trying to keep oxygen in your body. You have no business traveling anywhere. Besides, the snowstorm has dropped quite a few inches on us already, and snow is still falling. It's much too dangerous to travel. I think it's safe to say by now that we're in the midst of a blizzard. Josiah and Dr. Stanton are outside shoveling even though the snow is falling as fast as they can clear a path."

Guilt visited him faster than the storm. "I should help," he said, even though he knew he couldn't.

"Are you insane? Of course not. They understand. Do you want me to keep the steam going?"

He took in a breath. "I think I can make do without it."

Thalia's voice softened from competent nurse to dainty woman. "I feel terrible that all this happened."

"No, I should have known not to eat anything questionable after I knocked over that pepper shaker." He took a breath.

"What?"

"Spilling pepper is a bad omen. You know that."

"I know no such thing. I rely on God to keep me safe." She placed her hand on top of his. "But I don't want to argue. I'm sorry."

"I don't think I ever told you I was allergic."

"Maybe not. Now that makes me feel better. You always were considerate of others' feelings." She smiled.

Despite her attempt at cheer, he could see tiredness in Thalia's eyes. "Please go and get some rest yourself. There's no way you had a peaceful night sleeping in your party dress in a chair. Your dedication to me went far and above the call of duty of any hostess. I thank you."

She glanced demurely downward. "I—I think I will take you up on your offer to get into some fresh clothes and take a nap. I'll see you later this afternoon."

I'll see you later this afternoon.

He hadn't imagined such words when he arrived for the party. Regardless of what Norma had said so long ago, he yearned to see Thalia again. Her sweet face had not disappointed. And now he would be staying even longer. The miserable illness was almost worth it. Could it be a sign he was supposed to remain in Colorado after all? Confusion left him feeling disconcerted.

Lord, help me figure this out.

Bored yet restless, he took a few moments to appreciate his surroundings. As might be expected from the fine furnishings in the rest of the house, Thalia's guest room was well appointed. The cherrywood dresser, vanity, and wardrobe, each mellowed to a reddish brown with age, featured carved magnolias that told a bit about the Bloom family's history.

Snow still fell outside, but inside the steam kept him warm.

"Thank you, God, for Thalia," was the last thing he muttered before falling asleep.

Chapter 5

After a long nap, Maximilian awoke in a strange room. Within a flash, he remembered everything that happened—the party, the tart, the violent illness, and Thalia. Thalia. She had been there for him, nursing him throughout the night. If only he didn't still feel so wretched. Sweating despite the cold, he threw off the coverlet. Ah. Relief.

"Just what do you think you're doing?" The questioning voice didn't belong to sweet Thalia but to her aunt, Dorcas.

"Where's Thalia?"

"Where's Thalia indeed? In bed where she belongs. She stayed up all night with you. She's getting some rest now. I'm taking over." Dorcas pulled the coverlet over him. "Do you want dinner? You missed breakfast and lunch."

He shook his head.

"Well, that's too bad, because you're getting it anyway. Eliza is bringing in warm broth."

"Warm broth? That doesn't sound too appetizing, but I

suppose it's best since it seems I've picked up a cold."

"True. Dr. Stanton said to force fluids. You must drink some broth. You need the nourishment in it for energy." Dressed as she was in a no-nonsense gray house frock and wearing a stern expression, Maximilian didn't doubt she knew exactly what she was talking about.

"Thalia? Where is Thalia?"

"Now don't get too attached to the idea of Thalia being your nursemaid. I'm up for the task, and she has other guests to attend to. They're in the drawing room piecing together a jigsaw puzzle now. Never liked puzzles much myself. Besides, I'm old, and no one will miss me. Tending to you is the least I can do for poor little Norma. She would have wanted me to take care of you, I know."

Maybe so. But he liked his other nurse much better.

If he had to get sick and be embarrassed, now that he was out of the makeshift tent, at least he couldn't have chosen a more comfortable place. He looked through a window framed by brocaded draperies at snow still falling outside. From all appearances, the blanket of snow had grown deep enough to cause considerable trouble walking through it.

"Looks as though there's no letup on the snow. I guess we're shut in today," he speculated.

"Yes, I suppose anyone can look outside and see there's not much traveling today. I just pray that those who left last night got where they were going."

"Me, too. I'm sure they did." He heard voices coming from the dining room. "Apparently not everybody left."

"You really are out of it, aren't you? Rose and Dr. Stanton are here. And Josiah." Dorcas sat on the nearby chair and took up some knitting.

He held back a grimace. Of all the people he wished had gotten out in time, Josiah was top on his list.

"I'm glad Josiah stayed," Dorcas said as though she had heard his thought and wanted to debate. "He's the perfect match for Thalia, don't you think?"

"The perfect match? What, has one of Thalia's hands turned into a baseball mitt?"

"Don't be silly. All men have interests that don't relate to women. She can't expect to love everything he does. For comparison, I wouldn't expect you to be interested in my knitting project." She held up a square of green yarn with two needles wrapped up in it. How those needles and thread ended up in a sweater or whatever garment the women wanted, he would never know.

"There's interest in a subject, and then there's obsession. I don't think Thalia likes to be bored."

"She won't be bored long. The Billings family has plenty of money, and she will be happy and secure. And she'll have plenty to do, especially once the babies start coming. Can you just imagine redheaded little imps?" She chuckled and kept knitting.

Maximilian could imagine them, but he didn't want to. The combination of red hair and imps conjured up little devils in his mind. The thought of Thalia having Josiah's children made his fever rise. Too distressed to pay attention to his breathing, he coughed.

Dorcas dropped her knitting and rushed to his side. She slapped him on the back. "Now, now. Let's not make your cold worse on top of everything else."

Her worried look concerned him. Still, he desperately wanted to return to Aurora, but how could he with snow falling so hard one could hardly see the sky? He tried to rise, but apparently his motions caused a stir, as Thalia entered, leaving the door open behind her. "Maximilian, what are you thinking? Don't you dare try to get up!"

"But I feel so much bet—" His spinning head forced him to realize that indeed he did not feel better. He lay back.

Thalia set a tray on the bedside table.

"Thalia, what are you doing with that tray?" Dorcas asked. "You're supposed to be in bed yourself."

"I couldn't let my guest go without a bite to eat."

"Eliza can bring his meals to him."

Maximilian wondered why Dorcas's tone was so grumpy. "She was just trying to do me a good turn. Thank you, Thalia."

"You don't look so good, but the hives seem to be gone," Thalia answered. "If you have a cold—and I think you do—Dr. Stanton will try his best to keep you comfortable."

"Thank goodness for him."

"It's fine that you want to be a good nurse, Thalia," Dorcas interrupted, "but you're not being a very good hostess, are you? You should be tending to your other guests."

"But Maximilian is a guest, too."

"You shouldn't argue. It's not becoming of a lady," Dorcas cautioned. She turned to Maximilian. "You must excuse her, dear.

She's been in a state with this party."

"No doubt."

Thalia blushed and, without a word, excused herself. Maximilian wondered what had gotten into Dorcas for her to be so willing to reprimand her niece in his presence.

Putting down her knitting, Dorcas got up from her chair and approached the patient's bed. "I'm so sorry this party had to be spoiled by a horrid fruit tart. After all, this was your first time out socially since Norma's death, wasn't it?"

He swallowed. "I—I suppose so."

"Dear, dear Norma." Dorcas clucked. "She was a jewel, one of a kind. No one can ever replace her. Her death was so tragic."

"Yes."

Dorcas placed her hand on his. "I know life alone will be hard. I've lived as a spinster all these years, and though it gets lonely at times, it's never too much to bear. But keeping Norma's memory enshrined, as if it were a pearl set in prongs of gold, will honor her and your marriage."

Maximilian wanted to point out that he never said he wanted to live life alone, but considering Dorcas's wistful demeanor, decided against it. He thought back on his brief marriage. Norma had been one of a kind, with many good qualities. If only she'd been as perfect as Dorcas thought. Maximilian had been taken by her charm and beauty, but as soon as they married, Norma's pettiness and jealousy revealed themselves. He wondered if she loved him at all. If only he had chosen Thalia when he had the chance. But Norma had said that Thalia didn't love him—that her true love was elsewhere. And Thalia never did anything to dispute Norma's claim. If only Thalia had loved him, things would have been so different. Sure, she'd been a wonderful nurse the previous night, but a display of sympathy to an ill guest wasn't the same as giving the commitment of a lifetime love.

"Even once you're better, I hope you'll avail yourself of our hospitality as long as possible. We enjoy having you around. It's been too long. Having you near reminds me of my dear Norma."

Maximilian couldn't bear Dorcas's reminiscences much longer. Cold or no cold, he would rise out of his sickbed and leave as soon as he could. Thalia had already told him that she couldn't bear to lose Dorcas's love, and the more Dorcas spoke, the clearer it was that he could never have Thalia and her aunt's approval at the same time.

The sign he had asked for had happened. He would be heading for California as soon as the snow cleared the mountain passes on the Union Pacific Railway.

Chapter 6

The next afternoon, Thalia, wearing a fresh dress with a pattern of roses, entered the drawing room.

Josiah shuffled Flinch cards for the group at the game table. "Good. Now we have a foursome."

"I'm afraid not. I'll be taking care of Maximilian today."

"Aw, come on, Thalia, you don't have to stay by that baby," Josiah chided. "You've been with him all day. Stay with us awhile."

The last thing Thalia wanted to do was play, even the most popular card game of the day. "Aunt Dorcas is much better at cards than I ever could be."

"He doesn't need you to watch him sleep." Josiah grimaced. "You should have some fun."

"I think it would do you good to play," Dr. Stanton suggested.

"Can't argue with doctor's orders, can you?" Josiah gave the physician a satisfied grin and shuffled the deck of cards once more.

Recalling how groggy Maximilian had been when she last checked on him, she reconsidered. "Oh, all right. I suppose I can join you for a few hands."

She sat at the table with the others and took a hand. Before long, she got caught up in the spirit of fun competition and for the first time since Maximilian had taken ill, enjoyed her own party. Even the snow falling outside no longer bothered her.

"Beat you again!" Josiah said after a particularly lively and close round.

"You are demonstrating talents beyond baseball," Dorcas observed, knitting in the corner.

Thalia knew the remark was aimed at her but decided not to comment as she dealt the next hand. She created the stockpile, dealt the hands, and set the stack. The players organized their cards, and Dr. Stanton started the play.

"Flinch!" Maximilian cried as he entered the room.

Thalia's heart jumped upon hearing the now familiar voice. Without rising from her seat, she swiveled to see that her patient not only stood before her, but had shaved and dressed. The hives had disappeared, and he looked like his handsome self.

"May I join in the fun?"

"Maximilian, what are you doing out of bed?" Thalia scolded.

"I felt better, so I decided it was high time for me to join in the fun." He stifled a cough.

"Are you sure you're well enough to be up?" Rose queried.

"Yeah, maybe you should go back to bed. We have enough hands to play Flinch," Josiah urged. "Isn't that right, Doc?"

"We have enough to play, but if he feels like staying up, it would be better than becoming weaker by lying in bed so long." The doctor smiled. "I'm glad to see you up. For a while there, you were in grave danger."

"Not anymore. I'll join you, then." Maximilian pulled up a chair to sit by Thalia.

"Here," Josiah intervened. "Sit here instead." He made a dash to occupy the seat by Thalia and left Maximilian with the empty spot between him and Dr. Stanton.

Thalia waited for Maximilian to comment, but he acquiesced without a murmur. As she dealt cards, she resolved to thank him later for letting Josiah get away with his childish behavior. Josiah would never change, so there was no alternative but to give in so they could keep the peace.

She stole a furtive glance at Aunt Dorcas. The older woman, rather than pursing her lips in disapproval, smiled at what she must have perceived as a victory for Josiah. Would she ever get through to her well-meaning but stubborn aunt?

During the game, Thalia noticed that Josiah was more competitive than he needed to be, especially with Maximilian. The fact that Maximilian showed good sportsmanship and gentlemanlike conduct, in spite of holding back coughs and sniffles, did not escape her notice.

"Everyone ready for a bit of cocoa?" Thalia asked after several hands.

Maximilian peered out the window. "I think more shoveling might need to be done before dark. Then cocoa would be more than called for."

"That's a fine thing for you to say," Josiah scoffed. "You

haven't had to do any work."

He stood. "That's where you're wrong. I plan to shovel right along with you and Dr. Stanton."

"We only have two shovels," Aunt Dorcas pointed out.

"In that case, I'll take a short turn since I still haven't totally shaken this cold. But I do want to contribute. After all, I owe the doctor a break after he took such good care of me."

His firm resolve worried Thalia. Maximilian always struggled with pride, and now it looked as though he wasn't going to let a cold keep him from facing hard work in freezing, snowy weather. "I don't think it's a good idea." She looked to the expert for help, making sure a pleading light showed in her eyes. "Do you, Dr. Stanton?"

"I think waiting at least until tomorrow is well advised under the circumstances."

"I know you mean well, Dr. Stanton, but I'm over the allergic reaction. As long as I don't touch more rhubarb, I'll be fit as a fiddle." Without waiting for more arguments, Maximilian rushed to the coat closet.

Thalia rose to try to stop him, but Aunt Dorcas placed a firm hand on her shoulder. "When a man is that determined to do something, there's no stopping him. If you try, you'll be viewed as a nag."

A quick glance in Rose's direction told Thalia she'd get no help from her friend. Thalia held back a grimace. "I guess you're right."

Josiah stood. "I'll go help him and make sure he doesn't keel over and fall in a snowdrift." The sardonic expression on his face took away any hint of real compassion for the other man.

Thalia let Josiah exit without protest, but then she turned to the doctor. "Can't you convince Maximilian not to go out in this?"

"I did my best, but short of tying him to the bed with a rope, there's nothing I can do to force any patient to follow my orders. If his cold symptoms get worse, common sense will prevail and he'll come in. And I'll be sure to go out soon to relieve him. I think he wants to prove to us he can do his part. Maybe letting him have that will do more than any amount of steam and hot soup."

"How can I argue with that?" Thalia smiled. "You're a good doctor."

"I think so, too." Rose's soft expression led Thalia to believe that her words were a shallow veil for deeper feelings. The thought of Rose and Dr. Stanton becoming a couple seemed sweet to Thalia.

"You know, I think I'll have a bit of tea." Aunt Dorcas placed her knitting in her basket. "Could you help me in the kitchen, Thalia?"

Thalia knew her aunt needed no help and wondered why she wanted to speak with her. "Okay. Excuse me, will you?"

She followed Dorcas into the kitchen. No matter how many times she entered the room, Thalia always noted how the yellow walls projected a summer feeling regardless of the weather. Cook was on break, so they had the room to themselves. Thalia closed the door behind them so the others wouldn't hear. "What is it?"

"You are being entirely too hard on Josiah." Aunt Dorcas reached into the cabinet for a teacup and pulled out one with a daisy pattern.

"What do you mean? He practically ran over Maximilian to get to his seat and then wasn't a very good sport over cards. Really, Aunt Dorcas, I need you to get over any thought of us ever being a couple." Thalia leaned against the counter and crossed her arms.

"But the only reason he stayed here was because of you. And I'm glad he did. I can see you are getting entirely too attached to Maximilian. He is not for you, Thalia. He's not for anybody." She set her cup down in a matching saucer with more force than needed.

Thalia knew that her aunt meant well, and she didn't want to sound snappish with the older woman. "I know your fond desire is to see me make a match with Josiah, but I just don't feel he's the one for me. Even with us being in close proximity, I don't long to be near him."

"You feel nothing for him?" Hurt, surprise, and disappointment evidenced themselves in her tone. "After all, he is attractive."

She had to stand her ground. "Yes, but still I feel nothing more than the blessings I would want for any brother in Christ. I'm sorry, Aunt Dorcas."

"Fine." She poured water into the teakettle. "What about the other men who looked your way at the party? Why, there was Andrew Stallings, Ned Jones, Thomas Callahan, even Whit Tanner."

"Whit Tanner? That scoundrel? Please, Aunt Dorcas." Exasperated, Thalia took a seat at the worn but serviceable kitchen table.

Aunt Dorcas tightened her lips while she stuffed a silver steeper full of loose black tea leaves. As soon as she was done, she covered the tea tin. "Oh, all right. I admit I have heard a thing or two about him I don't like. But the others are more than respectable. They come from fine families and would make a wonderful match for you."

"I know it seems that way, but none of them touches my heart."

Dorcas let out a harrumph of disgust as she dropped the steeper into her empty cup. "Fine then. But that doesn't mean you should go running after your deceased cousin's husband. Sullying her memory in such a way would raise a few eyebrows."

Thalia wasn't sure she agreed with her aunt, but she decided not to argue. "I have already given the situation over to the Lord. I don't want to hurt anyone, either. Please, let's see how His plan unfolds."

The steaming water Aunt Dorcas poured was no hotter than her anger. "As long as it's His plan and not yours."

"At the rate you're going, we'll be here all day," Josiah chided as Maximilian shoveled.

Maximilian didn't want to admit how tired he was. Each shovelful of snow seemed heavier than the last. The coal shovel was already heavy. Almost from the moment he ventured outside, he wished he had heeded the doctor's advice to take it easy. But pride had forced him to shovel. Each day he learned more about how foolish he had been to cling to his pride. With God's help, he tried to let go. Though their efforts didn't reveal bare ground for long, at least by removing snow as more fell, a pathway remained visible.

"I'll try to move faster," he shouted to Josiah. With determination, he picked up the pace.

"You'll never beat me."

Maximilian had only been near Josiah a couple of days, and he'd been out of commission most of that time. Yet the jerk got on his last nerve. He moved toward Josiah and set his shovel in the snow, leaning ever so lightly on the handle. "Josiah, why is everything a competition with you? Life is not one big baseball game."

"Everything is not a competition with me. But Thalia's different. I may court her."

"Is that so?" he challenged. "You've had all this time to ask. And obviously Miss Dorcas has no intention of standing in your way. So what are you waiting for?"

Josiah hesitated. "I—uh, I hadn't thought about it. I—I reckon there's no good reason not to ask."

"Is that so? I think in your heart of hearts you know the reason. She's not interested in you, at least not in a romantic way."

Josiah's face blazed crimson, and not from the cold. "What makes you think you know so much? And why do you care?" He frowned. "I know. You want her for yourself, don't you? That's why you came to the party."

"Not exactly, I—"

"I'll show you who's boss."

Before Maximilian realized what was happening, Josiah punched his face, knocking him off balance and into the snow.

"Ha-ha!" Josiah pointed at him and laughed. "You deserve a comeuppance!"

Maximilian recovered as quickly as he could, staggering to his feet. He could taste blood, but a quick lick on the inside of his mouth told him his teeth were intact. Anger swelled in him. "Why, you—" He raised his fist to retaliate.

"Maximilian! Stop!"

Both men turned to see Thalia, without a coat, racing toward them.

Immediately Maximilian felt remorse. He never should have let his pride get the best of him, even to argue with Josiah, much less come at him with a fist, bloody lip notwithstanding.

"Thalia, get back in the house," Maximilian insisted. "You'll catch your death of cold."

"I saw you out here, and I could tell by the way you looked that you were arguing. What's wrong with you? Two grown men should know better."

"I'm sorry. Please go in the house." Maximilian looked skyward. "Shoveling is a waste of time for now anyway. Let's go in." He realized he had something else to say. "Josiah, I'm sorry."

"You sure are."

Ignoring Josiah and his attitude, Maximilian took Thalia by the elbow in a deliberate fashion and guided her back to the house. He noticed she seemed to hold back a grimace.

"He got you good," she said. "What were you arguing about?"

Running up beside them and keeping lockstep, Josiah glared.

Tempted though Maximilian was to tell all, he decided that to declare victory in an argument—especially over her—could do him more harm than good. "Never mind." He took her by the arm to help her up the icy porch steps. "Let's get you back inside. Dr. Stanton has all the patients he needs."

Chapter 7

After nearly a week of falling, the snow stopped. With an accumulation of forty-five inches, the area stayed shut down far beyond anyone's guess. Rapid winds pushed most of the accumulation into high drifts. For the remainder of the time they were stranded, Josiah and Maximilian lived under an unspoken truce, which relieved Thalia. Once the trains resumed running, Thalia bade good-bye to Dr. Stanton and Rose as they left her house. Judging by the way they looked at each other, she could tell romance brewed.

Though happy for Rose, Thalia felt wistful for herself the day after they departed. In the early morning, sitting alone in the library with her Bible and cup of tea, Thalia realized that the city's ability to spring back meant one thing—that Maximilian would be leaving. She never thought she'd mourn his departure, but she realized that after almost losing him, she didn't want him out of her life again. She wasn't ready for courtship as long as Maximilian's relationship with God appeared weak, but she could stay on friendly terms with him. She would have to make herself content with that.

She turned to the fifth chapter of Matthew: *And if ye salute your brethren only, what do ye more than others? do not even the publicans so? Be ye therefore perfect, even as your Father which is in heaven is perfect.*

If she didn't follow Jesus' guidance and forgive Maximilian, and even Norma, was she better than any garden-variety pagan? How could she serve the Lord as a faithful servant if she couldn't let go of past romantic disappointments?

She turned to one of her favorite verses, Psalm 86:5: *For thou, Lord, art good, and ready to forgive; and plenteous in mercy unto all them that call upon thee.*

Had Norma ever expressed a shred of remorse for ruining her chances with Maximilian? No. At least she never shared regrets with Thalia, even on her deathbed. Perhaps Norma's vanity and pride wouldn't allow her to see how much she had hurt Thalia. But she couldn't lay all the blame at Norma's feet. Maximilian had chosen her cousin, breaking Thalia's heart as easily as a toothpick.

She expected anger to surge at such distressing thoughts. But it didn't. Maybe Maximilian's appearance at her party, seeing him again, proved to be the best thing that could have happened.

Lord, is it true? Have I forgiven them both long ago, in my heart?

Thinking about her reaction to Maximilian, she realized that spinsterhood was not her desire. He was. But could he ever be hers?

A silent prayer entered her mind. She shut her eyes. "Lord, I know my thoughts about Maximilian and Norma have been unkind, but I have come to full and complete forgiveness of them. You know my sadness over Norma's death is genuine. I do miss her, in spite of everything. Please forgive me for being so hard-hearted toward her—and Maximilian."

Josiah interrupted. "Thalia, I want to speak to you."

Jumping a little, she opened her eyes and threw her hand to her chest at the same time.

"Did I scare you? Sorry."

"A little, but I'm fine." She rested her hand on the doily-covered armrest of the couch to show she had relaxed. A flash of thought that she hoped he planned to bid her good-bye occurred to her, but she squelched it. "Sure, we can talk."

Thalia could feel his anxiety as he sat by her. His twitching foot made her wonder why the usually brash Josiah seemed nervous. "I—I have something to ask you. And since I've got to get back home, I don't have much time, so I'll make it quick. I–I'd like to court you. I know your aunt approves."

Not a shred of happiness visited Thalia. Surely when a man asked to court a woman, her heart should beat strong with love. Though Josiah's appearance pleased her, she couldn't imagine being his bride. If only he had seen the signs she tried to give him. Though always civil and polite, she'd done nothing to encourage him toward romantic thoughts.

He didn't wait long to prod her. "Well? Aren't you going to say anything?"

"Uh, I'm sorry. I—I didn't mean not to answer."

"Happiness does that to a woman, right? Makes her at a loss for words?" Hope in his voice made it harder for Thalia.

"Maybe sometimes, but I'm afraid not this time." The urge to take his hand seized her, but she knew that any touch would only make matters worse. "I have no plans to marry. Ever. I'm sorry, Josiah. I know you'll make some lucky girl a very good husband someday. She just needs to be the right girl for you."

A flash of hurt crossed his face before he screwed his expression into a snarl. "It's that dandy, isn't it?"

"Dandy?"

"Yeah, Maximilian." He narrowed his eyes when he said the name.

"He's made no move toward me, if that's what you mean."

"Oh, but he will. You can count on it." He rose. "Go ahead. Stay with that sickly fool. You'll play nursemaid your whole life with that one."

Unwelcome feelings roiled within Thalia. Josiah's venom resulted from jealousy, and she knew Maximilian's illness was a unique occurrence, never to be repeated as long as he shied away from rhubarb. But the truth about Maximilian's lack of faith in the living God bothered her, enough to keep her from acting on any romantic feelings she harbored for him.

"And to think I gave him a bloody lip over you."

So the fistfight did happen because of her. She didn't respond.

"Never mind. Well, you had your chance. Don't come crying to me when you're tired of nursing that dandy back to health.

Good-bye." Josiah turned and left the library. As though to emphasize the end of their friendship, he shut the door so the thud resounded throughout the house.

Thalia knew he meant what he said. She would never have another chance with him. For some reason, the thought left her sad.

She didn't have time to think about Josiah before Aunt Dorcas rushed in. "What's the matter? Josiah ran out of here as if he were a fox with hounds on his tail."

"I don't think we'll be seeing much of him around here anymore." Realizing she'd never be able to return to her Bible reading for the day, she shut the book and set it on her lap.

Aunt Dorcas gasped as she took a seat beside Thalia. "Did you discourage him?"

"I did more than that. I told him I don't want him to court me. I'm sorry, Aunt Dorcas. I know you were hoping for us to make a match."

"I just hope you won't live to regret that decision."

"If I do, I'll know the consequences are my own doing. Try not to worry about me so much. I know my life will turn out just fine, regardless of whether or not I marry."

"But once I die, you'll be alone without me."

"Is that what this is about? You're afraid for me?" Touched by her aunt's concern, Thalia softened her voice.

"I've lived my life—or most of it, anyway. Spinsterhood suited me. I had my brother and sister-in-law for company, and now you," Aunt Dorcas pointed out. "And now, I'm not afraid of death. But you, on the other hand, have no one but me. I don't think you should live your life alone. I may seem stern, but I want you to be happy."

Her aunt's unselfish sentiments made Thalia's eyes mist. She took her hands. "I'll be fine. I promise."

Maximilian wished he didn't have to go back to Aurora. He enjoyed staying at Thalia's too much. Family and friends kept life at the Blooms' exciting. Never did he feel a pall about the place. Superstitions and darkness were swept aside. Maximilian contemplated the reasons for Thalia's successful home. Could her success be attributed to her faith?

Seeing Thalia again brought back so many unresolved feelings—feelings he had long forgotten. The desire to go to California had lessened since he arrived at the party. He had to tell his cousin whether he wanted to join him. The time for a final decision had come. He had to talk to Thalia.

A quick survey of the house revealed her in the library, sitting with her Bible and tea.

She greeted him when he entered. "I'm quite popular today, it seems. You're my third visitor, and I've only been here an hour."

He stopped short at the doorway. Never could a woman but Thalia make an everyday housedress appear to be a heavenly robe. Even Norma, deservedly considered a great beauty, couldn't have compared to Thalia. "I see you have your Bible. Am I interrupting your devotions?"

Her smile sweetened her face even beyond its usual angelic

appearance. "They've been interrupted so many times I've given up for the day. But don't worry. God has heard my concerns." She set the Bible on the end table.

He approached her and sat on the sofa. "I wish I had such faith."

"Such faith can be yours if you trust and keep the lines of communication open with God."

"I heard you praying for me while I was ill." Maximilian wanted to reach for Thalia's hands but decided the gesture might be too bold. "Just thanking you seems so inadequate."

"I don't need your thanks. I know God's providence is the reason you recovered."

"I guess it didn't hurt."

"Your lucky rabbit's foot didn't seem to do you much good." Though her words chastised, they didn't sound harsh.

"Maybe it kept me from dying."

Thalia sighed. "Maximilian, why do you hold on to silly superstitions? You go to church—" She paused and leaned a few inches toward him, enough that he could inhale the pleasant scent of tuberose. "You do still go to church, don't you?"

He nodded. "Of course. And of course I do believe in God. I'm just not as sure as you are that He answers prayer."

"Maybe that's because you don't talk to Him enough." Her eyes glinted with sadness.

So many things he wanted to say ran through his mind, but he stopped. He couldn't say how he really felt. Not now. Clearly Thalia wanted her God more than she wanted him. Norma must have been right. Thalia never did love him. He would have to live with that.

"I—I wanted to say good-bye, and to thank you again for everything." He rose from the couch.

She followed suit. "I'll miss you. I'm sure Aunt Dorcas will want to invite you over for dinner now and again, especially since your official period of mourning is over."

"That would be nice." He paused. "I should say good-bye to Josiah."

"He's not here. He already left."

"Oh." Though he could hardly say he made friends with Josiah while they were snowed in, courtesy called for a farewell. "I'm sorry I missed him."

"He left in a hurry."

Maximilian knew his next query was nosy, but since he still considered going to California, he figured he might as well go for broke. "That's strange for a man who told me he wants to court you."

"He told you that?"

"Yes, right before he punched me in the lip." Maximilian's hand involuntarily touched his mouth at the painful remembrance. "No doubt your aunt is dancing a jig."

"I turned him down. She's not too happy with me." Thalia sighed and stared at the fireplace. "I wish I didn't have to distress her so. I don't want to lose her love, Maximilian. She's the only family I have."

Desperately he wanted to reach out to her, to take her in his arms, to tell her he could give her all the love she would ever need. But he couldn't. Dorcas had made her wishes clear.

For him to marry anyone would be upsetting enough to her, but he couldn't risk pursuing Norma's cousin, the very woman who lived under her roof. He had to find the strength to remain quiet.

Chapter 8

Maximilian trudged through the snow to his motorcar. He dreaded going home. Snow still covered the ground, and driving the vehicle through it would be tough. He had never tried such a feat with the motorcar. A hay burner would have served him better. But another reason for his despair pulled at his heart. He didn't want to leave Thalia. Despite his efforts to look for signs that he should stay, he saw none.

He opened the livery barn door. His motorcar waited for him on the left, covered by a canvas tarp. He pulled off the frozen material and sat down in the cold leather seat. He grabbed the starter crank and engaged the switch, then proceeded to the engine block and inserted the crank.

The engine failed. He tried again.

It still failed. No matter how much he tried to start the Studebaker, the engine refused to turn over.

He got out of the automobile and made his way back to the house. *Lord, why are the signs so hard to read?*

Thalia greeted him at the door. "What's wrong? I thought you'd left."

He scowled even though he hated for her to see him in a bad mood. "I can't get the Studebaker to start. I need to get home. I don't know what to do."

She flitted her hand at him to dismiss his worries. "That's easy. We'll take you in our sled."

Why hadn't he thought of the obvious? Still. . . "I hate to inconvenience you in such a way."

"It's not an inconvenience. Let me get my coat and some blankets for the journey. Aunt Dorcas will want to come along. We're so tired of being confined to the house."

"Okay, but I insist you both stay the night at my house in return for the favor."

"Are you sure we should stay, considering your cook serves up raw potatoes?" Her eyes sparkled, and her mouth curved into a mischievous line.

"Maybe you'd be better off hungry." He grinned.

"Hmm. Maybe not. We'll accept your hospitality. And our driver, Jonas, is here today. He just dug out of the snow at his house himself. Now that he's here, he can drive us."

Soon Thalia and her aunt joined Maximilian just outside the carriage house. Jonas pulled the sled out with ease.

"Told you there's nothing better than horses for transportation," Dorcas declared, not bothering to conceal her glee as she settled into her seat. "You young people will rue the day you decided to rely solely on motorcars for transportation."

"I think I might already be sorry," Maximilian said only

half-jokingly, remembering how he'd already had to fix a flat tire on the way to the party, and now this. Chilly, he checked to make sure all the buttons on his coat were fastened.

"Oh, my!" Dorcas exclaimed during the trip as they traveled by mounds of shoveled snow in front of homes and businesses. "Look at this mess. We weren't the only ones who had trouble digging out."

"We'll have a winter mess for quite some time," Maximilian agreed. "Until spring, at least."

"Hope we don't get more snow anytime soon, but I imagine that's a dream," Dorcas ventured.

Glancing at Thalia, he noticed that though she nodded in agreement with their various observations, she remained strangely quiet.

"Maybe the blizzard, my illness, and the trouble with my motorcar are signs that I should head out to California after all," he mused aloud.

"California?" Dorcas asked. "Whatever do you mean?"

For the first time during the trip, Thalia turned her full attention to the conversation. "I want to know, too."

"I didn't tell you? My cousin has asked me to go in with him on some orange groves out there. I thought the warm weather and change of pace might do me good, what with everything bad that's happened."

"I wouldn't put so much stock in signs." Dorcas wagged her finger. "Just because your mother believed in old wives' tales, doesn't mean you need to stay in bondage to them."

"His mother?" Thalia asked.

Dorcas's eyebrows rose. "Didn't you know? Lily Newbolt was the most superstitious woman in town."

"She had reason to be," Maximilian noted.

"Why?" Thalia's voice heightened with curiosity.

"I thought everyone in the family knew that story." Dorcas jumped in. "She was supposed to go back East to some fancy school to study music. She wanted to be a concert pianist, you know."

"Really?" Thalia gasped. "Maximilian, why didn't you ever tell me that?"

He shrugged. "It never came up. She didn't enjoy talking about her past, so I never dwelled on it."

"So what made her superstitious?"

"I'll tell you as much as I know. On the day she was supposed to leave for school, she was on her way to the train station and spotted a penny, faceup," Maximilian answered. "Of course, if you see a penny, you're supposed to pick it up for good luck. Well, not putting any stock in superstition, she ignored it. She ending up missing her train, and when she went home, she found that her sister—Aunt Nettie—you remember her. . ."

"Oh, yes," Thalia said.

"Well, Aunt Nettie had suddenly taken ill, and she had to stay home—she was the only other woman in the house, you know—and nurse her back to health. Once the opportunity was missed, she never had another chance to follow her dream. To the day Mother died, she swore that if only she had stopped and picked up that penny, she would have been a famous concert pianist."

"That is the silliest thing I ever heard," Thalia blurted.

"She didn't think it was silly," Maximilian pointed out. "She taught me every superstition she knew and taught me how to look for signs."

"That hasn't helped you much, has it?" Thalia kept her voice gentle. "You've been so busy looking for superstitious signs that you may have missed true signs you could have read from real people."

Maximilian flinched. Was she telling him that if he had paid closer attention, he would have seen her true feelings for him and not listened to Norma?

"Is that true, Maximilian?" Dorcas asked. "Do you really believe in those things? Norma never mentioned it."

"I'm not surprised. Norma was very attentive to me during our courtship, but once we were married, I could have worn a powdered wig and tights, and she wouldn't have noticed." He shrugged. "It seemed as though since she'd won me, she didn't care after that."

Thalia paled.

Dorcas snapped back as though she had been walloped. "Is that so?"

He hadn't meant for his confession to upset the older lady. "I'm sorry, Dorcas. Please don't mind me. I'm not myself. I know how much you loved Norma."

"Things would have improved once children arrived," Dorcas said decidedly.

"Maybe, except she didn't want any. She told me she was too busy enjoying herself to be tied down to a brat."

Dorcas gasped. "I don't believe it!"

"I have no reason to lie. I'm sorry if I upset you with these truths, but I only have revealed them to you. . .her dear relative."

"Aunt Dorcas knows Norma wasn't perfect," Thalia said. "Don't you, Aunt Dorcas?"

"Of course," she answered with an unconvincing tone. "But we're talking about superstitions now. I don't put stock in those. I listen to God's leading."

"I try to," Maximilian answered, "but He's not always clear. I can't see God, but I can see my rabbit's foot. It's clear to me that I can avoid spilling pepper and crossing paths with black cats. I can pick up that penny rather than passing it by."

"Do you realize how ridiculous that is?" Dorcas managed to reprimand him without a tone of condemnation. She leaned over and placed a maternal hand on his knee. "If you ask God to release you from the bondage of superstition, you'll be able to hear Him."

"Wise words, Aunt Dorcas." Thalia looked thoughtful.

"I do pray to God, but I honor Mother's memory by following what she taught me."

"Your mother was no fool, but superstition was not her friend. And it's not yours. I think you want to honor her, but you can do so in other ways," Dorcas suggested.

Maximilian decided not to answer. But he resolved to give what Dorcas said some thought.

Chapter 9

Thalia couldn't digest everything Maximilian had said during the ride to Aurora. So Norma really never cared about him. She knew her cousin had been vain, but she never considered she would give up the blessings and joys of motherhood for parties. Poor Maximilian. How brokenhearted he must have been.

Soon they reached the outskirts of Aurora, and the sled pulled up to the gate of the Newbolt home. Maximilian's eyes held a longing light. She could imagine how touched he must be to return home. Surely during the darkest hours of his illness, he may have pondered never seeing his childhood home again.

"The smoke really is thick today," Dorcas noted. "Everybody must have their fireplaces going trying to keep warm."

"I don't think that's it." Maximilian's happy expression soon turned to one of fear. "What's that?"

Thalia saw smoke and flames streaming from what remained of the house. "Oh, no!"

"At least the Aurora fire department is here!" Maximilian exclaimed.

As soon as the sled stopped in front of the house, the passengers jumped out and ran to the flaming structure. Maximilian's valet, maid, and a young girl Thalia assumed to be the new cook, watched as the firemen did everything they could to stop the destruction. Thalia wished there was something she could do. Maximilian stood as still as a statue. No doubt he felt helpless watching every memory of his life destroyed by vicious flames.

A woman who appeared to be in her thirties, with three young children in tow, approached. "I'm so sorry. You can stay with us as long as you need to."

"Thank you, Mrs. Daily." Maximilian introduced his neighbor to the Blooms.

"That's okay. He can come back home with us," Thalia told her. When he smiled at her answer, she knew he needed the comfort of those who really loved him and was glad she had made the offer.

After the crowd dissipated amid many other offers of kindness and shelter, the Blooms and Maximilian were left standing in front of the destruction.

Thalia looked at the rubble and noticed a singed oil portrait of Norma. "Maybe if we go through this mess, we can find a few things that were spared."

Maximilian shook his head. "I'll go through everything on my own time. But I don't care about things. I kept most of my money in the bank, so I'll be okay. And the Studebaker is at your house, for all the good it did me today. The main thing is the people. All my staff is well, and that's what matters. Maybe they can tell me how this happened."

"I think I'd rather go back to the sleigh where I can sit, if it's all the same to you," Aunt Dorcas said.

Thalia didn't want to leave. "Do you mind if I go with you to talk to the staff? Maybe you could use the support."

Maximilian nodded. They didn't have to approach them. The valet and a pretty maid walked toward them. Thalia knew them as Addison and Minnie.

Addison spoke first. "I'm sorry, sir. This is unforgivable. I don't know what happened except it was near breakfast time, and the fire started in the kitchen. I have no choice but to think Cookie started it. That girl has got to go, Mr. Newbolt. She's nothing but trouble."

The young girl ran up to them. "I heard that. I did not start that fire. I know you want to think I did since I'm new and I'm not a very good cook yet, but I had nothing to do with it. I promise."

"How dare you," the valet snapped.

Cookie flinched and blushed but stood her ground. "The fire started in the parlor, where Minnie was dusting."

"Not true," Addison insisted.

"Yes, it is," Cookie protested. "Oh, I know no one will believe me." Tears fell from her eyes, though she covered them with her hands. Her body shook.

Thalia couldn't help but feel compassion for the girl. She wrapped a maternal arm around the bony shoulders, calming her. "I believe you." To emphasize the point, she looked up at Maximilian with a strong countenance.

"I believe you, too."

The frightened girl looked up at her employer. "You—you do?" Her voice trembled.

"Yes." Maximilian turned a sharp expression to Addison. "What is the meaning of trying to make me think Cookie started the fire?"

Minnie flushed red. "He—he was protectin' me."

Addison's eyes narrowed. "Stop it, Minnie."

"No, I'm going to tell him. I wouldn't feel right if I didn't. I dropped a lit lantern and it broke. Fuel spilled on a stack of papers on your desk, and the fire caught on. There was nothin' I could do but get out of there. I don't have the money to replace what I damaged, and I'm sorry." She looked at the ground. "I know I'm dismissed. I'll be leavin' now."

Maximilian held up his hand to stop her. "No, I am not dismissing you, Minnie, because you told me the truth. Granted, I don't have a house right now for you to dust, but as soon as I get my life back in order, you can come back."

Addison spoke. "Thank you, sir."

Maximilian's countenance didn't seem benevolent when he turned to his valet. "Addison, you're dismissed."

"What?"

"I know you're sweet on Minnie, but trying to blame the cook for something she didn't do was wrong. I can't trust you. Don't look to me for future employment or ask me for a reference. Good-bye."

Thalia wasn't surprised when Addison said nothing but glared and stomped away. Minnie didn't speak but ran after Addison.

"So—so I can stay?" Cookie's voice sounded weak with happiness.

"Yes, you can stay. I'll pay your wages while you wait to come back into my employ."

"Oh, thank you, sir. I don't deserve such generosity. I promise to practice making lots of dishes while I wait to come back."

He smiled. "That's a good idea."

"Promise not to put a trace of rhubarb in anything," Thalia cautioned. "Mr. Newbolt is deathly allergic to rhubarb, and not the first stalk of it should be in his house."

"Yes, ma'am."

Maximilian smiled. "Now run along home, Cookie. I don't want you to get sick out here in this cold."

She nodded and complied.

Thalia gave him a sardonic smile. "I hope you won't be sorry about these decisions you just made in your heightened state of emotion."

"No, I won't."

"I think you did the right thing."

He pulled the rabbit's foot out of his pocket. "And now I'm going to do something else you'll think is the right thing."

He tossed the rabbit's foot on top of Norma's half-burned portrait. "This never did me any good. I can see that now." He looked heavenward. "From now on, it's just you and me, Lord."

Chapter 10

A week later, Thalia sat at the baby grand piano in the music room and stared at the sheet music for an Irish ballad enjoying newfound popularity, "Danny Boy." Her plan had been to learn it by that evening, but her mind betrayed her, forcing her to focus on Maximilian.

The past few days, she had watched him seek the Lord with an eagerness she hadn't witnessed from any other Christian in a long time. Throwing the rabbit's foot on the burned rubble had only been a start. She could see him embracing the faith of his childhood, returning to familiar Bible passages and talking with her about their significance. And while she didn't see him pray except to bless each meal, she sensed his prayer life had increased. Truly the fire had set Maximilian free from the bondage of his past so that he could walk with the Lord in the future.

Such happy thoughts encouraged her to play.

"That sounds pretty good."

She jumped and swiveled on the piano bench. "Maximilian, what are you doing sneaking up on me? I didn't think you'd be back from Aurora already."

"I didn't mean to scare you." He grinned. "I was called by the siren song from your beautiful piano."

"You are so silly." In spite of her teasing assessment, he looked anything but silly. With his straight, tall bearing, warm brown eyes, and comely face she could stare into every day for the rest of her life, he made her wish she were a sculptor so she could preserve an image of him forever. The picture in her mind would have to suffice.

She rose from the bench. "Come into the parlor. I'll ask Eliza to bring tea. I want to catch up on how your week went."

"Very well, though I missed you. I finished my Christmas shopping. There are now a few gifts for you and Dorcas under the tree."

"You didn't have to do that, with everything you've gone through. You'll find a gift or two from us as well, though," she noted. "So were you able to save anything from the fire?"

"Yes, a few things."

"Good. I'm glad you will have some memories to hold on to."

Moments later, they sat in the parlor and waited for tea to be served. "So have you thought about rebuilding the house?" Thalia asked.

"I haven't decided yet."

"Oh." She became conscious of her heartbeat. He had mentioned going to California. Was he planning to leave Aurora after all?

"A lot of my decision depends on you."

"On me?"

"You told me to start looking at people for signs instead of trusting in superstition. That was good advice. It's been freeing. Similar to losing almost everything in a fire." His mouth twisted into a rueful line.

Thalia thought about his words. "Perhaps losing everything did offer you a way to begin fresh."

"I'll say. I've been watching you as I recovered."

"Oh, you have, have you?" She wasn't sure what to think.

"I hope I'm not too weak at reading people now that I've thrown away my talismans. I—I'm hoping you've changed your mind about me."

"Changed my mind?" She paused. "Well, I'm glad you're looking toward the Lord now, of course. But other than that, I don't have any idea what you mean."

"Don't be coy. You know why I didn't choose you over Norma all those years ago." He seemed more hurt than angry.

Shock bolted through her. She leaned closer. "Uh, no, I don't."

His eyes widened. "Why, Norma told me the truth about you—that you didn't love me."

Taken aback, Thalia gasped. Her head spun. How could her cousin tell such a lie? Even worse, how could Maximilian believe it? "When did she tell you that?"

"Why—I—I—I don't know. Sometime before I decided to start courting her in earnest. Does it really matter when?"

"I knew she wanted you, but I didn't think she'd resort to lies." Thalia didn't know whether to laugh or cry.

"Lies? You mean you did love me?"

"Couldn't you tell?"

"I guess I should have. But Norma seemed so sure of herself. And you were so reserved and so much closer to God than I ever was. I am hoping I can follow your example and become closer to God, too."

"I know." The thought filled her with joy.

At that moment, Eliza brought in tea. The maid couldn't take her gaze from them, but Thalia didn't want to satisfy her curiosity. The couple remained silent until she exited.

Sweet tea, with its spicy aroma, would have been appealing any other time, but Maximilian and Thalia were too preoccupied to enjoy it.

He took her hands in his. Their warmth sent a tingle through her. "I don't want to talk about the past. I want to talk about the future. Do you still love me?"

Her voice came out as a whisper. "Yes."

"And I love you now more than ever. You have changed my life for the better."

"With God's help. I do nothing good alone."

"I know how important your aunt is to you. You want to stay here in Colorado, near her."

"Yes." She hoped her answer wouldn't ruin her chances with him, but she had to speak the truth.

"If that is what you want, that's what I want. I would love to build a new house for you, in any style you like, if you would live with me in Aurora."

The thought left her dizzy. "A one-room cottage would be enough, if I was with you." She paused. "But Aunt Dorcas. . ."

"I spoke with her. She knows about this, and in light of how dramatically my attitude toward God has changed, plus everything we confessed to one another on the way to Aurora that day, she has given her approval."

"I might have been surprised by that only a few weeks ago, but no longer. I know she really does want me to be happy."

Nodding, he reached into his suit pocket and took out a small box. "In the midst of all that rubble, I found a link to the past that I do want to remember. Surely the preservation of this treasure is a Christmas miracle. This is a way that I can honor my mother. Here." He handed her the box.

She opened it to discover a gold-filigreed ring with a large marquis-shaped diamond flanked by two emerald baguettes. "Oh, I've never seen a ring so beautiful!"

"I know Mother would want you to have it. Will you wear it as a token of our engagement?"

"Our—our engagement?" She wondered at how such words fell from her lips. But saying them felt fantastic beyond belief.

With a gentle motion, he took the ring out of the box and placed it on the third finger of her left hand. "There. It fits perfectly."

"It's gorgeous."

"Not as gorgeous as you. So you'll wear it?"

"I'll never take it off. Ever!"

His lips moved toward hers, and she looked into his eyes. As they kissed, everything faded into oblivion. Everything except the fires of love.

TAMELA HANCOCK MURRAY

Tamela lives in Virginia with her real-life hero and their two daughters. Tamela and her heroic husband learned the game of Flinch from a missionary, Matilda Alexander, and passed on a love for this game to their family. When not writing or playing Flinch, she enjoys time with family and friends. Prayer is a vital part of this story and also of Tamela's life. Find out more at: www.tamelahancockmurray.com.

The Best

Medicine

by Lena Nelson Dooley

Dedication

This book is dedicated to my writing teammates: Tamela Hancock Murray, Susan Page Davis, and Darlene Franklin. Working together on this collection has been a lot of fun.

Thank you, Rebecca Germany, for giving us this chance.

Very special thanks to Dr. Richard Mabry, a friend in Dallas. Richard owns antique medical books and was able to give me authentic practices from the time period as well as symptoms. This is the second book he's helped me with. Any errors are mine and not Richard's.

And as always, I dedicate this book to my wonderful husband, James. When I married you almost forty-four years ago, I loved you with all my heart. You brightened my life with your love. Through all we've experienced, the good and the bad, that love has grown stronger and deeper and provided a beacon in this topsy-turvy world for our daughters, sons-in-law, granddaughters, grandsons, one granddaughter-in-law, and now one great-grandson. Welcome to the family, Sebastian Alexander Van Zant.

A merry heart doeth good like a medicine:
but a broken spirit drieth the bones.
PROVERBS 17:22

Chapter 1

December 1913

Metallic tapping awakened Rose Fletcher. She stretched then got out of bed, but she couldn't identify exactly what startled her. Of course not. She wasn't in her family's home in Breckenridge, or even at the house out on their ranch. Another soft clang came from the steam radiator. She hoped these knocking sounds wouldn't keep her awake after she went to bed tonight.

Rose picked up the dainty timepiece her father had ordered from France for her last birthday. She should have heard it ticking, but no sound emanated from the jewel-studded brooch. As she began to turn the stem, it felt loose. The instrument had completely run down because she had forgotten to wind it. No way to tell exactly how long she'd been asleep.

Glancing at the window to estimate how late in the day it was, Rose noticed snowflakes dancing in the dwindling winter daylight, casting a white haze over everything outside. She rushed through her ablutions and donned the new emerald green dress she'd had made just for this party. The dressmaker in Breckenridge had copied the style from *Harper's Bazaar*. The magazine kept Rose aware of what was going on in fashion even when it was *Harper's Bazar*. After Randolph Hearst bought the magazine from the Harpers and changed the spelling, the coverage improved. This lovely dress was the perfect example of how they presented up-to-date fashions. She slid her hand down the other sleeve, enjoying the soft feel of the lightweight wool.

Rose tilted the pier glass up to make sure her new coiffure was not mussed. Quite a departure from the Gibson-girl pouf she had worn all through finishing school. She felt her hair to make sure the figure-eight chignon was secure. Then she tilted the glass down so she could see all the way to the hem of the dress. Tiers on the skirt gave it definition without adding width. She turned her back and glanced over her shoulder. The gown fit like a soft kidskin glove and made her feel like a princess.

When Rose arrived downstairs, Thalia and her aunt Dorcas once again made her feel welcome. Why hadn't she made more opportunities to spend time in the city with her friends?

"Dr. Stanton has arrive," the maid announced.

He must be new. Rose couldn't remember a doctor by that name being in Denver. When Thalia had taken ill at school, she'd lamented the fact that Dr. Wetherby wasn't there to take care of her. He'd looked after her family since before she was born, and she trusted his wisdom.

Rose couldn't keep her eyes away from the stranger. He doffed his hat, took off his muffler, and handed them to the waiting servant, leaning toward the young maid and speaking softly to her before he turned toward the parlor. Surprise blossomed within Rose's chest as she beheld the handsome man. Tall with broad, muscular shoulders, he looked as if he performed hard physical labor instead of the less strenuous profession of caring for the sick.

While she stood spellbound, the man pushed at unruly dark curls, trying to make them lie down. The effort was in vain, for one drooped across his broad brow like an errant child. Dr. Stanton shrugged out of his coat and handed it to the maid before striding toward their hostess.

Rose took a deep breath and slowly let it out, more to calm herself than for the needed air. Why hadn't Thalia told her about the arrival of this young doctor in Denver? Surely she could have mentioned it in one of her letters.

Thalia glanced up, and her eyes twinkled. "Rose, I want to introduce you to the doctor who has joined old Dr. Wetherby in his practice."

The man turned intense gray eyes toward her. For a moment, they seemed familiar, but nothing else about the man did. Perhaps she had met someone who shared the same kind of serious expression. He never took his gaze from her, making her want to squirm. She pressed her hand over the bottom of the V-neckline of her dress. Hopefully, he didn't think it too daring.

Thalia slipped an arm around her waist. "Rose is one of my dearest friends."

Rose smiled at the tall man. She held out her hand for him to shake, but instead he lifted it and barely pressed his lips against the back of her fingers.

For a moment, she stared into his eyes. When his hand encountered hers, heat from his body infused the connection and began a slow journey up her arm. At the same time, a blush rushed up her neck and into her cheeks, causing them to burn. She wished she carried a fan. So much for looking poised.

After he raised his head, he continued to hold her hand captive. "I'm charmed by your presence." The tone of his words was almost familiar.

"Nice to make your acquaintance" was all she could think of to say after his greeting.

A twinkle lit his eyes, and once again she felt as if she should know this man, but no real remembrance came to mind.

Thomas held Rose's hand a little longer than decorum allowed from a stranger, but he hoped she would recognize him. It had been years since he left her father's ranch to go to Harvard Medical School. Back then, Rose had turned longing eyes toward him, almost as if she didn't want him to go.

After a blush befitting her name suffused her cheeks, she tugged her hand from his. He raised one eyebrow, gave her a nod, and waited for her response. At any moment, she'd realize who he was.

"Rose!" The newest arrival rushed toward her, and the young women threw their arms around each other and started talking at the same time—in exclamations.

Thomas moved away but kept his attention on Rose, studying all the ways she had changed. A sophisticated hairstyle in dark auburn replaced her carrot-colored braids. The waves framing her face ended at the nape of her neck with a soft bun like one of the nurses at the hospital wore below her cap. He'd heard her tell one of the other nurses that it was the latest style from France. A spark of fire burned on the crests of those dark red waves. He wanted to reach out and touch one to feel its warmth. Quickly, he shoved both hands into the pockets of his slacks.

Even her freckles had faded. He'd heard her father call them her pennies from heaven that were scattered across her cheeks and forehead when she was younger. Now her skin looked translucent, like creamy porcelain. When he'd worked on her father's ranch, the girl had idolized him. She made his life miserable. The young hoyden who followed him around the ranch, riding her horse with reckless abandon, was gone. Little Rose had grown up while he had been away, and he wanted to get to know her as a woman.

The other young woman turned to take off her coat, and Rose finally noticed that he still stood close by.

"How long have you known our hostess?" He hoped his question would keep her near him until she realized who he was.

"Thalia and I were roommates in boarding school." Rose's smile lit her face like the electric lights that had come into general use in many areas of the country.

"Where did you go to boarding school?" Thomas didn't want this conversation to end too soon.

"Outside New York City." Rose glanced around the room as if looking for someone else.

What would it take to keep her attention on him? "I returned to Colorado from back East a few months ago. I attended Harvard Medical School."

That caught her attention. "You did? I know someone who is going to—"

"Thomas." Thalia's voice interrupted as she stopped beside them. "I have someone else I want you to meet. Can you come over here, please?"

At the first sound, he'd looked at their hostess. When he turned back to Rose, her brow puckered. "Thomas?" The word sounded almost strangled.

"Yes, Rose. Thomas Stanton."

A myriad of expressions that he couldn't decipher raced across her face.

"Are you coming, Thomas?" Thalia's insistence urged him along with her hand on his arm. "Rose, please excuse us."

He leaned toward Rose. "I need to go now, but we will continue this conversation later."

While Thalia took Thomas from group to group, introducing him to the other guests, a special awareness of Rose went with him. When she finally started a conversation with another young woman, he was able to concentrate more on the people he met.

Rose watched Thomas walk away with Thalia. How could she not have recognized him? Evidently her heart did even though her mind hadn't. Those gray eyes and that voice, though the timbre had deepened with maturity. Her heart fluttered as butterfly wings danced in her stomach, making her breathless. What was wrong with her? This was just Thomas. She'd fancied herself in love with him when she was in pigtails, but she never really expected to see him again after he left for medical school. He hadn't even returned when his father died. She had been sure the lure of the big cities back East held him there.

They hadn't held her, either. She'd enjoyed finishing school, but the Rocky Mountains called to her heart, and she'd gladly returned to Breckenridge.

"Rose!" Natalie Daire was taking off her long coat and gloves as she hurried toward her. "I've been anxious to see you."

And she was glad to see Natalie. Now all four of the girls who had been so close at school were at the party.

"Daring Natalie, what's this I hear about you having one of those Cadillacs?" Rose's question brought a sparkle to Natalie's eyes. Her nature fit her last name so well.

"You'll have to go for a ride with me while you're in Denver." Natalie laid her coat across one arm. "I wore my driving duster and hat. There isn't any dust this evening, but it helped keep the snow off my new dress and out of my hair."

"Do you really like driving that thing?" Rose had a hard time keeping her attention on Natalie. Her gaze kept returning to the tall, handsome man across the room.

"So have you met our new Doctor Stanton?" Evidently Natalie noticed where Rose's gaze wandered.

Rose smiled at her friend. "Actually, I've known Thomas for

years. His father was the foreman on my father's ranch. Thomas worked there, too, before he went to medical school."

A knowing smile crept across Natalie's face. "So that adds to his fascination, doesn't it?"

For the second time tonight, Rose felt a blush stain her cheeks. "I wouldn't say I find him fascinating. I just didn't expect to see him after all this time." In her heart, she knew she was more interested in him than what she professed to her friend.

Chapter 2

How was Thomas ever going to keep all these new people straight? His inability to remember names had plagued him all his life, and it wasn't a desirable trait in a doctor. Patients felt more comfortable with a physician who called them by name every time he met them, in the office or out in public.

No matter where he was in the house, somehow he sensed Rose's movements as she went from group to group of her friends, always staying on the opposite side of the room. A fact that wasn't lost on him. When he meandered toward the fireplace, she drifted through the archway into the dining room where the table stood laden with so many good things to eat that everyone here would probably gain a pound or two.

He, as graciously as possible, ended his conversation with those near him and headed toward the punch bowl on the sideboard near the food. By the time he arrived, Rose stood at the bottom of the staircase, talking to three other young women of similar age. After filling his cup once more with the delicious beverage, he headed toward the cluster of giggling femininity. Before he took two steps out of the dining room, the group broke apart and scattered toward other people in the parlor.

Rose began talking to a tall, thin man. If Thomas remembered correctly, his name was Newbolt. . .Maximilian Newbolt, to be exact. And if he had all the details right, the man was a young widower with no children. Could Rose be interested in him? Maybe he should mosey over and check out the situation.

The two were deep in conversation as he approached. He didn't think they noticed him until Maximilian smiled toward him.

"Rose, have you met Dr. Stanton?"

When Newbolt turned his gaze back toward her, did Thomas see a hint of proprietorship in his face? After a moment, Thomas was sure he only imagined the extra connection.

She swiveled and glanced toward Thomas. "Yes, Maximilian, I've known the doctor for a long time."

That seemed to surprise the man. "I thought he was new to Colorado."

"No." Thomas moved halfway between the other two. "I actually lived here before I went to medical school."

"Here in Denver?" Creases between Maximilian's eyebrows signaled his puzzlement. "Should I have known you?"

"No, to both questions. I lived near Breckenridge." Thomas hadn't felt this gauche since he was in his teens. He stuffed his hands in his pockets, because he couldn't think of anything else to do with them. "My father was the foreman on the Fletcher ranch."

A slow smile spread across Newbolt's face. "No wonder Rose knows you."

She peered at a young woman on the other side of the room. "Excuse me, but I need to ask Patricia something."

The object of Thomas's sensory attention turned and walked away. His gaze followed her until he heard a deep chuckle.

"So that's how it is." The twinkle in Newbolt's eyes didn't bode well for Thomas's peace of mind.

Thomas glared at the other man. "I don't know what you mean." He knew he would be considered rude, but this was the last time Rose would get away from him. "Excuse me." They needed to finish their previous conversation.

Rose had worked hard to stay as far away from Thomas as possible. She didn't really want to converse with him until her mind was settled. This wasn't the boy she'd longed for as a girl in her teens. This man was even more imposing, and his effect on her was hard to understand.

She'd matured and learned how to be gracious, but all her graces fled when he came near. Disturbing, because deep in her heart of hearts, she knew there could never be any kind of romantic relationship between them—no matter how much she wished otherwise.

A scene from her childhood returned to her thoughts. She had finished a thrilling ride then cooled down her mare. Next she lovingly brushed her best friend's hide, using just the right amount of pressure to give the chestnut the most pleasure.

Thomas came through the barn door, leading his mount. "How you doing, squirt?"

How Rose hated for him to call her that. "I'm taking care of my horse." She patted the mare's flank before moving to the other side with her brush. "I think horses are some of God's greatest creations, don't you?"

A harsh laugh burst from the young man. "God? You don't believe all that stuff, do you?" Derision dripped from every word. His attitude had caused the first bit of doubt about him to enter Rose's heart.

Over the next few months, she had tried to bring up God's goodness, but only a few times. His response remained much the same. The man was not a Christian, and he didn't sound as if he would ever change his mind.

Those memories warred with the strong attraction she felt toward the mature man across the room. His reactions to her attempts to talk to him about God had made her mad when she was younger. Now his lack of interest in the Lord grieved her heart.

How could they ever really be friends, much less anything more?

Rose stood beside the heavy green draperies and gazed almost unseeing at the snow filling the scene outside. She'd always loved winter when she was home. Getting snowed in didn't have to be a problem in the house in Breckenridge, or even the log one on the ranch. Father and mother kept both stocked with games and books, plenty of things to do indoors during the extended bad weather.

No matter how much she tried to turn her thoughts to other things, they winged back toward Thomas Stanton. She didn't remember ever hearing his last name when she was growing up. Dad always called his foreman Farley and the son Thomas. No wonder she didn't recognize his name when she first heard it.

"Rose?"

Her whispered name on his lips so close to her ear made her gasp for breath. How had he come so near without her hearing him? She turned slightly. "Yes?"

Thomas moved around until she could see his face. "I'd like to continue our conversation. You didn't recognize me when I arrived, did you?"

She glanced down at her clasped hands. "Not at first."

"I immediately knew who you were." His voice carried a husky tone, entirely too intimate. "But you were no longer the boss's young daughter. I want to get to know the woman standing before me."

The heat returned to her cheeks, and she glanced back toward the window. "I'm not sure that's a good idea." Her words trailed away.

This was not the reaction Thomas expected. He conjured up the memory of her beseeching eyes following his departure when he left for Cambridge, Massachusetts. Why wouldn't she want to get to know him better now?

Walking in a resolute manner, she opened the door and floated out onto the porch.

He followed before she could shut the door behind her. "Have I upset you?"

She crossed her arms and whirled to face him. "Seeing you again after all this time has somewhat unbalanced my emotions. I'm trying to calm myself and cool off."

He smiled to himself. *So she felt something, too.*

The frigid wind cut through his suit. Surely her dress, as pretty as it was, wouldn't keep the air from chilling her. "You should be cool now."

"You're right. Maybe I should return to the house." She started to go around him.

He moved one step over to keep her in front of him. "Here, take my coat. We need to finish this subject." After slipping off the garment, he snuggled it around her shoulders.

Rose clutched the lapels and pulled them together. "Thank you. That feels better. But aren't you cold?"

"I'll live." Thomas leaned toward her. "Why are you shying away from me?"

"Father will want to know you're back in Colorado." The wind blew a wave of auburn hair across her forehead, and Rose brushed it away.

She hadn't answered his question. He'd have to practice patience to give her time to feel comfortable with him again.

Thomas placed his arms loosely around her and leaned his chin on the top of her head. "This should help keep you warm." He wanted to enjoy holding her in his arms for as long as he could, even if it wasn't a romantic tryst. "I'll have to go to Breckenridge to see him soon."

She pulled away, and he wondered if he'd made her feel uncomfortable. That hadn't been his intention.

Rose turned toward the snow that had grown so thick Thomas couldn't even see the iron fence at the edge of the front yard. "Thomas, I'm worried about the weather. We could end up being snowbound."

He took her hand and led her back through the door into the heated house where she relinquished his suit jacket. "Let's warm up by the fireplace. Then we'll find Thalia and share our concerns with her."

How easily Thomas had moved beyond her defenses. Rose followed him toward the blazing logs. For those few moments when Thomas sheltered her from the harsh wind, she'd felt protected. . .and even almost cherished. But that could never be.

After he stopped on one side of the fireplace, she took up a position as far from him as she could, while still taking advantage of the warmth. Her fingertips felt like icicles. She held her hands toward the flames and kept her attention on the dancing colors. She'd always been fascinated by the way fire moved and glowed.

"There you are, Rose." Thalia joined them. She looked at Thomas standing nearby. "I wondered where the two of you had gone. Catching up on old times?"

Rose glanced at her friend then back at her hands, which tingled as the warmth infused them. How could she answer without letting Thalia know how much his presence rattled her?

"Trying to." His strong baritone held a hint of laughter. "We seem to be always talking to other people."

"Didn't I see you come in from outside?" Thalia placed her hand on Rose's arm. "Weren't you cold?"

Rose nodded. "That's why we're warming up now." She peered into Thalia's eyes. "Actually, we're concerned about the weather. Thomas and I spoke about it while we were on the porch. People might have trouble getting home tonight."

"Oh pooh, Aunt Dorcas said it's just a Denver winter storm. We always have snow." Thalia's bright smile could light up a whole room. "Besides, you don't have to worry about that, since you're staying overnight."

Rose moved back from the heat, which was becoming overwhelming. "It could be snowing even more up in the mountains. What if it covers the railroad tracks?"

Thalia looked up at Thomas. "Has she always been such a worrier? I know she did a lot when we were in school."

He chuckled. "I don't remember that about her. Maybe it came later."

They were talking about Rose as if she weren't standing there. Although she didn't know what to say right now, their conversation made her feel uncomfortable. She might as well go get something hot to drink.

Thomas watched Rose glide across the floor, wishing she would come back so they could finish their conversation.

"Don't worry." Thalia's voice pulled his attention back to

her. "I think the storm will be over before morning."

"Dr. Stanton!" A girl named Nanette hurried toward them. "We need your help. Maximilian is having a problem breathing!"

Thomas followed her as they hurried to the library. Maximilian's breathing was even. He didn't seem to be in imminent danger, but his skin had red splotches all over. Deciding that a better plan of action would be to have all his implements and medications with him when he examined the sick patient, Thomas wanted to get his satchel first.

"Please try to keep him quiet. I'll be with you in a moment after I retrieve my medical bag from my buggy." Thomas hurried from the library.

He shrugged into his overcoat and slapped on his hat, then slung his scarf around his neck before going out into the storm to retrieve the medical equipage from his buggy. Thankfully his vehicle was parked in the carriage house.

Why hadn't he brought his medical bag in with him? Of course, he hadn't really expected to need it, but he never left home without the black leather satchel. Much simpler to bring it in with him and leave it with his coat, hat, and scarf. A lesson learned.

At Nanette's words, Rose forgot she was peeved at Thalia and Thomas. She turned back before she reached the hot chocolate and watched people scurrying around. Thomas hurried outside, and others flocked to see what was happening in the library. Why did people always want to gawk at someone who was in distress?

She knew something better to do. Not wanting to kneel in her party dress, she dropped onto an upholstered wingback chair near the fireplace. After folding her hands in her lap, she closed her eyes and began to pray silently.

Her prayers were interrupted when Thomas returned from outside. The amount of snow that had accumulated on him the brief time he was gone shocked her. She peered outside but could see nothing but white. Her father called this a whiteout. Snow so thick it was almost impenetrable. How ever did Thomas find his way back to the house? For a moment, her heart almost stopped beating when she thought about him lost in the snowstorm. No matter how much she told herself that she couldn't have feelings for the man, her heart didn't listen.

When he returned to the house, he realized that even though he and Rose stood on the porch only a few moments ago, that wouldn't be possible now. Icy wind swirled the flakes, flinging them against the windows and door with a fury. He couldn't get back into the house without bringing windy swirls with him.

Thomas opened the door and entered as quickly as possible, slamming it behind him. He glanced around and found everyone looking at him while he brushed the accumulated snow from his hat and overcoat. "The storm doesn't seem to be letting up."

Varying reactions answered his pronouncement. A few of the guests talked about leaving before the conditions worsened. Thomas didn't agree that was a good plan, because the weather already looked dangerous, but he couldn't think about that right now. He needed to get to his patient. They'd have to make their own decisions without his input.

A rumbling murmur that started while partygoers watched Thomas remove his outer garments grew to a dull roar. Everyone was talking at once. Many said they wanted to try to get home.

"I don't think that's a very good idea." Rose tried to make herself heard above the others, but no one paid any attention.

Soon most of those at the party were donning their coats, gloves, hats, and scarves and setting out through the dense storm. Now Rose had something else to pray about.

Evidently, everyone except Thomas, Maximilian, Josiah, and herself had started home. Josiah stood in front of the fireplace to chase away the chill caused by the door being opened so many times. Rose stayed where she sat and once again prayed for Maximilian. . .and those who ventured outside.

Thomas hurried down the hallway to the library where Newbolt sat on a sofa in front of the fireplace. Other people gathered around him.

"Move aside everyone, please. I need to see the patient."

Red splotches scattered across Newbolt's face and neck—and even on his hands.

Thomas set his bag on the table at the end of the sofa and pulled his frigid stethoscope from the interior. The instrument felt much too cold to touch anyone with, so he started rubbing it with his hands. He was glad to see that everyone had left the room. "Can you breathe okay?"

Newbolt shook his head.

"Has anything like this ever happened before?"

Newbolt squinted his eyes and stared at the mantel. Thomas could tell he was thinking, maybe trying to remember.

"Has there been another time?" Thomas needed to know before he proceeded.

The other man sighed. "Fruit. . .rhubarb."

"With the rash and difficulty breathing, I thought this might be an allergic reaction to something. Is your throat closing up?" Thomas certainly hoped not. That could be really serious.

Maximilian shook his head. "Throat's sore and a little tight."

"We can take care of that." Thomas hoped he could keep the patient calm. That often helped in situations like this. "Have you eaten rhubarb today? I don't remember seeing any on the table."

Newbolt shook his head.

The culprit might be something else. Thomas needed more information. "How many times has this happened to you in the past? Do you recall? You don't have to speak, just hold up your fingers to indicate the number."

Newbolt once again stared toward the fireplace while he pondered the question. Finally, he held up one finger.

The door opened, and Miss Dorcas Bloom entered. "Can I get you anything, Dr. Stanton?"

Thomas looked at her. "Not right now, but you could wait a minute while I question Mr. Newbolt."

She glided through the door and gently closed it behind her.

"Maximilian, when did you first notice your symptoms?" Thomas studied the man's face as he prepared to answer. Sometimes he learned as much from a patient's expression as he did from the words he spoke.

Newbolt shook his head slightly as if trying to remember. "About. . .fifteen. . .or twenty minutes ago. . .itch in my throat. . . nose started running." He reached into his pocket, pulled out a rumpled handkerchief, and blew his nose.

Finally the chest piece of the stethoscope felt warm enough to use. Thomas slid it inside his patient's jacket and pressed it against his shirt. "When did you first notice the rash?"

"A few minutes later." A croupy cough punctuated the answer, followed by a gasp that ended in a wheeze.

Thomas didn't like the way the man's lungs sounded, and his throat might be closing up. "Does your throat feel full?"

This time Newbolt nodded instead of answering.

"We need to figure out if you had rhubarb." Thomas put the stethoscope into his jacket pocket. "If not, we have to find out what else you're allergic to."

He called in Dorcas, who appeared with Thalia.

"Ladies, was there any rhubarb in anything you served tonight?"

Thalia blanched. "Yes. Why?"

"From the best I can tell, Mr. Newbolt is allergic to rhubarb, and he has had a reaction."

"Oh, no!" Their hostess gasped. "Maximilian, did you eat one of the tarts with red filling?"

"Yes. . .strawberry, Edith said. Delicious. I had. . .another."

"It's all my fault." This time she wailed. "That was a new recipe that called for strawberry and rhubarb preserves. Oh, what have I done?"

Thomas turned toward their hostess. "We need to get him into bed. Could we move him to a guest room?"

"Of course, we have several bedrooms. Actually, one is on the first floor. It would be easier to put him there. I'll have Eliza start the fire." Dorcas moved toward the door.

"After he's in bed, we need to make a tent out of a sheet and fill it with steam. You do have a teakettle on the stove, don't you?" He helped Newbolt to stand.

"Yes, I can get whatever you want." Dorcas clasped her hands as if trying to keep them still. "Perhaps you could take Max down the hall and help him get into bed. There's an old nightshirt of my brother's in the top drawer of the bureau."

"I'll do that, and Miss Bloom, please bring a glass of water and a spoon when you return."

The bedroom was easy to find, and very soon Thomas helped Newbolt get undressed and slip between the sheets on the bed. When he was settled, Thomas checked his pulse rate. The rapid staccato didn't bode well. Thomas knew this night was going to be a long one. He'd heard of people dying from a severe allergic reaction, but that wouldn't happen to Newbolt. At least, Thomas would pour every effort into preventing such an outcome.

Chapter 3

Whena the door opened, Thomas glanced up, surprised. Miss Bloom shouldn't be back so soon.

"Is Maximilian going to be all right?" Thalia's brows knitted in concern.

Thomas quickly stood. "Oh, it's you, Thalia. I thought you were your aunt returning with the things I requested. Yes, I believe Maximilian will be all right." *At least I hope so.*

Thalia peered at Newbolt's still form. "Is there any way I can help?"

"I've been thinking about the best way to tent him for the steam." Thomas studied the headboard of the bed. "Maybe you could get us a sheet. And bring a couple of towels and a bowl. Miss Bloom is bringing the teakettle and a glass of water."

"I think there's an extra sheet in the bureau." Thalia opened one of the drawers.

Thomas once again checked his patient's blood pressure, pulse, and respirations. No change. At least the man was resting right now. He'd even slipped into slumber.

Thalia started toward the door then stopped. "I wonder if he'll sleep through the night."

"I wouldn't count on it, although I'll make him as comfortable as I can."

After pulling a chair close to the bedside, Thomas sat down and pondered the situation. He hadn't read about any recent developments that would assist him in treating an allergic reaction. Medical professionals actually didn't know a lot about what to do with them. With all the modern advances, he wished one of them had been for situations like this one.

A quick knock sounded, and the door opened again. Thomas turned to see both of the Bloom women carrying a number of items. He crossed to the door and relieved Miss Bloom of the tray she carried.

Noting that it contained what he had asked for, he set it on the bedside table. Thalia still had a folded sheet across her arm. He reached for it. "Probably the best way to do this is to tuck this behind the headboard and drape it across Mr. Newbolt."

He leaned toward his patient and gently shook him. "I really hate to disturb you, but we need you to sit up in the bed."

Miss Bloom assisted Thomas as they arranged the pillows behind the patient's back so he would be comfortable.

When Thomas turned to call Thalia forward, he found her right behind him. He took the towels, folded them, and laid them across Newbolt's lap, then placed the bowl on top of the towels.

"Before we finish making the tent, I want to give him some bicarbonate of soda." He took the glass and spooned the powder into the water. After stirring until it dissolved, he gave the elixir to the patient. "Drink this right down."

Newbolt took a tentative sip then made a wry face.

"I know it doesn't taste good, but it should help you. If you drink it fast, you won't taste it very long."

After a brief hesitation, Newbolt chugged it down. When he was finished, he couldn't contain a loud burp.

"See." Thomas had to force himself not to laugh. "It's already helping some."

Newbolt glanced toward the two women, and his face turned crimson. "Pardon my faux pas."

Thalia smiled at him. "Think nothing of it."

Thomas picked up the teakettle and carefully poured the hot water into the bowl. Miss Bloom helped him drape the sheet over Newbolt and the headboard of the bed to form the tent to keep the steam inside.

"Breathe in as much as you can." Thomas picked up the patient's wrist and checked his pulse, which was still too rapid for his liking. "Try to relax, but don't fall asleep. And if you get too hot inside there, let us know. We can raise one corner of the sheet so you can have some fresh air." *This had better work.* If it didn't, getting Newbolt to the hospital in this snowstorm could prove impossible.

After spending more than an hour with the patient, Thomas stepped out for a break, leaving Thalia sitting with Newbolt. Her aunt came out with him.

Miss Bloom looked at the parlor with only a couple of people in it. "Where are all the others?"

Rose raised her head and stood. "Miss Dorcas, most of them tried to get home. I just hope they make it."

Thomas recognized the tremble in her voice. She sounded ready to cry. He walked toward her. "I'm sure they'll be fine."

Her hazel eyes had darkened to brown, and tears wet her lashes. "I hope you're right. I tried to tell them it wasn't a good idea to leave, but I don't think anyone heard me. Everyone was talking at once."

Thomas wanted to take her in his arms and comfort her. If only he had the right.

Miss Bloom clapped her hands to get their attention. "No one else is going to leave tonight. We have plenty of bedrooms. Come with me, and I'll show you where you'll be staying."

Josiah followed her out of the room as if she were the Pied Piper, leaving Thomas with Rose.

"Aren't you going to see where you'll be staying?" Rose smiled up at him, making his own heartbeat accelerate, but not as much as Newbolt's.

And Thomas's wasn't from an allergic reaction. Just the opposite. He'd better stop this line of thinking before it got him into trouble, encouraging him to do something that would make her shy away from him even more.

"I'm not sure I'll be sleeping tonight anyway. I have a patient to take care of. The first twenty-four hours are the most critical. If he pulls through that, he should be all right." This wasn't what he wanted to be talking to Rose about, but he couldn't decide how to turn the conversation to the subject he did want to approach. Would she be offended if he asked her why she kept running from him at the party?

Rose laid her hand on his arm, and he felt the heat clear to his heart. "I'm going to retire to my room, Thomas. It's been a very long day."

Before he could answer, she was walking up the staircase. After a few steps, she stopped and turned around. "I'm so glad you were here. I don't know what we would have done about Maximilian if you hadn't been." With a brief smile, she continued out of sight.

He wanted her to be glad he was here for another reason—because she really wanted to see him again.

When Rose awakened the next morning, the steam radiator had kept her room comfortable all night. Although she loved watching the flames in the fireplace, this was much better for a bedroom. Even the water she used for her ablutions wasn't too cold. Sometimes at home in the winter, the water in the pitcher would have a thin film of ice on the surface.

She arrived in the kitchen in time to help Thalia's aunt Dorcas set the table for breakfast. Even though the Blooms had several servants, the two women often worked right beside them.

Rose stood in the dining room, counting out silverware for the table settings. "Thomas, Maximilian, and Josiah stayed over. Do you think they'll all come to breakfast?" She hoped Miss Dorcas could hear her question.

"I know I'm hungry." The deep baritone voice was hard to

mistake, and it didn't come from the kitchen.

Rose whirled toward the doorway. "Thomas, how is your patient?"

Although he was fully dressed, his hair was disheveled. "Maximilian made it through the night. I'm hopeful for a full recovery."

"Did you sit up all night with him?" Rose started pulling linen napkins from the top drawer of the sideboard but turned at an angle so she could watch him.

"No, Thalia helped me a lot." His smile reached across the room to her heart. "I actually was able to get a few hours of sleep. Have you checked the weather this morning?"

"I did peek outside. Nothing has changed. Will Maximilian join us for breakfast?" Rose wanted to be sure to set him a place if he did.

"I don't think so. He had a rough night. Perhaps he could have some broth. I think I'll go ask if they have some in the kitchen." He walked through the room and out the other door.

When he was gone, Rose felt as if the morning had lost some of its brightness. She would have to stop reacting to Thomas every time he came near. She took a deep breath and slowly let it out.

"Is something the matter, dear Rose?" Miss Dorcas came to her and patted her shoulder. "Didn't you sleep well? Was your room too cold?"

Rose smiled at the older woman. "Yes, I slept well, and the room was just right."

"I only hope we can keep it that way. If the snowstorm

goes on too long, we might run out of coal for the boiler." A frown marred Miss Dorcas's appearance. "Of course, we have the fireplaces, but they aren't as efficient as coal for keeping the house warm."

Leaving the silverware and napkins, Rose went to look out the front window. The snowstorm hadn't let up one bit. This would be a second day of snow. How long would it last? Hopefully not long enough to cause too many problems.

After breakfast, Josiah and Rose went into the parlor. She wondered what they should do today.

Josiah turned from where he stood staring into the fire. "Why don't we play charades?" Had he been reading her mind?

"Do we have enough people?" Rose knew Thalia, Thomas, and Maximilian were in the house, but they hadn't rested as well as she and Josiah evidently had.

"There aren't as many as last night, but we only need two or three on each team." He started looking through the writing desk and took out pencils and paper.

"I don't think Maximilian is well enough to participate. And Thalia and Thomas took turns staying with him. They're probably both too tired." Rose didn't want to close the damper on their fun, but the playing field had just been diminished.

"Do you want to play checkers, Rose?" Josiah wasn't going to give up. His pleading expression brought a smile to her face.

"Okay, but I'm very good." She taunted him. "I haven't been defeated in a long time."

Josiah took up the gauntlet and started setting up the game on a table he pulled near the fireplace. "We'll see about that." He was much too serious about his games.

Rose decided to make it fun. Soon the two of them were making almost as much noise as the party last night.

"What's all this racket?" Thomas stood in the doorway.

Chagrin cloaked Rose as silence descended on the room. Why hadn't she remembered there was a patient in the house? "We're sorry, Thomas. Did we disturb Maximilian?"

He strode across the Persian carpet and stopped right beside her. "He's taking his first serving of broth. With the bedroom door closed, I doubt he even heard it. I just didn't want to miss whatever is causing all the merriment."

Josiah groaned. "Rose thinks she can beat me at checkers. She's telling a lot of funny stories. Probably hoping it'll take my mind off of what I'm doing."

She giggled. "It's working, isn't it? Who has the most checkers left?"

Josiah gave a loud groan. "I may be down, but the game isn't over." He picked up a checker and jumped one of hers, which took him into the last row on her side of the board. "King me!"

"Good move, old man." Thomas pulled up a chair and sat back to watch the rest of the game.

For some reason, Rose couldn't even remember the strategy she was using to win. In less than five minutes, Josiah held all her checkers.

He jumped up with his fists pumping the air. "I won! . . . I won!"

"So you did." Rose couldn't think of anything else to say.

"How about you playing checkers with me?" Thomas gave her an enticing smile.

She rose from her chair and offered it to him. "Since Josiah was the winner, you should play him. I'm going to see if I can do anything to help Miss Dorcas."

Thomas liked this relaxed, fun-loving Rose much better than the reserved Rose of last night. He watched her leave the room as if she was fleeing something. Probably him. Were they back to her staying away from him as she did last night? He'd planned to let her win the first game so she would play a second with him. They could converse while they played. Maybe she would warm up to him being here.

"Your move." Josiah leaned back and smiled.

Knowing he couldn't gracefully get out of playing, Thomas decided to win as quickly as possible. Very soon, he realized that he'd underestimated the skill of his opponent. Even though he tried to keep his mind on the board, his thoughts often strayed to the auburn waves and hazel eyes that beguiled him. Now that he was a doctor, surely he was good enough for the boss's daughter.

What a thought! Maybe that was the problem. Rose still thought of him as the foreman's son. Her father had never treated him as if he wasn't equal to them. And Rose hadn't when he had worked on the ranch. Maybe that boarding school back East had given her other ideas.

Chapter 4

Since Newbolt was no longer having trouble breathing and his rash was almost completely gone, Thomas spent the next night in his own room. He sorely needed the uninterrupted sleep. Arising before dawn, he stared out his window at the continuing snowfall, clearly visible against his window. Three days was fairly long for a storm to rage, and this one showed no signs of letting go of its fury. He should get back to the clinic in case Dr. Wetherby needed him, but traveling the streets in this mess would be next to impossible, and Thomas didn't want to subject his horse to the torture and risk losing her. He hoped the snow would let up today so he could get home.

When he descended the stairs, he realized the fire had gone out in the parlor. Already cold drafts of air were chasing the warmth from the room. He had noticed the firewood stacked on the back porch when he went out to retrieve his medical bag. After being in this house so long, he needed more exercise than climbing stairs.

The back door was frozen shut, and he had to pull hard to dislodge it. While making his way the ten feet across the porch toward the stack of split logs, he wished he'd returned upstairs for his overcoat. The wind whipped and howled, blowing drifts across the expanse of porch as well as the yard. After loading his arms with icy logs, he hurried through the door to the back hallway. When he tried to close the door, he bumped it too hard with his hip, and the door slammed behind him.

Oh, no. He hoped the noise wouldn't awaken anyone else. The other people in the house needed sleep, too.

He stacked the logs in the woodbox beside the fireplace in the parlor. He needed to get the fire started before he could put any of them in the grate. A bucket of kindling and newspaper sat on the opposite side from the firebox. Beside it rested a package of safety matches by the Diamond Match Company. All the other matches being made in the United States were poisonous because of the phosphorous. After treating various patients suffering the effects from breathing the fumes, Thomas always bought Diamond matches.

Building a fire that would start quickly was an art he learned as a young boy. Soon all the kindling caught fire, so he placed pieces of split wood on top, careful not to inhibit the fire. When the flames finally leaped and danced, Thomas added more logs. He stood and turned to warm his back, clasping his hands behind him.

"Good job, Stanton." Josiah leaned nonchalantly against the door facing. "I'll wager that's not the first fire you've built."

Thomas grinned. "You're right."

Josiah joined him beside the fireplace.

"Couldn't you sleep?"

"I slept fine." Josiah turned around so he could warm his back, too. "I hardly ever sleep longer than six hours."

"I was afraid the back door slamming woke you."

"No, I was already dressing by then."

Thomas stared into the flames. "This isn't the only fireplace I'm worried about."

"I'll help you bring in more wood to build the other fires. I'd enjoy having something productive to do."

The two men grabbed their coats and headed out to the woodpile. They soon had plenty of wood beside each fireplace in the main rooms downstairs. While they were at it, they built up the fire in the kitchen stove, which had been banked last night.

After they finished the last fire, Thomas stood. "I've been wondering about the coal supply for the boiler. I'm sure the wagons won't be making deliveries in this storm. I'm going to take a lantern down to the basement to see about it."

Josiah rubbed his hands together. "I'll go with you, but I want to put on a coat first."

As Thomas feared, the coal bin was less than half full. "Do you know how much coal a boiler this size needs in a day?"

Josiah stomped his feet, probably to keep them from getting too cold. "I'm not sure. The one at our house is smaller."

Thomas walked around to the other side of the huge furnace. "I've never seen one this big in a private home either."

He picked up the padded glove on the workbench and used

it to open the metal door to the firebox. Josiah helped him load more coal into the boiler without dousing the fire. After they finished, they climbed back up the stairs.

Rose was thankful that the fire in the kitchen stove was already burning. She started a pot of coffee so that soon the hot beverage could warm her insides, too.

She went to the window to check the weather. Nothing had changed since yesterday. How long would this blizzard last? Her thoughts leapt over the peaks to the valley high in the Rocky Mountains. Did Father stay in Breckenridge, or had he gone out to the ranch? If he was at the ranch, she hoped he wasn't alone in the big log house. Maybe some of the hands had gone up there for the evening. They'd be snowed in, too. Of course, they used a system of ropes and pulleys they attached to the structures at the first sign of snowfall. With them, they would be able to get around to the other buildings near the ranch house. Too bad something like that wouldn't work in town.

Behind her, the door to the cellar opened, startling her. She pressed her hand to her heart and suppressed a scream as she turned around. "Thomas, what are you. . .and Josiah doing?"

Thomas's long strides ate up the floor as he approached her. "We wanted to see how the coal is holding out."

He towered over her, the gaze from his steel gray eyes never leaving her face. The room that had felt cavernous a moment ago had shrunk with his presence. The man was just too handsome for his own good. . .or hers. She'd never known his mother. When Farley came to work for her father, he was a widower. Thomas must look more like his mother, who surely had been a beautiful woman. Farley's grizzled appearance didn't resemble his son in any way.

"And is it holding out? The coal, I mean." She felt like a stammering child around him. And yet not quite. This man standing before her made her aware that she was a woman.

Thomas blinked, releasing the hold his gaze had on her. "I'm not sure. The coal bin was not even half full."

Rose realized she still had her hand on her heart. She dropped it to her side. "The snow hasn't let up."

Thomas gazed outside for a moment. "I don't like the looks of the storm. If we run out of fuel before this stops and the coal wagons can't get through, we could be in trouble. This far from the center of town, no one will be digging us out anytime soon."

That was not what Rose wanted to hear. Once again her thoughts flew to her father. She'd worried about him ever since her mother died. Even with his housekeeper and ranch hands, he would be lonely because she hadn't returned home as planned. He probably was worried about her.

Thomas noticed the sadness that invaded Rose's expression. While they were talking, Josiah had slipped from the room. Maybe Rose would open up to him now. "What's troubling you? It's more than just the weather, isn't it?"

"I'm concerned about my father. I only meant to leave him for a couple of days." Worry lines crinkled her brows.

"He's not alone, is he?" Thomas knew Mr. Fletcher had a number of employees around him, unless things had changed a lot since he left.

Her spine stiffened, and she lifted her chin. "No, but he has no family near him." With those words, she turned and left the room.

Thomas stared after her retreating figure. *What was that all about?* The pleasant aroma of coffee teased Thomas's nostrils, leading him toward the pot on the stove. Since the coffee hadn't been there before he and Josiah went to the cellar, Rose must have made it. Yet she left the room without getting a cup. Every time Thomas tried to talk to her, Rose withdrew from him. Why was she acting that way?

When Rose and Josiah played the game last night, Thomas had caught a glimpse of the Rose he had known. He wanted to see her flashing hazel eyes and the high color on her smooth cheeks. Where was the Rose Fletcher who loved spending time with him?

Chapter 5

Finally the storm was over. It had continued for six whole days, almost driving Thomas crazy. At least the coal supply hadn't run out. The men shoveled snow during the storm to keep too much from building up around the house and the carriage house. The social interaction at other times gave a pleasant break, but he'd made little headway with Rose.

Today he had to try to get to the clinic. Even though he'd washed out some of his clothes and hung them on the radiator in his bedroom overnight, he was ready for more than just what he wore to the party. And he wanted to check on Dr. Wetherby. With the storm finally over, people who were sick would find their way to the clinic.

With Josiah and Maximilian's help, Thomas dug the snow from the front sidewalk and the street along the whole block in front of the house. Other people worked on the connecting streets. By midafternoon, he hitched his horse to his buggy and set out. The trip should have taken less than half an hour, but he didn't arrive at the house until past suppertime. Exhaustion and the extreme cold weighted him down, so he could imagine how tired his horse had to be. When he unhitched the animal, he gave her a good rubdown and a bucket of oats. She deserved the extra treat.

Thomas entered the back door of the house. Silence greeted him. He wandered through each room, but no one was there, not even Dr. Wetherby. Thomas opened the front door and tested the porch to see if ice made it hazardous to cross. He found no evidence of anyone having been there during the storm. A piece of paper tacked to the front door fluttered in the gentle breeze. *If you need a doctor, come to my house.* The older physician's signature was scrawled across the bottom.

Alone, Thomas headed toward the stairs that took him up to his quarters but then turned back. He'd have to start the boiler to take the chill out of the house, and he needed to bring in wood for the fireplace and stove. Since no one had been here for the duration of the storm, his supply of coal wasn't depleted.

Two hours later, Thomas sat in his favorite chair with his Bible open on his lap. A bath, clean clothes, and a shave made him feel like a new man on the outside. Now to take care of the inside. Too many days lately, he'd let busyness crowd out his private times with the Lord. In his silent apartment above the empty clinic, this was the perfect time to reconnect.

Thomas read then reread two chapters in the New Testament, letting the words burrow themselves deep inside him. One of the doctors he'd interned under had introduced him to Jesus, and he still felt like such a baby in Christ. He closed his eyes and prayed for a long time until his spirit finally felt refreshed. Why did he so often neglect his time alone with the Lord?

He foraged in the pantry for something easy to fix. All he could come up with was a can of Campbell's Pork and Beans and a can of peaches. He opened the beans and dumped them in a pot on the stove. While they warmed, he opened the peaches and set the can on the table. Why get a bowl dirty since he was alone? He stirred the beans to keep them from sticking and set the pan on a folded towel on the table to prevent a scorch mark.

He bowed his head and thanked the Lord for the food, such as it was. Eating alone had never been his favorite activity, even though he often had to while he was in Cambridge. This meal looked meager after the abundance at the Bloom house.

His thoughts turned to Rose. He couldn't understand why she was unapproachable most of the time they were snowbound at the Blooms' home. He stuffed a spoonful of hot food into his mouth and chewed away. *Could you give me some discernment here, Lord?*

Another bite of beans was followed by a thick slice of peach. They tasted better together.

Give her time. The words resounded inside his head.

"Okay, Lord, what does that mean?"

After they repeated again, he heard nothing more, even though he tried to listen while he finished consuming his meal.

He washed the pot and spoon and pondered the phrase. What could it mean? Give her time for what?

By the time he finished cleaning up his mess, he'd come up with a plan.

After Thomas left the Bloom house, Rose missed him. Every room she entered held memories of his presence. His smile, the laughter they shared over games, even his caring ministrations to Maximilian. Everything pointed to what a wonderful person the man was. If only he were a Christian, she could stop fighting her attraction to him.

Not even wanting to spend time with anyone else, Rose went to her room. She pulled out her well-worn black leather Bible. The book had been such a comfort to her while she was in boarding school—almost like a real live friend.

She sat in the wingback chair by a small round table. Letting the book fall open in her lap, she started reading in Proverbs. The verses found in this particular book of the Bible had affected most of her life. Her parents started reading them to her when she was very young. Probably one of the reasons she'd wanted to learn wisdom and discernment. But her powers of discernment seemed to have deserted her. Or the desires of her heart overruled them.

If she didn't gain control of her wayward emotions, she might be tempted to forget the admonition not to be yoked to an unbeliever. *Father God, please help me.* Rose spent a long time communing with her heavenly Father, asking Him to help her close the door on her attraction to Thomas.

Maybe it was a good thing he left today. She wouldn't see

him again unless he waited to go to Breckenridge to see her father until after she returned home.

She felt the need to read one of the wonderful stories about a woman who listened to God instead of her own desires. The much-loved story of Queen Esther thrilled her with every word she read. When she finished, Rose knew that like the woman who saved her people, she could control her emotions and follow the path God set before her.

Before she finished with the Bible, she turned to Ephesians 4. The last verse caught her eye. *And be ye kind one to another, tenderhearted, forgiving one another, even as God for Christ's sake hath forgiven you.*

Kind. . .tenderhearted. Rose knew she had used the excuse that Thomas had scoffed at her belief in God all those years ago to turn a cold heart toward him. She knew she did it to protect herself, but she hadn't been showing God's love to him. How could he come to know the Lord if every Christian treated him the way she had the last few days? With her new resolve to keep a tight rein on her emotions, she wanted to express God's love to Thomas, to draw him into the fold.

After lunch the next day, Rose decided to get out of the house for a while. She bundled up in her coat and scarf and pulled on her gloves. When she reached the front edge of the porch, she held on to the column and took in all the surroundings. The men had dug a deep path to the street. As she contemplated strolling down the walkway, someone entered from the street end.

If she hadn't glimpsed his face before he trained his eyes on the ground, Rose would have known who he was anyway. His every movement was familiar. "Thomas, what are you doing here?"

He looked up as he took another step. His foot slid before it found traction, and one arm windmilled to compensate. Finally, both feet were stationary. A smile lit his face. "Rose, I came to see how you're doing."

She clutched the column even tighter. "I just wanted a breath of fresh air. I was trying to decide whether to venture down the walk. Maybe I should just stay here since it's so slick."

"There are icy patches you have to avoid." He continued toward the house, this time missing all the other slick places. "Why don't you have a hat on? It's too cold to be out here without one."

Rose laughed. "Is that the doctor talking or just the friend?"

He stood beside the bottom step and stared deep into her eyes. "Which one do you want me to be, Rose?"

The way his voice caressed her name sent chills up her spine that didn't have anything to do with the temperature. She couldn't stop the shiver they brought.

Thomas climbed the few steps to the porch. "Are you too cold?"

If only he knew, his presence caused warmth to invade her whole body. "Not. . .really." Why did she stammer so much around him?

"We can go in." The concern in his tone tugged at her heartstrings.

"I've been in the house so long." She pulled one end of the

long scarf up around her head and tucked the end into her coat. "I'd rather stay here."

Thomas blew out a deep breath that instantly became a white cloud before it dissipated. "Fine. Are you doing okay, Rose? Do you need anything?"

Rose laughed. "This storm has really changed all my plans."

He leaned closer to her, and she could feel the warmth emanating from him. "What plans?"

"I would already be home by now. I had planned to go shopping here in Denver before returning home, but that wouldn't have taken long." Rose wanted to stand this close to him for hours. *Lord, I asked you to help me with my emotions.*

"I could take you shopping tomorrow." His murmured words surprised her.

"You like to go shopping?"

He chuckled. "I didn't say that. I just offered to accompany you. We could go to Daniels & Fischer department store."

"I'd like that. I need to get some more clothes. I've been washing things out at night." Rose wondered if she should have mentioned that, sure he'd know the type of clothes she was talking about. A blush brought even more heat to her face. "But I also want to get some candy and other things to take back home."

"Let's make a day of it." Delight twinkled in his gray eyes, lightening them. "Then when the railroad is cleared, you'll be ready to head to Breckenridge."

As Thomas walked back home, he whistled "Sweethearts." His

heart was light, and the future looked promising. The time he spent with Rose today gave him hope. Not once did he sense her retreating from him. Tomorrow would be a wonderful opportunity to do what he'd been wanting to for a week. Get to know her as the woman she'd become.

Even though he slept well that night, he awoke far too early. So after he ate a quick breakfast of a bowl of cornflakes, he sat down with his Bible again. Usually he didn't have any trouble concentrating on the words before him, but a beautiful face crowned with glorious auburn waves kept intruding. Finally he closed the book.

Lord, forgive me for not finishing the chapter. Once again, he poured out his heart to God then listened in his spirit. He didn't feel God cautioning him about his interest in Rose.

Thomas dressed with care, wanting to look dapper for her. He carried a hot brick wrapped in a blanket out to the carriage house. Before he hitched up his horse, he placed the bundle in the floor of the sleigh. He even placed a second heavy blanket on the seat.

Rose was ready when he arrived to pick her up. Thomas helped her into the sleigh before unwrapping the brick and placing it under her feet. He gave her one blanket to wrap up in and placed the other around her skirt.

"Thomas, how thoughtful of you, but we won't be traveling that long." Rose smiled down at him.

He hurried around the front of the sleigh, only giving his horse a cursory pat before he climbed up beside Rose. "Can't have you getting too cold."

First they stopped under the clock tower of the Daniels & Fischer department store. Immediately, the clock chimed ten times.

Thomas helped Rose alight from the sleigh then held out his elbow. She slipped her gloved hand into the opening and rested it on his forearm. He could get used to the feel of her hand on his arm.

Knowing that she might need to buy some personal items, he turned toward her after they entered the imposing front door. "I have a few things I need to pick up, so why don't we meet here in half an hour?"

How thoughtful of Thomas to suggest this. Rose had decided not to buy more unmentionables, since he accompanied her to the store. Now she could make her purchases freely. If she wasn't careful, she'd find herself caring far too much for him. He was not at all like the boy she had known before he went to medical school. Over the last few days, she'd seen his kindness exhibited in many ways. Thomas had been funny and serious, and he put the good of others in front of seeking his own needs. So many wonderful qualities, but the one missing was the most important. She would continue to pray for him to find the Lord.

Thomas waited near the front door with several bulging paper bags. "Are you finished shopping here?"

"I have all I need." Rose held up her purchases.

"Let me take them to the sleigh." He put his bags under one arm and hers under the other. "I'll put our sacks on separate sides so we won't be confused and get the wrong purchases."

Rose watched him through the glass in the door, knowing she'd be terribly embarrassed if he opened hers. As promised, he kept the bags separate. She heaved a sigh of relief.

Thomas returned. "Would you like to walk around and see what else they have in the store?"

She agreed, and they sauntered through several different departments. The store even had a rather large book section. "I want to look at some of the titles. I love to read."

"I do, too."

They walked along the shelves, commenting on books they'd read. Thomas picked up a book before Rose could read the title. "I've heard about this one. I think I'll buy it."

"What is it?" Rose craned her neck, trying to see.

Thomas turned the spine toward her. "*The Secret Agent* by Joseph Conrad. I read *Lord Jim* when I was younger and have been wanting to read this one."

Rose didn't think she'd try either of them. She lifted a volume from the shelf. "This one looks more interesting to me." She turned it over in her hands. "*A Room with a View* by E. M. Forster."

Thomas held out a hand. "Let me see." After she gave it to him, he studied the first few pages. "How about if we buy both of the books? Then when we are finished with reading one, we exchange them."

"That sounds good to me." Not the only thing that sounded good to Rose. Evidently, Thomas expected them to see each other again later.

After strolling through the store, they went to the counter to pay for the books. Thomas hadn't given hers back, and she expected him to when they got there. But he didn't. He paid for both of the books.

They arrived back at the sleigh, and Thomas settled her into the seat. After he climbed in beside her, she asked, "Why didn't you let me pay for my own book?"

"I wanted to give you a little memento of the day." He picked up the reins and clicked at his horse. "Where else did you want to go, Rose?"

"I really wanted to buy a few special things. Some tea bags for Mrs. Barclay. You remember our housekeeper. She has really taken a liking to them. Some Hershey bars. I like the plain ones, and Daddy likes the newer ones with almonds in them."

"Let's go to the emporium." Thomas turned the corner and headed another direction. "They'll have those things and much more."

Rose loved going to the emporium when she came to Denver, so she laughed and agreed. They walked up and down the aisles looking for the tea and candy. Rose bought several Hershey bars while Thomas looked at other confections. He had another clerk measuring out some bulk candy for him while she paid for her purchases.

When she turned away from the counter, Thomas stood beside her. "I have something else I want you to try."

"Okay." Rose waited expectantly.

He took out a small piece and slowly unwrapped it, never taking his gaze from hers. "Open your mouth."

She complied, and he dropped in a lump of chocolate that immediately started melting. Her lips tingled where his fingers had brushed them. She savored the sweetness until the confection had completely dissolved. "What was that?"

"A kiss, Rose." Thomas paused a moment. "A Hershey's Kiss."

Rose loved the chocolate, but his words caused a riot in her emotions, and her lips still felt his touch. *A kiss indeed!*

Chapter 6

Rose sat beside the dressing table and brushed her hair, arranging it into her favorite chignon at the nape of her neck. The past week since the storm ended had been full of activity. Besides the times she spent with Thalia and her aunt, she enjoyed Thomas coming in the evenings. The knowledge that he was a thoroughly nice man grew with every visit.

When she allowed her thoughts to dwell on the man, she had to admit he was more than nice. Such an insipid word, falling far short of describing Thomas. Thoughtful…handsome…intelligent. She could compile a long list of adjectives if she had time.

She heard a knock on the front door, and soon a timid tap on the door to Rose's room. "Miss Fletcher, that nice Dr. Stanton is here to see you."

Thomas was here? *But it's morning.* "Thank you, Eliza. I'll be right down."

Rose slipped the last hairpin into her coiffure and studied her reflection in the pier glass. She pinched her cheeks and rubbed her lips together several times to bring more color into her face. Then she went downstairs.

Thomas waited at the foot of the steps with his hat in one hand. "Good morning, Rose. How lovely you look."

She held out her hand for him to shake, but as he had done at the party, he lifted it and pressed his warm lips to the back of her fingers. She held her breath for a moment and felt a blush stain her cheeks. Why had she pinched them? Now they were probably too red.

"Thank you, Thomas. What brings you here this morning?" Her gaze traveled up his broad chest to the twinkle in his gray eyes.

"Isn't it enough that I wanted to see you?" His deep chuckle rumbled around her.

She extracted her fingers from his clasp and nervously brushed both hands across the front of her skirt. "Yes. . . Did you just want to see me?" She liked this teasing exchange.

"Actually, I came to get you and take you to the train station."

"The tracks are clear?" Rose almost shrieked. However, her training came to the fore, and she was able to maintain decorum. "After all the trouble with the railroad this year, I was afraid they'd use this storm as an excuse to shut down service to Breckenridge. Of course, I could at least get to Frisco and take a horse from there."

He brushed the brim of his hat with his other hand. "One of the workers brought his sick wife to the clinic late last night. He told me service is restored all the way to Breckenridge."

"I wonder if I can make the morning train." Excitement at the possibility of seeing her father today warred with disappointment that she wouldn't continue to see Thomas every day.

"That's why I'm here, Rose. Hurry and pack your things. I'll accompany you home."

Relief flooded through her along with a sense of panic. How would they ever get to the station in time? "Won't Dr. Wetherby need you?"

Thomas shook his head. "I've run the clinic the last week. He said he could take over now, and I could go with you."

Rose turned and almost ran up the stairs. She'd quickly pack then tell her hostesses good-bye.

Thomas drove the horse-drawn sleigh as fast as he felt was safe, but they barely made it before the train was scheduled to pull out from the station. The livery would send someone to retrieve the conveyance. The conductor agreed to hold the train while Thomas ran in and purchased two tickets. Thomas boarded and found Rose seated halfway down the car. By the time he dropped into the seat beside her, the wheels were already turning and the engine building up steam.

The conductor, who had continued down the car, returned and took the tickets from Thomas.

"Why is the train so short?" Rose smiled up at the man.

"With all the bad weather, miss, not too many people even know that the tracks are cleared. They decided to just pull two passenger cars besides the caboose. I think they only brought the second one in case more people wanted to take the return trip to Denver." He tipped the bill of his cap and continued on.

Even though the passenger car was heated, the extreme cold seeped in. Thomas took a blanket from his bag and offered it to Rose. "I brought this for you to use. I know how cold it can get on the trip over the mountains."

"How thoughtful of you, Thomas." She spread the cover around herself and clutched it tight.

When she gazed at him, his heartbeat accelerated, and he felt as if he could lose himself in the depths of her eyes. Today they took on a dark blue hue to match her traveling coat and hat, and golden flecks sparkled in their depths. Since their shopping trip in Denver, Thomas had enjoyed the change in Rose. He'd begun to hope that soon she would have the strong feelings for him that he experienced every time he looked at her. Actually, he didn't even have to be in her presence to feel the depth of his emotions and longing for her. Could this be love?

If love was more intense than what he felt now, he wasn't sure he could handle the emotion. *Love!* This was the first time he'd actually allowed himself to dwell on that word. In his mind, love led to marriage, and that was what he wanted. To marry Rose. Even though he had dismissed the crazy idea he had earlier about him not being worthy of her because of his father working for hers, he wanted to proceed with caution. He had to be sure she felt the same way.

"Miss Dorcas gave me a package of food." Rose tipped her

face toward Thomas. "She said we'd need to eat before we arrived in Breckenridge."

Thomas didn't want to think about food. He wanted to lean his head toward hers until their lips met. The day he'd fed her the chocolate kiss often lingered in his mind. The velvet touch of her lips on his fingers made him want to experience their touch on his own lips. He jerked his attention away from the temptation.

"The mountains look beautiful, don't they?" That should be a safe topic of conversation.

Rose glanced at the glass window veiled with moisture that clung to the inside. How could Thomas see a thing through them? "I've always loved the textures of the trees against the thick blanket of snow. Each trunk and limb outlined by the stark white. Of course, the evergreens add a welcome touch of dark green." Why was she babbling?

When she looked up at Thomas a moment ago, she felt a strong connection. Although she wanted to feel only tender-hearted toward him until he came to know the Lord, controlling her emotions was hard in the close confines of the railroad car. And as the train went around curves, their shoulders often touched. Each time, tingles went all the way through her. Maybe his ploy of conversation would keep her mind off her emotions.

The farther they went, the more questions Thomas asked, and Rose told him more about herself than she had ever told anyone else. How she worried about her father now that her mother was gone. How much she enjoyed living at the boarding school back East. How much she missed seeing friends on a more regular basis. Even how she wondered about her future, how out of place she sometimes felt. He kept her talking about herself, but she had a hard time turning the conversation toward him and his desires. He was closemouthed on that subject.

Rose leaned toward the window and rubbed the glass, clearing away the mist. "Look at that, Thomas."

She could hardly believe what she saw. Where the Keystone water tank should have been, she saw a wondrous frozen waterfall cascading to the ground and down the incline away from the tracks. She noticed the conductor making his way through the car.

She leaned around Thomas and waved toward the other man. "Sir, what happened here?"

"The blizzard was a real doozy, miss. The workers were able to keep most of the water tanks from bursting, but they didn't make it to this one soon enough."

"Many of them leak." Thomas stood beside the man. "We've seen the large icicles hanging from all the others."

Rose once again glanced out the window. "I know that's a problem, but the icy sculpture is beautiful."

The man ducked his head and squinted against the vast whiteness. "I guess you could say that. Most people would only see the damage though."

He continued on down the car, and Thomas returned to his seat. "Since this is Keystone, we're not too far from Breckenridge."

She grasped his hand. "Oh, Thomas, I will be so glad to see my father. I hope he hasn't been too worried about me. And I'm sure he'll be glad to see you."

When they arrived at the station in Breckenridge, Thomas shoved one of Rose's traveling bags under his arm then picked up the other one as well as his suitcase.

"Thomas, I can carry my own bags."

"There's no need. I already have them."

He led the way down the car to the landing where they could exit the train. After his feet touched the platform, he set down the baggage and offered her a hand for the last long step. He'd like to do things like this for her for the rest of their lives. He cleared his throat and turned back to pick up the luggage.

"I'll get you settled in the station, Rose. Then I'll go to the livery and get a sleigh to take you home."

Thomas watched Rose stare around at Breckenridge as if she hadn't seen it for years before heading toward the station door. "Okay, the sooner I get home the better."

He left her and hurried down the street. He didn't want to be out in the bitter cold longer than he had to. Right before he reached the livery, he encountered one of the ranch hands who'd worked for Mr. Fletcher when Thomas's father had been foreman.

"Petey, do you remember me? I'm Thomas Stanton." He held out his hand for the man to shake.

The old-timer looked him up and down before he gave him

a crooked smile. "Wal, I wouldn'ta known you if you hadn'ta said somethin'. Yur all growed up."

Thomas laughed. "That I am."

"What ur you doin' here in Breckenridge since yur Pa's gone?" Petey pulled his hat off and placed it over his heart. "God rest his soul."

"I've accompanied Rose Fletcher home from Denver. I'm heading to the livery for a sleigh. She's real anxious to see her dad." Thomas hoped the other man understood his need to hurry away.

"Wait a minit there, son. The boss's out t' the ranch." Petey scratched his bearded cheek.

"Thanks. I'll get horses instead, so we can ride out there."

When Thomas arrived back at the station with two horses in tow, Rose stared at him. "How are we going to carry these bags on horses? I'm not dressed to ride."

Thomas explained about meeting Petey.

"This suit has a full skirt. I could ride in it." Rose glanced down toward the bags. "What will we do with these?"

"I have enough rope to tie them on the horse." Thomas squatted and started tying her two bags together. "These will balance my bag, so I'll tie them on behind me. We only have a few miles to ride."

Even though the ride wasn't long, Rose felt like that frozen waterfall back in Keystone by the time they reached the ranch house. Thomas dismounted and helped her down, bringing the blanket he'd insisted she wrap around her as protection from the icy breeze. Her stiff legs almost gave out, and she slumped. He pulled her against him and slipped his arms around her back.

"Can you walk, or should I carry you into the house?" His breath against her hair infused her with warmth.

She leaned back so she could see his face. "I can walk now. I was just a little stiff."

He released her, and she hurried up the walkway to the front porch, clasping the blanket around her like armor. Her heart needed protection.

Before she reached the door, it flew open, and Mrs. Barclay gave a shout. "Land's sakes, come in here, child. It's freezing out there."

Rose fell into her waiting arms and returned her bear hug. "I'm so glad to be home." When the older woman pushed the door closed, Rose shook her head. "You'll need to see if Thomas could use any help with the bags."

Mrs. Barclay pulled the door wider. "Is that Farley's Thomas?" The smile she turned on the man should have blinded him it was so bright.

Thomas came in and set down the bags he carried. "Is that your famous stew I smell, Mrs. B.? I hope so, because I'm starving."

The housekeeper led the way to the kitchen and poured them each a cup of steaming coffee before she reached for the bowls to serve the stew.

Rose had always loved this homey kitchen, but one thing

was missing. "Where's Daddy, Mrs. Barclay? I expected him to meet us at the door, or at least join us in here."

"Oh, Miss Rose, it's so sad. Your dear father has been sick in bed for several days. It's all I can do to get him to drink a little broth." She tsked and shook her head.

Rose's heart dropped to her stomach. She had a hard time remembering the last time her father was sick, and she knew he didn't stay in bed more than one day. *Please, Lord, don't let anything happen to him.*

Chapter 7

Rose slammed her steaming cup down, sloshing coffee on the table and rushed out the door of the kitchen. "He has to be all right."

Thomas went to his suitcase and extracted his medical bag, then followed her. "I'm sure he will be. I'll check him out."

She stopped and whirled around. "I'm so glad you came with me." She grabbed him and gave him a big hug before continuing up the stairs and down the hall.

When she reached the closed door of her father's bedroom, she gave a gentle knock.

"Come in, Mrs. Barclay." The thready voice didn't even sound like her father's. "I'm not asleep."

Rose pushed the door open and gasped. Her father looked old and frail. She'd never seen him like this.

"Is that you, Rose?" This time his voice carried a little more strength.

Before Rose could step into the room, Thomas stopped her. "I don't want you in there if this is what I think it is."

"Thomas?" Her father tried to raise his head but quickly dropped back on his rumpled pillow. "Is that. . .really. . .you?" He had a hard time getting the words out.

She wanted to go to him, but she knew Thomas wouldn't have prevented her from doing it if it hadn't been important. She put her hand on Thomas's arm. "Please take care of him."

Thomas put his arm around her and gave her a comforting squeeze. "Wait out here. I'll let you know what I find."

Thomas closed the door behind him, thankful he'd left Rose in the hall when a paroxysm of coughing came from the older man. After hurrying to the bedside, Thomas pulled up a chair and sat beside his patient.

When the coughing spell ceased, Thomas placed his hand on Mr. Fletcher's forehead. The man definitely had a fever. "Mr. Fletcher, how long have you been feeling bad?"

The older man swallowed then croaked, "About. . .a week. . . Is Rose. . .okay?"

"She's fine. I just want to take care of you before she comes in here. When you got sick, you didn't stop working right away, did you?" Thomas studied the sick man's flushed face and watery eyes.

Mr. Fletcher shook his head a little but quickly stopped and closed his eyes as a tear trickled down one pale cheek.

"Does it hurt to move your head?"

His eyes slowly opened. "Yes."

"I heard your cough. Does your chest hurt?"

The older man placed a trembling hand on his chest. "Yes." The word came out on a whisper.

Thomas took out his thermometer and shook the mercury down before placing it under the patient's tongue. He didn't like what he saw. The Spanish flu. Every year many people contracted the disease. He had treated a number of them, and some of them didn't survive. Without a doubt, Mr. Fletcher was suffering from influenza. No matter how much Thomas learned about different ailments, he often felt helpless against them. But he would use everything he knew to save this man who'd had such a profound influence on him.

He took the instrument from the man's mouth and frowned at the high number that registered. First he'd have to get the temperature down, if he could, but he also needed to use steam to break up the congestion in his chest. The dilemma all physicians faced. What was the best way to treat this patient? And such an important one, at that.

After sterilizing the thermometer with alcohol, he returned it to his bag. Thomas would need to get help, but he didn't want Rose in the room with her father. He wanted to protect her from the disease. Although he and Rose had slowly drawn closer, he hoped they would develop a deep and abiding love. He knew he already had.

Trying to picture what could be going on in her father's bedroom, Rose paced the hallway and prayed. *Lord, please don't let Daddy die. I need him. He's all the family I have left.* As if

God didn't know that.

Memories of the way Thomas cared for Maximilian flitted through her mind. Thomas was the best thing that could happen for her father. *Give him wisdom, Lord, even if he doesn't know You.*

Mrs. Barclay came up the stairs then approached down the hallway. "Rose, I brought your coffee. You're probably still chilled."

Rose took the proffered heavy mug and wrapped her fingers around its warmth. "Thank you. I really did need this." She took a sip of the steaming liquid, finally realizing just how cold she was, even though the log house kept them snug from winter's cold winds.

"So how's your father?" Worry brought deep grooves to the older woman's brow.

"I don't know. Thomas wouldn't let me go all the way into the sickroom." Tears breached her lower eyelids and slid down her cheeks.

Mrs. Barclay wound her arms around Rose and held her close against her cushiony bosom without spilling the coffee Rose clutched between them. "The good Lord's watching over him."

Rose nodded. "And Thomas is a very good doctor."

"And how do you know that for sure?"

Maybe telling her about what happened at the party would make the time pass more quickly. "He was at Thalia's party when one of the guests became sick. He knows what he's doing." Her words brought herself comfort, too.

"I hope you're right. I have been real worried about your father."

The door opened, and both women turned toward it. Thomas stepped through and closed it behind him. "I believe that Mr. Fletcher has the Spanish flu."

The women gasped in unison.

"I know, it's serious, but I'll do everything I can to help him." He raked his fingers through his dark hair, making it stand out in all directions.

Rose had never seen him like this. His coat and tie had been discarded, and his sleeves were rolled up, revealing muscled forearms. A stethoscope hung around his neck. He'd never looked better to her, because this was who he was—a doctor through and through. A glimmer of hope for her father entered her heart.

"How can we help?" Mrs. Barclay stood with her fists pressed against her ample hips.

"Have you given him any aspirin?"

She shook her head. "I don't think we have any out here on the ranch. I have some at the house in town. I could make sure one of the hands brings some back the next time anyone goes to town."

"That's okay, I have some in my bag." He took a deep breath and huffed it out. "I need a washbasin of cold water and some cloths to help me bring down his fever. After we get that lowered, we'll use steam for the congestion in his chest."

"I'll get them right away." Mrs. Barclay hurried toward the stairs.

Rose marched over and stopped so close she could almost feel his heartbeat. "I want to see my father now." She started to go around him, but he gently held her arm.

"I can't take a chance on you getting influenza. I'll take care of him." His gaze bored into her, making her feel as if he could see everything in her heart.

"You don't understand." She heaved a deep sigh. "I will stay with him and help you. I don't want to be anywhere else." Her emphasis on the last words echoed in the silence of the hallway.

Thomas stared at her; then his frown softened. "All right, Rose, you can come in, but you must do everything I tell you."

She nodded. If that was the only way, so be it.

For hours, Thomas watched Rose sit beside her father's bed and bathe his face and chest with cool water and then place the folded cloth on his forehead until the fabric warmed. Over and over she repeated the process until the cloth finally remained cool to the touch.

Thomas wondered exactly what time it was. Midnight had passed long ago. "Rose, you need to get some rest."

"And what about you? You've been here longer than I have." Her eyes looked strained and weary, and her pale face had a pinched look about it.

"I'm used to taking care of patients." His reminder didn't seem to shake her resolve.

Another bout of deep coughing wracked the patient. Thomas didn't know how long Mr. Fletcher could keep this up. He looked so frail, not the strong man Thomas remembered so well.

"We have to ease that congestion in his chest." Thomas

brushed thick black hair peppered with gray from Mr. Fletcher's forehead.

Rose stood, but didn't let go of her father's hand. "How do we do that?"

"With steam."

After sending Rose for the teakettle, a bowl, and some towels, Thomas studied the bed. Built differently from the one where he took care of Newbolt, this bed would be harder to tent.

The older man's hand snaked out and latched onto Thomas's. "Should. . .my Rose. . .be in here?"

Compassion touched Thomas's heart. "I know what you're thinking, but Rose wouldn't stay away. I'll just have to pray that the good Lord protects her."

"Good. . .Lord? When did. . . ?" The man's eyes begged for an answer.

Thomas dropped into the chair Rose had vacated. "Yes, I know Jesus now."

A faint smile veiled his old mentor's face.

"Because of all the things you told me, I was finally ready to listen when one of the doctors I interned under shared the Lord with me." Thomas clasped the other man's hand. "But I wouldn't have listened to him if it hadn't have been for you and your influence. And I don't mean the money to go to medical school. The most valuable thing you did for me was prepare me to hear Dr. Denison's words."

"I'm. . .glad." Tears squeezed out of the older man's eyes after he closed them.

Thomas loved this man, but he loved his daughter even more. If he had thought about it before, he would have admitted he had loved Rose as a girl, but that early love was more as he'd love a younger sister. The love he felt for the woman she had become had nothing brotherly about it. He loved her as he would love the woman he married. A forever kind of love.

When Rose arrived at the top of the stairs, she wondered how she would open the door. Her hands were full. She walked carefully so none of the boiling-hot water would spill from the teapot.

The bedroom door opened, and Thomas glanced out. "There you are, Rose." He hurried to take some of her burdens.

They placed the items on a table near the bed.

"We also need a sheet." Thomas couldn't keep his eyes off Rose. Even after staying awake most of the night, she looked beautiful to him. He wanted to brush back a loose auburn curl that probably tickled her cheek.

As if she felt his glance, she whisked the offending lock of hair back and stuffed the end behind her bun. "Has he been awake since I left?"

"Yes, we had a short discussion."

"That's a good sign, isn't it?" Her pleading expression almost broke his heart.

"I certainly hope so." He watched her leave the room to fetch the sheet.

While she was gone, he folded the towels into thick pads.

When she returned they worked together to help her father sit up, then draped the tent over him with a steaming bowl of water resting on the padded towels in his lap.

For the next couple of hours, they continued to change the water in the bowl so her father breathed in the steam. Finally, most of his coughing settled down, but the heat had brought back the fever.

Rose only left the sickroom for short periods of time. Thomas spent all the time she was gone in fervent prayer for his patient and the man's daughter. By midafternoon the next day after a long bout with chills and fluctuating high temperatures, the fever finally broke.

Thomas sent Rose away and cleaned up his patient, dressing him in a fresh nightshirt. He helped the man sit in a comfortable chair while Mrs. Barclay changed the sheets on the bed. After Thomas returned Mr. Fletcher to his bed, Rose walked into the room.

Remembering the verse in Proverbs about a merry heart being good medicine, Thomas started regaling them with funny stories from his days in medical school. Soon the room rang with laughter. The laughing Rose he remembered had returned. Her laughter blessed his heart. Even her father roused much of the time and joined in. Could things be looking up for Thomas?

Chapter 8

Rose hadn't wanted to leave her father's room, but now she agreed that Thomas was right. After a hot bath and a long nap, she felt refreshed. She wouldn't have left if her father hadn't been better. Even though she'd been afraid she'd sleep a long time and miss something, she awoke early in the evening. She dressed and fixed her hair quickly so she could get back up there and be sure Daddy hadn't had a relapse.

When she started up the stairs, she heard Thomas talking to someone. She knew she shouldn't eavesdrop on a private conversation, but she didn't want to miss any detail about her father he might not want to share with her. So she crept quietly up the stairs, skipping the third one from the top that always squeaked. Thomas's voice receded then moved toward her. He must be pacing the hallway.

"Father God, I praise You for the miracle You worked in this house. Thank You for healing Mr. Fletcher. I wasn't ready to let him go, and I'm glad it wasn't Your will to take him right now. And thank You for protecting Rose from this dreaded disease. Lord, my medical degree can't do a single thing to heal anyone, but with You, I can help people. Thank You for being with me this time."

Once again his voice faded away until she couldn't understand the words. How could she have been so wrong about him? Those memories from childhood when he jeered at her for her faith in God had colored her perception of him far too long. She had changed. Grown and matured. Why hadn't she considered the possibility Thomas could have learned to love the Lord during those years he was away?

The spark of love she kept trying to extinguish in her heart became a flame, fed by the knowledge that Thomas was a true man of God, someone she could spend her life loving. Knowing she didn't have to hold a tight rein on her emotions made her heart light and brought a smile to her face.

She stepped into the hallway and found it empty. Where was the object of her affections?

He'd been up longer than she had. Maybe he was in one of the other bedrooms. She hurried to the door of her father's room and knocked before opening it. Her father sat in a chair near the window, and Thomas stood beside him.

"Well, look who's here." This time her father's voice sounded strong, and no cough punctuated his words.

Rose rushed across the room and threw her arms around him, careful not to be too rough. "Daddy, I'm so glad you're better." She planted a kiss on his leathery cheek.

"I'm right as rain now, thanks to Thomas." Her father shook his forefinger at him. "He's a really good doctor."

"Because of you and Harvard Medical School." Thomas's laugh rolled around the room.

"You don't have to tell anybody else about that." Her father sounded stern. "It's just between you and me."

Rose looked from one man to the other. "What's going on here? What did I miss?"

Both men started talking at once.

She threw up her hands. "Wait. . .wait! One at a time, please."

"I said, 'Nothing,'" her father growled.

"And I was trying to tell you that your father paid for me to go to medical school."

Rose crossed her arms and gave her father her full attention. "Is that so?"

He clasped his hands in his lap. "I could see the potential in him, and we needed a doctor in Breckenridge."

"But Dr. Whitten came about a year after Thomas left." Rose was trying to figure this all out.

"That's why I went to Denver when I came back, instead of Breckenridge." Thomas stuffed his hands into his pockets and gave her a tight grin.

She leaned down and kissed her father's other cheek. "You're really an old softie under all that gruffness. I'm proud of you, and I agree that no one else needs to know."

Rose hadn't noticed how tense Thomas had become until he relaxed at that last statement. She turned toward him. "It's time you got some rest, too." She shooed him out. "I want to spend time with Daddy."

After Thomas left, Rose pulled a chair beside her father and sat down. "How do you really feel?" Her hands itched to touch his forehead to make sure his fever hadn't returned.

"I'm fine. Just a little weak. Won't be long until I get my strength back." He tried to look stern, but she could see right through his ruse. "Now tell me about your trip to Denver."

For the next few minutes, she regaled him with tales of the party, the storm, Maximilian's illness, and even about Thomas taking her shopping. Of course, she left out a few details of that trip. Especially about the Hershey's Kiss. Too much emotion was attached to that moment.

When she was talked out, her father's eyes roved over every feature of her face. "Something's different about you. You've changed somehow. . .even since you came home. You have a glow that you didn't have yesterday." Shrewd eyes peered from under his thick brows. "Want to tell me about it?"

What was there to tell besides how she felt about Thomas? Did she really want to talk to her father about that?

He waited patiently at first. Finally, he said, "You won't be able to keep it from me very long. We've always talked about everything."

Rose knew he was right. She started with the party. How Thomas had affected her. Then she recounted how he scoffed at her faith years ago before he went away to medical school, so she tried to hold her emotions in check.

He laughed when she said that. "So what changed your mind?"

"When I came up the stairs just now, I heard Thomas

praying, thanking God for healing you and protecting me from the Spanish flu. The way he was talking to the Lord, I could tell He was an old friend to Thomas." She stopped and looked down at her hands folded in her lap.

"So do you love him?" Her father had always been direct with her.

"I think so." She looked up at him. "How can I know that I'm truly in love?"

He started to laugh but stopped after the first hoot. "You'll know. No mistaking how I felt for your mother, and she returned the feelings."

Rose remembered how the love they felt for each other gave them a glow anyone could see. She wondered if she had a radiance like that.

"Just trust your instincts and let the Lord work it out for you. You know you can trust Him."

That's what she really wanted. To experience the love God ordained between a man and a woman. She was more than halfway there. If only she knew what Thomas felt for her.

Thomas awakened to the enticing aromas of frying bacon and baking biscuits. He'd slept all night. Evidently Mr. Fletcher hadn't needed him. A good sign the crusty rancher was on the mend. After dressing, Thomas stopped by his old boss's bedroom and knocked on the door.

"Come in." This time the voice sounded strong.

When Thomas opened the door, Mr. Fletcher sat on the

side of the bed, fully clothed. "It's good to see you, sir. Especially since you dressed yourself."

"I don't see any sense in lying in bed all day today." His patient huffed out a breath. "Took me longer than usual, but I managed."

"Maybe you could take breakfast up here before you tried to venture out. I'll bring it to you." Thomas knew he would help Rose's father down the stairs if he insisted.

"Sounds good to me. I'll be waiting for you." The older man stood and slowly made his way over to the chair near the window.

When Thomas arrived in the kitchen, Rose was setting four places at the table. "How did you sleep, Thomas?"

"Very soundly."

She looked rested, too. Instead of her usual waves and bun, Rose had pulled her hair back and braided it. Wisps framed her face like a halo of morning sunlight.

"Is Daddy coming down to eat, or do I need to take him a tray?" She placed the last utensil beside a plate.

"If it's all right with you, I'd like to take the tray up to him. I know he's improved today, but I'll eat with him. It'll help me evaluate how much better he really is."

Rose agreed and started fixing a tray with two breakfasts on it. When she finished, Thomas took it upstairs. This time when he knocked on the door, Mr. Fletcher opened it.

Thomas carried the tray to the table. The two chairs had been placed on opposite sides. While they ate, he observed the vast difference in the rancher. Although the man hadn't regained all his strength, Thomas was amazed at how far he'd come. After they finished with the food, they lingered over heavy mugs of coffee. Thomas lifted his to take a drink of the fragrant brew.

"So, Thomas, what are your feelings for my daughter?"

Thomas sputtered and almost spit out the liquid. How did the man know?

"Did you really think I couldn't see the way your eyes follow her every move?"

Thomas tried to detect any censure in the question but found none. "I like her very much."

Mr. Fletcher's eyes narrowed. "Is that all?"

Thomas shifted in his seat and placed one ankle across the other knee, resting his forearm on the raised knee. He tried to relax. "Actually, sir, I think I'm falling in love with her."

"You think?" The older man snorted. "You really need to know, son."

Thomas dropped his foot to the floor and stood, then rubbed the back of his neck. He turned to face Mr. Fletcher straight on. "I love Rose, sir, and would like your permission to court her."

"All right!" The old man slapped his knee. "It took you long enough to tell me." He cackled. "I'd be right proud to have you for a son-in-law."

Thomas laughed right along with him. Relief felt good.

Now that her father was well, Rose remembered the presents

she had bought. She went to her bedroom and returned to the kitchen with the tea bags for Mrs. Barclay. "I picked these up while I was in Denver."

"You always were such a sweet girl." The housekeeper gave Rose one of her famous bear hugs. "Should we try some of these now?"

"No, you go ahead. I bought Daddy some Hershey bars with almonds. I'll take them upstairs."

Before Rose could knock on her father's door, she heard a loud hoot of laughter. She wondered if she should bother the two men, but then she decided she wanted to know what that laughter was about. She waited until the noise quieted down, because she knew they would never hear her knock through all the racket.

"Come in." Her father's voice still contained a remnant of mirth. That was a good sign. She opened the door. Thomas stood beside the table with both hands shoved in his pockets. She'd noticed he did that when he was agitated or nervous. For a moment, she wondered which one he was this time.

"Hey, girl, come on over here." High color marked her father's cheeks, and his eyes twinkled. He peeked at Thomas. "You want to tell her, or do you want me to?"

"Tell me what?" Rose would have put her hands on her hips if she hadn't been holding the chocolate bars. She studied each man in turn. Something was up. That was for sure.

Thomas cleared his throat. She'd never heard him do that before. Maybe something was wrong with him. "Your father and I were discussing. . ." He left the sentence hanging while he expelled a deep breath. He crossed his arms and stood tall. "I want to court you, and he's given me his blessing."

Everything around her faded away while Rose stared at the man she loved. "Court? . . . As in?"

Thomas dropped his hands to his sides and took a step toward her. "As in learning whether we could love each other."

Her father harrumphed in the background, but she didn't take her eyes from Thomas. "Love. . .each. . .other?"

Thomas reached for her and gently clasped her shoulders. "Rose, may I court you?"

All she could do was nod.

The next day Thomas rode into Breckenridge. He wanted to buy some small gifts for Rose. Something to give her every day. The mercantile contained a large selection. He perused the displays and bought a book of poetry and a copy of *The House of Mirth* by Edith Wharton. He hoped she'd like them. In another section, he found a display of the new teddy bears named for Teddy Roosevelt, so he purchased one. He knew Rose liked to sing, so he bought sheet music to "Sweethearts" by Robert B. Smith. The words should tell her how he felt. He picked up some of the new Crayola crayons, because he hoped their relationship would always be filled with fun.

"Is that you, Thomas Stanton?" A booming voice behind him alerted everyone in the store of his presence.

He turned around. "Brandon Stone, I'd know you anywhere,

but where are the overalls?"

Brandon laughed. "I could beat you in any footrace, even if I was barefooted."

"That you could." Thomas studied the man before him.

Now his school chum wore a suit and bowler hat. "I work at the bank. Just made vice president."

What a change.

"Congratulations."

"Didn't I hear you finished medical school and came back to Colorado?"

Thomas nodded.

"Why are you working in Denver?"

Thomas wasn't thrilled that everyone in the store had stopped what they were doing and eavesdropped on their conversation. However, it might not be considered eavesdropping, since Brandon talked so loud.

"You already had a doctor, so I'm sharing a practice—"

"Don't have one now." Brandon's assertion raised Thomas's eyebrows.

"What do you mean?"

Brandon removed his hat and circled it in his hands. "Doc Whitten left town on yesterday's train, and he isn't coming back. His father is very sick, and he asked Doc to come home and take over his business until he gets well. I told him if he left, we'd have to replace him. Didn't bother him a bit."

Thomas thought he knew where this was leading. What would he do if Brandon asked him to move here?

Rose accepted the mail Thomas brought home. She shuffled through the few pieces and found an envelope addressed to her. She tore it open; then a smile crossed her face.

"What is it, Rose?" Thomas leaned toward her and enjoyed the floral fragrance of her hair.

"An invitation from Natalie Daire. Her birthday is Christmas Eve, and she's having a party." She sighed.

"What's the matter with that?" Thomas wanted to slay dragons for her, or at least work out her problems.

"I'd like to go, but I can't be in Denver on Christmas Eve and at home on Christmas Day. That won't work."

Thomas took her hand and peered into her eyes. "Do you want to go to the party?"

"Yes, but—"

"No buts." He dropped a swift kiss on her forehead.

"Thomas, will you be back in Denver by then?"

He squeezed her hand. "Would you like for me to stay in Breckenridge?"

Rose took a deep breath. "How could you do that?"

His smile gave her hope. "I saw Brandon Stone at the mercantile. He told me that Breckenridge needs a doctor right away."

Rose heard her father get up from the squeaky leather chair across the room.

"What're you talking about?" He came to stand beside her. They both waited expectantly.

"The other doctor left, and Brandon asked me if I would take his place."

She wanted to shout, "Hallelujah!" but didn't. "Do you want to take the position, Thomas?" She held her breath.

"That's the main reason I went to medical school." He looked at her father. "So I could return to Breckenridge to practice medicine."

Her father let out a whoop then clapped Thomas on the back.

"So, Rose," Thomas asked. "What about the party?"

Her father smiled at both of them. "Why don't we just celebrate early, and then you two can go to your party?"

After they had read the Christmas story and exchanged gifts the night before Christmas Eve, Thomas watched Rose's father excuse himself and head upstairs to his room. She turned toward her own bedroom.

"Rose." Thomas stood beside the Christmas tree where he'd been blowing out the candles. "I have another gift for you. Can you stay a few minutes?"

She hurried to his side. "You've been giving me a gift almost every day. What more could you have left?" She stared up at Thomas. Her nearness almost made him speechless.

"This, Rose." He handed her a tiny package overpowered by a big red bow.

He leaned down so close that their foreheads almost touched. She fumbled with the wrapping, finally uncovering the small box.

Inside she found a gold ring with a pearl nestled on soft cotton.

She turned her gaze to his. "It's beautiful, Thomas."

He gently took the box from her and set it on the table. He lifted the ring and slid it on her ring finger while gazing deep into her fathomless eyes. "Rose, would you marry me?"

"Yes." The word came out on a breath.

He slid his arms around her and pulled her close. "I love you."

Just before his lips touched hers, she whispered, "I love you, too."

Her eager acceptance of his kiss sealed that love for all their lives.

Laughter isn't the best medicine—love is.

LENA NELSON DOOLEY

Lena loves the Rocky Mountains of Colorado in the winter—
the snow, the peaks, the trees, the frozen lakes. This collection is
her eighteenth book release. She's a full-time author who loves
to lift up other authors. You can read interviews on her blog:
http://lenanelsondooley.blogspot.com. She lives in Texas with
her husband, who has been the love of her life for more than
forty-four years. They love spending time with their extended
family, now including a great-grandson. Learn more about her
at her Web site: www.lenanelsondooley.com.

Almost Home

by Susan Page Davis

Chapter 1

December 1913

Patricia stared out the window of the train as it pulled into the depot at Colorado Springs. Snow fell fast, and she could barely make out the boardinghouse across the street. Her hopes of making it home to the Logan ranch tonight plummeted.

When she stepped down onto the platform, she didn't see John Ryder. She looked about anxiously until he suddenly appeared out of the driving snow.

"Mr. Ryder! Thank you for meeting me!" The wind snatched Patricia's words as she hauled her leather bag out of the passenger car.

"Glad you made it through, Miss Logan." Ryder reached to take her luggage, and Patricia pulled her wool scarf across her face. "This wind is mighty fierce. Just stick close to me, and we'll get over to the house." He set off with his head lowered.

Patricia followed, stepping in his deep boot prints in the snow. Even in the street, it was nearly a foot deep, and she felt the cold crystals falling down inside the tops of her boots.

They gained the porch of the Ryders' boardinghouse, and he slammed the door behind them, shutting out the storm. The quiet warmth of the entry enveloped her. Mrs. Ryder, plump and maternal, came to the front door to meet her. Patricia longed to remove her wraps, shake off the snow, and sit before the cozy fire she could see through the parlor doorway.

But an even deeper longing prompted her to ask instead, "Will we be able to leave right away?"

Mr. Ryder eyed her as he unwound his red wool muffler. Patricia almost laughed because she could see the snowflakes that had clung to his arched eyebrows melting as she spoke.

"Can't go anywhere tonight, Miss Logan."

"Are you certain?" She'd anticipated his answer, but that didn't ease her disappointment.

"Oh no, child," his wife said. "The storm is too wild. I misdoubt the car could get down Main Street in this weather, let alone all the way to your uncle's ranch."

"Not a chance tonight," John Ryder said. "Probably not tomorrow, either. You were lucky the train got this far."

"But I need to get home." She stopped, realizing the futility of her pleas. The conductor on the train had come through the car before they pulled up at the depot, advising all passengers to disembark as the locomotive would not likely go on tonight.

"We've got a room all prepared for you," Mrs. Ryder said.

Patricia nodded in defeat. "I appreciate that. And I expect

you'll have extra guests tonight from the train."

At that moment, a robust knock on the door sounded, and Mr. Ryder went to open it.

"Hello," called the new arrival. "Any chance of getting a room tonight? The train is stopping here until morning."

"Come on," Mrs. Ryder said to Patricia in a conspiratorial whisper. "I knew you'd be disappointed that you had to stay over, but I've kept the best room for you."

Patricia sighed and picked up her bag. Mrs. Ryder puffed up the stairs ahead of her and led her down the hall.

"Maybe a sleigh could get through tomorrow," Patricia suggested. "Does Mr. Ryder have a sleigh?"

Her hostess shook her head. "We don't keep horses anymore, Miss Logan, since we got the car. It's too bad your uncle doesn't have a telephone at the ranch so you could call him and tell him you're safe. Here now. Your room is all snug and waiting for you."

"Thank you." Patricia entered the bedroom and realized how tired she was. When she'd left the Christmas party at her friend Thalia Bloom's home, she rode to the train station in Denver with another friend, Natalie Daire, arriving on the platform at the last possible moment. She'd anticipated traveling late into the night, but now the four-poster bed with its handmade patchwork coverlet did look inviting.

When she was alone, she undressed and blew out the lamp. Pushing aside the ruffled curtains at the window over the street, she looked out. No automobiles or wagons traveled through the storm. The only movement was the blowing, drifting snow—

falling fast, in a thick, swirling mass. No one would leave Colorado Springs until the storm was over.

A gray light streamed in through the window when Patricia woke. She hopped out of bed and hurried across the cold, bare floor. The clouds lowered and light snow was still falling, but the wind seemed to have abated. The deep snow that drifted unbroken across Main Street looked daunting, but Aunt Edna needed her, and Patricia was determined she would get home today.

She dressed and packed her things then went downstairs to the parlor, where she waited impatiently for Mrs. Ryder to serve breakfast. The stranded travelers who had filled the boardinghouse to capacity the night before began to fill the dining room. Patricia joined them, and all made introductions and exclaimed about the inclement weather. When Mr. Ryder appeared in the doorway and greeted them with a cheery "Good morning, all," Patricia pounced on him.

"Mr. Ryder, is there any chance. . . ?"

"I'm sorry, Miss Logan." He gave a mournful shake of his head. "I don't expect to take that car out of the carriage house until spring."

"But. . ." Patricia stared at him. Her brained whirred, trying to come up with a solution.

Mrs. Ryder brought a platter of pancakes and a pitcher of warm syrup from the kitchen.

"You'd best hunker down here with us until your uncle Bill

can fetch you in his sleigh." She set the platter down before a hosiery salesman and a mine supervisor who had come in after Patricia the evening before.

Patricia sat down and ate her breakfast, thinking as she chewed. She refused coffee afterward and pushed back her chair. "I believe I'll walk down to the livery stable and see if they can help me."

Mr. Ryder blew on his steaming cup and sipped the hot liquid, then set it down. "Mrs. Ryder's right. You won't get out of this town today. It's still snowing."

"But it's not so bad as it was." Patricia eyed him, her hope shrinking like a snowdrift in bright sunlight.

He shook his head. "There's more coming, if you ask my opinion. Not that you did."

"Well, I'm going to give the livery a try." Patricia turned to her hostess. "Thank you, Mrs. Ryder. Breakfast was delicious. If I find transportation, I'll be back in a jiffy for my things."

"Surely you're not going out this morning," Mrs. Ryder protested.

"I'm sure I can make it a few yards down the street to the stable."

Mr. Ryder set his fork down and grimaced. "Won't nobody be leaving town today. I suppose they might break the roads tomorrow if it doesn't snow more."

She swallowed hard. "I really can't wait. My aunt needs me, and I promised her I'd only be gone two nights. I'm already a day overdue."

He winced and shook his head doubtfully. "You might hire

a sleigh from Ned Peakes at the livery. Perhaps. If the snow's not too deep."

"And a driver?"

Ryder shrugged. "Doubtful. Very doubtful."

She stood thinking for a moment. She didn't feel confident enough to set out on her own, driving a horse in winter, and she wasn't at all sure she could find her way home alone in the snow-covered landscape. If Mr. Peakes couldn't supply a driver, she would have to find someone willing to take her. She decided to face that hurdle when she reached it.

She went to the entry and wriggled into her coat, hat, and gloves, then opened the front door and ventured out into the glaring white world.

She would not allow herself to think that she would be stuck for another day in the town ten miles from Uncle Bill's ranch. Somehow she would get home.

Well, Lord, I guess this is when I should ask You to show me how to get home. She refused to consider that it might be God's will to delay her trip home. How could it be? Of course He wanted her at Aunt Edna's side. Uncle Bill had married late in life, and he and Edna expected the arrival of their first child any day. Aunt Edna was a sweet and wise woman and had become dear to Patricia in the three years she had been Mrs. Bill Logan. Now, at age thirty-eight, she faced her first delivery. Uncle Bill was ecstatic about the coming child but worried that Edna would have a difficult birth. Patricia knew she had to get home, as much for Uncle Bill as for Aunt Edna.

The livery stable down the street seemed her only hope, and

she headed toward it, wading through the deep snow. It came in over her boot tops almost at once and sent shudders up her spine, but she forced her way onward through the unbroken whiteness. A few flakes still fell, but surely they would stop soon.

Inside the stable was dim, and the warmer air smelled of hay, manure, and horses. Two men conversed at the far end of the building while one of them saddled a horse, and Patricia walked toward them.

"Help you, miss?" The older man turned toward her and left the other to finish his job.

The one who spoke must be Peakes, the stable's owner. Patricia walked toward him and put on the most confident smile she could muster. "Yes, I wondered if you had a sleigh and a driver available today. I need to get to my—"

"Nope."

She caught her breath. "It's very important, sir."

"Still nope."

"Mr. Peakes, I must get home today. It's only ten miles, and—" She shot a glance toward the other man and stared in disbelief. It was dim inside the stable, but still. . . Could it be?

"Jared? Jared Booker?"

The younger man turned toward her, and her heart pounded. Her mouth was suddenly dry, and her stomach turned hand-springs. She couldn't be mistaken, even in the poor light. His straight nose, his gentle brown eyes, the quirk at the corner of his mouth.

He studied her, a puzzled frown wrinkling his brow. "Patricia Logan?"

She laughed and hurried forward to grasp his hand. "Jared! Yes, it's me. And you used to call me Trisha."

She looked him over and shook her head. He had changed, gaining maturity, of course, and his form had a new solidity. His shoulders had broadened, and he was taller, too. Of course, he'd been only fifteen years old the last time she saw him. He looked wonderful, better even than her girlish memories of him.

She scowled at him. "Why didn't you write to me?"

Jared stared down at her and slowly began to smile. "I can't believe it! What are you doing so far from home in this weather?"

"I've been to a party in Denver. My old school friend Thalia Bloom threw an early Christmas celebration, and when I left last night, the storm was at its peak. The train barely made it this far. All the passengers had to stop here last night at the Ryders' boardinghouse."

"Imagine our meeting like this. I take it you didn't intend to stay in town last night?"

"No, Mr. Ryder had said he would drive me home, but the storm prevented that. Now he can't get his car out in the deep snow. He may not run it again until spring. So I came here to see if I could find some other mode of transportation to the ranch. I didn't see you at Ryders', though. Where did you stay last night?"

"I bunked here at the stable with Mr. Peakes. As a matter of fact, I was heading out for your uncle's place this morning."

She grabbed his arm and squelched a scream of joy. "That's perfect! Take me with you!"

"Oh, I don't know. It'll be hard riding. Do you have a horse?"

"No, and Mr. Ryder seemed to think the snow is too deep even for sleighs."

"That's true," Peakes said. "Can't send a team out in these drifts. They wouldn't get to the edge of town."

"Please, Jared?"

He opened his mouth then closed it.

"What is it?" she asked.

Jared looked uneasily toward the stable owner. "No offense, Trisha, but I'm not sure I'd want to be responsible for you. They say there may be more snow before the day's out."

She gulped down the lump forming in her throat. No matter what, she would not let Jared ride out of her life again so easily. "Perhaps we could go down the street to Ryders' and get a cup of tea, and you could tell me—"

"No time. The traveling's not good, and I want to get to the ranch before it gets worse."

"Oh, please don't leave me here! I need to get home."

Jared looked toward Peakes, as if hoping to be rescued from a snare, but the liveryman just spit toward a pile of manure and looked away.

"Mr. Peakes, do you have a horse she can rent?" Jared asked.

"Afraid not, in this deep snow. I gave you my opinion. You ought to wait here until the weather breaks. Likely your nags will get in a deep drift and flounder around 'til they exhaust themselves."

Jared sighed. "So you won't rent Miss Logan a mount?"

Peakes shook his head. "If you did get through all right, I wouldn't get him back 'til who knows when. Now, if you want to *buy* a horse—"

Patricia said hastily, "No. I'm sorry, I don't have the funds for that."

Jared pushed his hat back and scratched his head. "I need to hit the trail, Trisha. I'm sorry about your predicament, but maybe your uncle can send someone down for you tomorrow."

"Please, Jared!" She clutched his sleeve, unwilling to let him ride off alone. "There must be a way."

Again he looked down at her, and Patricia felt the strange, unsettled feeling she'd had when she recognized him. For hundreds of lonely evenings at the boarding school she had told herself that eventually she would hear from him and see him again. Uncle Bill and Aunt Edna would welcome him home. Thoughts of Jared had grown into dreams of a future together. She had allowed herself for a long time to dream of winning Jared's heart. In those reveries, he rode back into her life a beloved hero. They bought a ranch of their own and raised superior horses, and they were supremely happy. Obviously, those fantasies were far from the truth. He was heading toward the Logan ranch but not to see her.

Jared cleared his throat and looked at Peakes. "This one was my shadow when my father and her uncle ran the ranch together."

"I take it that was some time ago."

"Oh yes, she was just a half-grown tomboy. Wanted to be a cowpoke."

The livery owner smiled, and Patricia knew her face was beet red now.

"Well, I've grown up, Jared. I promise I won't be any trouble to you if you'll take me along."

"I don't see a way to do that, Trisha. I need to get moving."

"But. . .we haven't even had a chance to get reacquainted." She looked to Peakes for support. "Jared's father and my uncle were old army buddies, back in the eighties. They were stationed together at Fort Garland, and when they mustered out, they bought a ranch as partners."

Peakes nodded. "I heared your uncle tell about the old days."

She felt some encouragement and raced on. "Yes, well, Uncle Bill and Rupert Booker had a bit of a falling out ten years ago. Rupert moved his family to Texas, and Jared and I haven't seen each other since."

"I'm really sorry," Jared murmured. He moved toward the back of the barn, but instead of untying the horse he had saddled, he opened another stall door.

Peakes's eyes glittered, and for the first time he showed some enthusiasm for the conversation. "He's got some fine horses, Miss Logan. Now, Booker, if you ever want to sell one—"

"I'll let you know." Jared entered the stall and emerged leading a magnificent, coal black stallion. The young horse snorted and lifted his feet extra high as he pranced beside Jared.

Patricia stared at the black's fine head, the sculpted ears and bright eyes. His deep chest rippled as Jared led him toward the paint gelding and untied the saddled horse from the ring in the wall.

"He's beautiful!"

"Easy, now." Jared stroked the colt's neck, and the black nickered and snuffled his coat collar.

Patricia's heart leaped. "How old is he?"

Jared frowned. "I know what you're thinking, and the answer is no."

"But—"

"No."

She clamped her lips together to keep from arguing, but she couldn't help clenching her gloved hands into fists and giving a tiny stamp on the straw-strewn dirt floor.

Jared and Mr. Peakes laughed, and once more she felt a blush creeping up her cheeks, this time from shame at her childish frustration. If she wanted Jared to believe she had grown up, this was no way to show it.

Jared led his two horses toward the door, and when he was close to her, he stopped and smiled at her.

"Listen, any other time, I wouldn't mind taking you. In fact, I'd enjoy the company. It's really good to see you again."

Patricia felt her insides thawing in the warmth of his wistful smile.

"But with this snow, I can't risk it. This stallion is only three years old. He's barely saddle broke, and besides, he doesn't belong to me. I couldn't let you ride him."

"But you could ride him." Immediately she knew she should have kept quiet.

Jared's smile faded.

"No, Trisha. I'm sorry."

Chapter 2

Jared led his paint horse, Patches, toward the big stable door. The colt followed a few steps behind, as much following the gelding as he was responding to Jared's gentle tug on the lead line.

Trisha scrambled around to walk beside him.

"Aunt Edna is expecting a baby anytime now, Jared. I'd hate not to be there when she needs me."

"Aunt Edna?" Jared had no idea what she was talking about. Peakes eased past Patches and slid the big door open.

"That's right, you don't know. Uncle Bill got married at last!"

"Not really!" Jared couldn't help smiling. He remembered Bill Logan as a gruff old bachelor. Getting married was about the last thing he'd expect of Bill.

"Yes. Three years ago, almost. And Edna is as sweet as they come. But she's thirty-eight, and this is her first baby. The midwife woman said sometimes older women have a. . .a difficult time." Patricia's cheeks went scarlet, and she avoided looking toward Mr. Peakes, concentrating instead on Jared. "If I don't get out of here now, I may be stuck in this place for a week or more! Jared, please. I'm begging. It's very important that I get home."

Jared felt himself wavering. He looked out into the stable yard. It wasn't snowing at the moment, but the gray clouds still threatened more. Ten miles to the Logan ranch. They could do it in an hour in summer. But this time of year?

"This stud colt is really green, Trisha."

"But you're such a good rider."

He sucked in a breath, trying not to laugh. She'd always had a way of wrapping him—and Uncle Bill and all the ranch hands, for that matter—around her little finger. "Have you kept up your riding since I last saw you?"

Patricia lowered her lashes and eyed him cautiously. "Of course! I ride all over the ranch with Uncle Bill and Joe Simmons. You remember Joe?"

"Sure I do. He was always good to me when we lived at the ranch."

"Well, he's still an old softie. Takes me on rambles. And I'm a good rider. You know I am!"

Jared sighed. She was always persistent. Stubborn, her uncle Bill called it. "I suppose if I showed up alone and they found out I'd seen you here and left you stranded, it wouldn't set well with your folks."

Patricia's heart leapt. "Thank you! Oh, thank you, Jared!"

"But I can't let you ride the colt," he said quickly.

"That's fine. The paint looks steady."

Jared looked down into her vivid blue eyes—still as bright and lively as he remembered. He gave himself a mental kick. He had to be crazy to tell her he'd take her with him. But her face was so eager. How many nights had he dreamed of those china blue eyes?

"All right, little girl, I guess I have no choice."

"You won't regret it!"

He sensed a new layer of reserve behind her enthusiasm. In the old days, he reflected, she would have launched herself at him and hugged him ferociously. The years of separation had changed things, but they both remembered how close they had been. Those memories tipped his hand.

Jared looked over at Peakes. "I don't suppose you can let us borrow a saddle?"

Peakes closed the barn door. "Guess I can let you take one. I've got an old cavalry-issue rig."

Jared winced. "All right, if that's the best you can do."

"Can't let you take one of my good saddles. You got a bridle for him?"

"Yeah." Jared handed Patches's reins to Trisha and tied the young stallion to an iron ring in the barn wall. "Easy, Chief." He took the extra bridle from Patches's saddlebags and slipped it over the colt's face. Chief took the jointed bit easily—something Jared was proud of. He had trained all of his father's colts to let their trainers handle them easily and safely.

"You got your stuff?" he asked Trisha.

"I left it at the Ryders'."

"Well, get on over there and get it. You've got ten minutes.

If you aren't back, I'm leaving." He tried to scowl at her, but she laughed at him, handed over Patches's reins, and opened the big door just enough so she could squeeze through. As soon as she'd left, he regretted sending her for her luggage. He should have told her to leave it and let her pick it up later. He dropped Patches's reins. The gelding wouldn't go one step until Jared told him to.

Peakes brought the saddle and a worn blanket. Jared eyed it for a moment and took the military gear with distaste. Next to no padding in those old things. He knew he would be uncomfortable all day.

"You want me to pay you for this miserable thing?"

Peakes waved his hand. "I'll trust you or Bill Logan to get it back to me sometime."

Jared folded the blanket and smoothed it over Chief's withers. He slung the saddle onto the young stallion's back.

"You're asking for trouble, you know," Peakes said.

Jared grunted and tightened the cinch.

"Shoulda told that gal to wait here."

"Tell me something I don't know." Jared tried not to remember how close he and Trisha had been ten or twelve years ago. She was always a bit bossy, and he wasn't above giving in to her to keep peace when they played together. He suspected her uncle did the same thing. So she was a little spoiled. She had also become a beautiful woman. He tugged on the leather strap. The saddle would stay on Chief. Too bad he'd gotten so fond of Trisha when he was a boy. By the time he and his father moved away, when Jared was fifteen, he was even dreaming of marrying her one day.

"I never knew why Logan ended up raising that girl," Peakes said, sticking the end of a straw in his mouth.

"Her parents died when she was five. Her pa was Bill's brother. Someone shipped her out here to the ranch after her folks died. My pa and Bill were working the ranch together then. I was seven." Jared shook his head. "I recall when she came, I couldn't decide if I was glad to have a playmate or mad that someone else started getting all the attention."

"So you two grew up like brother and sister?"

"More or less."

Peakes shook his head. "Making a mistake, that's what I say."

Jared was surprised how quickly Trisha returned with her bag. He rolled the door open and led the horses outside. Her face glowed with the effort of hauling her bag, and Jared caught his breath. In all his dreams, she'd never grown to be this beautiful. Good thing he hadn't been around her lately. She probably had dozens of young men swarming about. The funny feeling in his stomach told him he would have been jealous if he'd seen it. He took her bag and tied it securely to the back of Patches's saddle.

"You ready?"

"Sure am."

She smiled up at him, and his heart beat a strange, quick rhythm. What would Bill Logan do to him if anything happened to her? Too late to think about that now.

She swung into the saddle without waiting for assistance.

Her skirt billowed for a moment in the wind. Patches stood rock still for her, but Chief pulled at his reins and snorted. Jared turned to speak to him, calming him down. He hadn't thought about Patricia riding in a skirt. She used to tear around the ranch in dungarees, but he supposed she didn't wear them anymore, now that she was a lady. He mounted Chief, and the colt pranced a little.

"Easy, now." Jared patted the horse's neck. He lifted a hand to Peakes. The stable owner waved back and shut the big door. "Will you be warm enough?" he asked Trisha.

"I'm fine." She smoothed her skirt and tucked it in here and there. "I'll follow you."

Jared nodded and turned Chief toward the ranch.

The snow began to fall again lightly as they trotted out of the stable yard. Someone had gotten out and rolled a short section of the street, but as soon as they hit the end of it and got into the loose snow, the horses slowed to a walk. The young stallion whickered and tossed his head. He had almost no experience in snow. If he didn't settle down, he'd quickly wear himself out.

Jared looked back at Trisha. He ought to insist they give up and go back to the stable. She smiled and waved, her eyes bright.

"I can't tell you how much this means to me," she called.

Jared turned forward and concentrated on finding the best path for Chief.

They followed the contour of the road, although Patricia

couldn't tell where the road ended and the prairie began. Jared seemed to observe every tree and house closely and to have an innate sense of where to guide the horse.

After they got out onto a flat stretch, the going was easier, though snow was falling again. The wind had blown all night, and in places the snow was only a few inches deep. Patricia realized that the snow must have drifted into hollows and piled up much deeper in other spots.

She urged Patches up alongside the black colt, and he responded to her eagerly. The young stallion gave a whicker from deep in his throat and eyed Patches, his ears twitching.

Patricia laughed. "He's absolutely gorgeous, Jared. And he's behaving very well."

"I hate to push him hard." Jared shifted in the saddle and stroked the colt's neck. "His mother was a thoroughbred."

"He's got the long lines. I'll bet he's fast."

He didn't answer but frowned up at the gray ceiling of clouds above them. "I think the snow's getting heavier."

"We'll just take it slow. We've got all day." She smiled at him, but Jared's worried expression didn't lighten. "I'm so glad we met up this morning."

Jared rode in silence for several paces, as though thinking it over. At last he nodded. "Me, too."

Her spirits lifted on hearing that declaration, and she nudged Patches a little closer. The black stretched his neck around and nipped at the gelding. Patches squealed and hopped to the side.

"You all right?" Jared stopped the stallion and watched her bring her mount under control.

"I'm fine. I just expected Chief to have more manners, I guess."

"He's still young. I've been working with him, but you know stallions are unpredictable."

She nodded. "You're right. I know better. We'll keep our distance. It's just so good to have you close at hand again. I've missed you terribly. Uncle Rupert, too, but especially you, Jared."

He looked off at the hills in the distance. "I thought about you some, too."

"If only Uncle Bill hadn't gotten so mad at your father."

"Well, he did." Jared sighed. "Pa was angry, too. And too stubborn to give in. So he up and moved us to Texas."

"Yeah." Patricia brushed a light coating of snow from Patches's mane. "Uncle Bill missed Rupert, but he won't admit it. For years he's complained about how he took the best horses with him when he left."

"Well, your uncle got the ranch. It was only fair for Pa to get a string of mares to go with the stallion he captured."

"I guess so." She sighed. "I always felt as though that fight tore our family apart. You and your dad were part of the family, as far as I was concerned."

"Yeah. Dad and Bill were like brothers." Jared turned and looked into her eyes. "I'll tell you something."

"What?"

"I believe this horse is a peace offering."

Patricia caught her breath. "You mean. . .Uncle Rupert sent that stallion to Uncle Bill?"

"Yeah."

"That's wonderful."

Jared pressed his lips tight together and stared straight ahead. He didn't speak for a long time. The snow grew deeper, and Patches stumbled. Patricia let him fall back behind the black and walk in Chief's footsteps. The snow pelted down in small, dry flakes now. She hoped the squall didn't last long. She couldn't see nearly as far ahead as she could when they headed out of town.

She could see Jared's ramrod-straight back, however. He'd always been a pensive boy, but now he seemed even more serious. Had he changed so very much? Surely he still had the same tender heart he'd had when he helped her rescue a motherless ground squirrel. Of course he'd grown up. But still. . . She didn't like the thought that her old, childish love for Jared still colored her reactions to him. Better keep a checkrein on those meandering thoughts.

Chapter 3

Patricia hadn't paid attention. The snow was deeper, and the path of the roadway was obscured now. Jared must be navigating by dead reckoning and what few landmarks he could see. The young stallion floundered into a drift and whinnied shrilly. Jared pulled Chief's head around, forcing him to move his front feet to the side.

"Easy, now. Get up, you."

Patricia's throat constricted as she watched. There was nothing she could do to help him. The black horse pawed at the ground for a moment, and she realized they had strayed off the roadbed and into a low spot.

In an instant, the black found his footing and leaped onto solid ground again. Patricia exhaled and rode up on the other side of the stallion.

"Are you all right?" she called.

"Yes, but Chief's getting tired."

She looked about, but the driving snow made it difficult for her to orient herself.

"Stay close to me," Jared said, "but not so close that you follow me into a hole like that."

"I will." If Jared were traveling alone, would he have reached the ranch by now? She felt like apologizing for begging him to bring her, but that wouldn't do any good now. She pulled Patches in behind Chief and tugged her scarf up over the lower part of her face.

The young stallion moved slowly, head down, putting one foot in front of the other. Jared looked back. Tricia and Patches had fallen behind, and he could barely make out the horse's bulk as he plodded along.

"Whoa." Chief stopped and gave a big sigh. Jared turned him so his tail was to the wind and waited.

Patches trudged slowly up to him and stopped. Patricia's muffled form was covered in snow. She raised a gloved hand and brushed the loose, white coating from the scarf that covered her mouth.

"I'm sorry, Jared. I promised I wouldn't slow you down."

"It's not your fault. But this storm isn't going to let up. I think it's time we admitted that and looked for a house where we can stop."

Her shoulders straightened. "I can keep on if you can."

Stubborn, as always. His attempted smile cracked his bottom lip, and he winced. "Trisha, I was wrong to set out when I did, with or without you. I'm sorry I led you into this."

She eyed him for a moment then ducked her head. "I put

you on the spot. That was really low of me. If you think it's best to find shelter. . ."

He thought she sounded relieved. "I do. We've been riding for more than two hours, but I don't think we're more than halfway to the ranch."

Her blue eyes flared for a moment. "I guess we could be in serious trouble if one of these horses plays out on us."

Jared nodded. "Let's stick close together. I think there's a fencerow off that way." He pointed to the left, where he'd been watching an erratic ripple in the snow a few yards away, but it was becoming less distinct every minute. "We can't be far from a house."

He turned Chief into the wind again and set out. The snow was up to the young stallion's knees, making progress difficult. At this rate, night could overtake them. He scoured the landscape for a building, but he couldn't see more than a few yards in any direction. His ears ached with cold, and his toes were starting to go numb. *Lord, we need some help here. Please guide us to shelter.*

After what seemed like a long time, he heard Patricia call out behind him, and again he stopped and turned his horse to face hers. Patricia urged Patches up close to Chief and pushed her scarf away from her mouth.

"Are you sure we're still on the road? Whenever we drive to town, we pass several ranches between Uncle Bill's and Colorado Springs."

He gritted his teeth. No use glossing over it. "I'm pretty sure we've lost the trail, Trisha."

She nodded. They sat in silence for a long moment. The wind howled around them, blowing clouds of snow about the horses' still forms.

"What should we do?" Patricia had to yell to be heard above the wind.

"We'll have to keep going in as straight a line as we can and pray for a place to take shelter."

"All right."

He hesitated, knowing she and Patches were both exhausted. Chief had stumbled several times, and if they got into a deep drift, he would be too tired to fight his way out this time. But what else could they do? He sent up another silent prayer and turned his horse toward what he figured was northwest.

Patricia's fingers and toes were numb. They'd been plodding along for what seemed like hours, but she couldn't tell if they were making any progress. They might be heading away from the ranch, for all she knew. At least the ground was fairly flat, but the horses had reached a dangerous level of fatigue. The gelding stumbled again, and she spoke to him, stroking his neck and giving him a minute to rest. When she looked up, she could barely make out the hindquarters of Jared's horse. She hated to push Patches any farther, but she knew she'd be left behind, alone in the blizzard, if she didn't.

"Up, boy. Come on. Just a little farther."

Patches lifted his right foreleg and pushed forward two steps then stopped again. Patricia's chest tightened.

"Jared!"

At first she thought he hadn't heard her, but slowly his horse turned and came back toward her.

"Patches is about done in," she yelled.

Jared looked around and waved at something off to her right. Patricia squinted and made out a small stand of pine trees. The stunted pines might offer slight shelter from the wind.

Patches floundered into deeper snow, and she sat still, speaking gently to calm him. Once he stopped thrashing, she stroked his neck and squeezed him with her legs.

"Come on, fella. See those trees? That's where we're going. You can do it." She urged him on in the messy path Chief had broken. Patches bunched his muscles and leaped forward. In just a few strides, they were among the trees.

Jared dismounted and let Chief's reins trail. The colt immediately lowered his head and turned his hindquarters to the wind. Patricia started to swing her leg over the saddle and realized how stiff and cold she was. Jared shuffled to her side and held up his arms. She slid down Patches's side, glad to have Jared steady her when she landed.

"I've got a tinderbox in my saddlebag," he said, close to her ear. "Help me break some small twigs off the low branches. We might be able to get a fire going."

Twenty minutes later, Patricia sat in relative comfort with her hands and feet extended toward the small blaze he had kindled. They had stomped the snow down in a circle around the fire, giving them a recess where they could huddle mostly out of the wind.

Jared waded back to the hollow with an armful of small pine branches. "These won't burn for long, but they'll get us warmed up," he said.

Patricia noticed that he didn't have to shout. The wind had eased, and the snowfall seemed lighter. She pulled her scarf away from her face.

"Any idea what time it is?" she asked.

He shrugged and glanced toward the sky. "Hard to say, but I'm hungry."

She smiled. "I hadn't honestly thought about it, but I am, too."

"I've got some coffee. Maybe we can keep this fire going long enough to melt snow and make a pot. We'd both feel better, I'm sure."

"Let me help." She started to rise, but he placed a hand on her shoulder.

"No, you stay there. Take your boots off and get your feet good and warm."

"Well, I . . ." She gazed up at him, certain she'd be blushing if she wasn't so chilled.

"Do it." He turned away to where the horses stood nose-to-tail, offering each other some body heat.

As he filled his small coffeepot with snow and worked to position it over the coals without putting the small fire out, Jared considered their options. They could hole up right here with the possibility of freezing to death—the limited supply of small branches dry enough to break off and burn wouldn't last through the night—or go on. He didn't really like that alternative any better. The horses were near exhaustion. It might be better to stop here than to ask more of them. If one of them went down out in the open, they would have small chance of survival.

Patricia seemed embarrassed at his suggestion that she remove her boots, but that was of little consequence. Jared was beginning to fear he had brought her into mortal danger. He returned to Chief's side and took his small sack of coffee from the saddlebag. He didn't dare unsaddle the horses. There was no place to stow the saddles, and he didn't want to put them down in the snow. Besides, resaddling them would involve working the stiff leather straps. The weather would not be generous.

He removed his gloves and warmed his hands over the flames for a minute before removing the lid to the coffeepot. The snow was melted, but now the pot was only a third full. He pulled on his gloves and scooped up more snow to add to it. They'd been stopped at least half an hour before he had a passable brew.

"Drink this." He handed Trisha his tin cup, half full of murky liquid.

"You go ahead," she said, arranging her skirt hem carefully.

He almost laughed. Was she still worried about showing off her ankles? "Drink it." The words came out gruffly, and he immediately regretted it.

She reached out and took the cup meekly. Jared smiled grimly to himself. Maybe he'd hit the right tone, after all. Her stubbornness and defiance seemed to have vanished.

"Listen, Trisha, I'm wondering if we should stay right here for the night and heap up the snow for shelter."

Her eyes narrowed. "Stay here all night?"

He nodded.

"Do you think. . ." She looked around. "Jared, we wouldn't be able to get enough wood to burn all night, would we? If we had a hatchet. . ."

A small stick of burning wood fell and rolled to the edge of the fire, and he edged it back in with the toe of his boot.

"You're right, but if we made a snow cave, it would protect us some. We could survive the night."

He could see the fear now. She stared at him for a long time. At last she squeaked out, "But what about the horses?"

He sighed. They might live through a night in this storm, but he doubted it.

Trisha rose to her knees and passed him the empty cup. "Jared, I'm ready to go on whenever you are. I don't think we should dig in here. It might mean our deaths, and Patches's and Chief's, too."

He took his time pouring his coffee then returned her gaze. "I can't guarantee getting us through, and once we leave these trees, we're in the open. We might not find another place to stay—or make camp—before dark."

She swallowed hard and looked up at him with those huge blue eyes. "I'll do whatever you think is best, but. . ."

"But what?"

"I think we should try. The storm seems to have slacked a

little, and we might be just yards from a house."

He sipped the coffee. Grounds floated in it, but he swallowed them down. "All right. But if you've got extra clothing in your bag, I want you to put it on. Extra stockings, another dress, anything you've got that you can layer."

He trudged through the loose snow again to the horses. He had to remove his gloves, and even then he couldn't work free the leather thongs that tied her bag behind the saddle. After a few fruitless minutes, his fingers were numb again. He pulled out his knife and sliced the thongs.

"Here." He dropped the bag beside her and went to the other side of the fire to warm his hands. "I mean it, Trish. Put on every stitch you can. If I had an extra pair of trousers along, I'd give them to you."

Her lips twitched, and she cleared her throat. "Can you, uh. . ."

He realized she wanted him to turn his back. "Yeah, I was going to try to get some more wood, anyway." He pulled on his stiff gloves and waded toward the few trees he hadn't already stripped of dry branches.

When he returned a few minutes later, she had pulled a fancy blue dress on over her wool traveling skirt. She looked funny with the shiny material showing below her coat. The skirts stood out around her, giving her a pouffy, round form. *Must have added a petticoat or two.*

"Do you have any extra clothing?" Trisha asked as he dumped his scant load of branches on the fire.

"Just a shirt, but I have a blanket I can wrap around me. He squinted up at the sky. "It's let up some." He could see a lighter streak in the clouds where the sun was lowering in the west.

He shook out his blanket and draped it over Chief's saddle, then turned to give Trisha a boost. When he mounted the young stallion, he took his bearings and made his best guess as to the direction of the ranch.

"All set?"

"Sure am." Trisha smiled, and his heart lurched. He had to have been crazy to bring her out here. How could he face Bill Logan if anything happened to her? He clucked to Chief and squeezed the horse's ribs with his legs. The black snorted and set out with his head low.

An hour later the light was nearly gone. The storm lashed out with new fury, throwing grainy snow in their faces. Jared no longer expected to find shelter. Only a tiny part of him cared. Chief's steps had slowed to a crawl. Jared reminded himself of Patricia and slowly swiveled to look behind him. He couldn't see her. Any part of him that wasn't numb ached. He couldn't feel his fingers or feet.

"Trisha?"

Out of the swirling snow in the blackness, something moved toward him. He realized it was Patches, with an inch of snow piled on his head and neck. Jared made out Trisha's bulky form on the gelding's back.

Her dull eyes peered at him from between the snow-caked folds of her scarf.

There was nothing to say. He turned forward and squeezed Chief's sides. The colt took a step then stopped. Jared squeezed harder but got no response. He kicked his mount, but Chief only drooped his head lower. Vapor rose from the horse's breath.

Jared stared ahead of him. Something about the snow had caught his eye. Just beyond Chief's nose, stretched out but covered in a thick layer of ice and snow, was a strand of what could only be barbed wire.

He stared at it stupidly for a long moment then slowly wormed around in his saddle. Patches was right on Chief's haunches.

"Trisha!"

She raised her chin and met his gaze.

"We've hit a fence."

Chapter 4

Patricia leaned forward in the saddle and raised her right leg behind her. Her thigh muscles screamed, and her leg seemed outrageously heavy. With a jerk, she got it above the saddle and pulled it over to the near side. She kicked loose from the stirrup and slid to the ground.

The soft snow engulfed her, and she sank to her knees, with her skirts spreading out around her.

"Are you all right?" Jared sounded more alert now, which was probably good. He stirred in his saddle.

"Yes," she said. "Don't get down. This is awful."

She grabbed Patches's mane and pulled herself forward, propelling one leg at a time in agonizing slowness. She reached the fence line and knocked the snow off with her hand. Her gloves were caked and stiff with it, but she was able to uncover a couple of the barbs that were spaced along the wire. In the twilight, she bowed to peer at them.

"Jared!"

"What is it?"

"I know where we are."

"You do?"

"Well, not exactly where we are, but within a couple of miles. This is Uncle Bill's fence."

"Are you sure?" He pushed Chief around and bent down out of the saddle.

"Yes. He bought new fencing last spring to enclose his south range. The barbed wire is different from the old stuff and different from any of the neighbors'. Everyone remarked on it at the time. See how it's got these flat metal slices twined in at every barb?"

Jared squinted. He was so stiff, he couldn't lean lower without falling out of the saddle. "If you say so."

"I do." Hope surged up inside her. "We're at the boundary of the ranch. I'm not certain where along that boundary, but if we follow the fence, we'll eventually get home."

Jared was silent for a minute. Neither of them spoke the thought that hung in the frigid air. The horses wouldn't last long enough to trace miles of fence around the Logan Ranch's outer boundary. They could freeze to death on Bill Logan's land.

"Can you get back on Patches?"

"I'll try."

Getting her foot up to the stirrup was a feat, but she managed. When she tried to swing up into the saddle, her heavy skirts weighed her down in the deep snow.

"Jared, I don't know if I can do it."

He nudged Chief up close on the other side of Patches and

reached across the empty saddle. "Take my hand."

She reached up and tried to grasp his gloved hand, but her cold fingers didn't want to bend around it. How would she ever hold the reins? He seized her wrist with icy, leather-covered fingers and hauled her upward. She gave a jump and sprang free of the drifted snow and almost overshot the saddle, but Jared steadied her.

"Here you go." He leaned down and snagged Patches's trailing right rein. "Can you keep on for a while?"

"We've got to." She eyed the black colt with concern. He stood with his head and neck lowered and his eyes closed. "Is Chief all right?"

"He's exhausted."

"Maybe Patches could go first for a while and break trail."

Jared hesitated then gave a nod. "He's a tough old cow pony. Let's give it a try."

Patricia lifted the reins, and without her guidance, Patches began to walk slowly along the fence. They traveled obliquely to the wind now, and it blew across her cheek, more gently it seemed.

They had gone only a matter of yards when she spotted a bulge on a fence post and leaned to examine it.

"Jared! It's a gate."

He brought Chief up next to Patches and bent low to work at the wire. It was only a spot where the wires were looped over the top of a fence post, so that they could be taken down if the ranch hands wanted to ride a horse through. He couldn't pull it free, so he dismounted. After a minute, he had worked it loose and laid the wire back toward the next fence post.

"Wait," he called. "There may be another strand lower down, under the snow."

She nodded and waited while he waded into the gap.

"I feel it." Jared shuffled to the fence post and dug down through the snow with his hands.

"Can I help?"

He shook his head and kept working. At last he straightened, holding another loop of wire. He carefully pulled it back, yanking it up through the deep snow.

Patricia urged Patches forward. A moment later they were inside the fence, on Logan land. *Well, Lord,* she prayed silently, *I wanted to be home for Christmas, and here I am. Thank You for getting us this far.*

Jared led Chief through and mounted. Patricia peered around but couldn't make out any landmarks in the darkness.

"What now?" she called.

"Follow the fence."

She turned Patches in the direction they had been traveling and sent up more soundless prayers. With each step, the horse dragged his feet up out of the snow. Once he floundered, belly-deep, in a low spot. Jared came alongside, grabbed Patches's reins and spoke to him. The horse calmed and found his way out. They went on for what seemed like hours, and Patricia became aware of something ahead—something large and dark in her path. Patches took two more steps and stopped. They stood outside a small structure.

Jared squeezed Chief's sides, but the colt refused to take another step.

"I think it's a line shack," Patricia yelled over her shoulder.

"Oh, thank You, Lord!" Jared slapped Chief's withers, none too gently. "Come on, boy. We're here." The colt pushed forward a few more steps.

Patricia swiveled in her saddle and screamed, "Smell that?"

Jared inhaled deeply. The cold air filled his lungs, and he caught a whiff. "Wood smoke!"

She laughed and turned forward, drumming Patches's sides with her heels.

A few steps closer, and Jared could make out a faint glow. The golden light seemed to come from a small window in the cabin wall.

"This looks like the shack in the south forty," Patricia said. "See the lean-to?"

Jared nodded and swung down off Chief's back. He remembered riding out here as a youngster with his father to check on the herd grazing the south range. Those were great times. This line shack was probably as far as it could be from Bill Logan's house and still be on his ranch. At least two miles, as the crow flew.

He tugged the reins gently, and Chief followed him into the dark lean-to. Only a few inches of drifted snow had made it inside. Using his teeth, he pulled off one glove and felt along the wall. *Thank You, Lord!*

He let Chief's reins fall and went back to the opening.

"Trisha! Bring Patches in here. There's hay and a barrel that might have some feed in it."

She plummeted to earth just outside the lean-to. Jared reached out to grab her by the shoulders.

"You all right?"

"Yes, but my legs are numb."

He pulled her farther inside, out of the wind, and she collapsed against him for a moment. He held her close just for a second. "We're safe now."

She pulled away. "What do you need me to do?"

"Nothing. Let's get you inside. These horses won't go anywhere." Already he could hear them munching the hay they'd found. "I'll come out and unsaddle them after I thaw my hands."

They plunged out into the blowing snow once more and around the few steps to the door of the shack. It bothered him that no other horses were in the lean-to. But someone had lit the fire inside.

"Hey!" Jared raised his fist and pounded on the door. A moment later, it was pulled open a few inches, and a weather-beaten, wrinkled old woman squinted out at him.

"Annie?" Patricia stared at the old woman who served the area as a midwife. A new fear grew in her chest with the realization that Aunt Edna must do without Annie's services, at least for tonight.

"Land sakes, child! Where did you come from? Get in, get in! Out of the storm. Quick, now."

Patricia and Jared tumbled into the cabin, and the old woman slammed the door on the wind. The quiet and warmth enveloped them. Patricia looked around. Two sets of bunks, a small table with benches, a box stove, a few wooden crates stacked for storage. She gravitated toward the woodstove and struggled to unwind her scarf.

"Let me help you, Miss Patricia." Annie tugged the uncooperative scarf around until it came free.

Patricia pulled off her hat. "Oh, we're getting snow all over the floor."

"Don't worry about that now. You must be half froze."

"More than half, I'm afraid," Jared said.

The old woman turned and looked him up and down. "Who might you be, mister?"

"Annie, this is Jared Booker," Patricia said. "You remember his father, Rupert Booker, was my uncle Bill's partner when he bought the ranch?"

Annie squinted at the tall, snow-covered man. "Don't look like that scrawny Booker boy to me."

Jared laughed a deep, rich chuckle that warmed Patricia more than the sputtering little stove did.

"Well, it's really him, Annie. He was on his way to visit Uncle Bill, and I tagged along, coming home from a trip to Denver. But what are *you* doing here?"

The old woman began to work Patricia's coat buttons. "Get your things off. We'll thaw you out. Why, don't you know,

I smelled the storm coming yesterday, and I set out for the ranch house. Thought I'd go over and stay with Edna in case she needed me. I know she's not due for a couple of weeks yet, but I didn't want to be stuck at my house three miles away when her time came. Might turn out that no one could fetch me when that babe took a notion to come."

"And so you're stuck here now instead," Jared said.

She nodded grimly. "That's right. The snow comes on sudden in these parts. Got so I could hardly see where I was going. Almost missed the fence and kept on out into nowhere."

"Oh, Annie! I'm glad you found this shack," Patricia said.

"Me, too. I decided to hole up here until the snow let up, and I've been here one night and the better part of two days." She pulled Patricia's coat sleeve. Patricia let the heavy garment slide off. "Sit down on that bench now, and let me get those boots off you." Annie pushed her gently toward the table.

Jared used his teeth to help peel off his gloves.

"Get your coat off, Booker, or whoever you are," Annie said.

"I'll just warm my hands up for a minute. Then I need to go out and tend to the horses."

"How many you got?" Annie asked.

"Two, in the lean-to outside."

"They'll want water. We'll have to melt lots of snow." Annie scooped up a clump that had fallen from Patricia's clothing and threw it into a steaming pan on the stove. "I've got two buckets. When you go out, you can fill them and set them inside. I'll work on melting it down while you tend your critters. Then, if you're not frozen stiff, you can get more."

"Sounds good." Jared flexed his fingers and then spread both hands again, closer to the stovetop. "I need to get their saddles off and bed them down."

Patricia winced as Annie eased her left boot off. "At least I can feel that one."

"You can't feel the other foot?" Annie asked. "I hope you ain't frostbit."

"Ouch!" Patricia gasped as the blood tingled her fingers. She rubbed her hands together. "Pins and needles."

"That's a good sign." Annie's face wrinkled into more canyons and valleys as she bent over Patricia's other foot. "I may not be able to untie this until the ice melts a bit."

"I could cut the lace," Jared said.

"No, but let's move this bench closer to the stove."

Jared worked diligently at the lacing until at last it loosened. He grasped the heel and pulled the boot off. "There! Now let Annie give you some of that tea she's fixing. I'll go see to Chief and Patches."

"I'll have tea and hot oatmeal ready for you when you're done," Annie said.

Patricia grimaced. "Oatmeal?"

"Can't be choosy." Annie's beady eyes sparked. "We've got some canned beans and peaches, too. If you don't like the vittles, tell your uncle Bill he needs to stock his line shacks better."

Chapter 5

Jared could see that Patricia was worried about her aunt, knowing the midwife hadn't made it to the ranch. Of course, for all they knew, Edna didn't need Annie's services yet. But babies were known to arrive at odd times. As he scooped snow into the two pails, he assessed the swirling, drifting flakes. A rip-roaring blizzard. He wouldn't want to go more than a few steps from the cabin. He sent up a swift prayer for the Logans. *You know what's best, Father. We'll wait on You for direction. Can't do much else. But I thank You from the bottom of my heart for letting us find this cabin.*

He set the buckets inside the cabin door and took the lantern from Annie. Wading through the thigh-deep snow to the lean-to took all his energy. Already the cold sapped his body heat. Both horses had their heads down and their hindquarters to the entrance. He called out to them and slapped Patches's white rump. The gelding snuffled and sidled over enough toward Chief to let Jared in beside him. The colt let out a soft whinny but returned immediately to munching hay.

If we'd been out any longer, these horses wouldn't have made it. Jared shook off the thought and felt about for the barrel he had spotted earlier. The top was secured with a clamp to keep animals from getting into it. He set the lantern down and quickly removed the clamp. The barrel was more than half full of crimped oats. He wished they had some sweet feed for the horses. He would have to ask Annie if their limited supplies included a jug of molasses. That would perk these animals up and give them a little more nourishment to fight the cold. He scooped out a coffee can full of oats for each horse and dumped the rations on the ground, on top of the hay they were nibbling.

The knots in the leather straps that held the saddles on were stiff. He held the lantern up close but despaired of warming the leather enough to make it pliable. His own hands weren't warm enough for that either. He considered slicing through the cinches, but when he got out his knife, he found he could dig at the knot on Patches's saddle with the tip, and though he gouged it somewhat, after several minutes he got it loose.

At last the horses were free of their burdens. He stored the tack on an overhead rack and plunged out into the storm again. The irregular mound to one side of the door must be a woodpile. With great effort, he dug the snow away. His hands were already numbing, but he managed to pull out several sticks of firewood. All he could think of was getting warm. He stumbled toward the stoop, wondering if he could make those few steps.

He couldn't open the door to the cabin with his arms full, so he kicked the lower boards. Patricia opened it.

"Oh, Jared, you're covered with snow. Come in, quick!"

A lovely smell of cooking food met him, and the interior of the little shack seemed overly warm. The snow on the roof and banked all around the cabin no doubt insulated it, and heating the twelve-by-twelve room was not a problem. He lowered his armful of wood into the rough box near the stove and stepped back nearer the door to remove his snowy outerwear.

"Don't want to get the floor all wet," he explained as he handed Patricia his hat and gloves.

"I'll sweep it down the cracks in the floor before it can melt," Annie said. She advanced with a sorry-looking broom and attacked the little clumps of snow that had fallen from his boots and coat.

The plain food filled his hollow belly, and afterward Jared sat on a bench with his back against the edge of the table and stretched out his long legs toward the stove. Patricia helped Annie gather up the dishes. All day, he'd thought of her mostly in terms of her danger and the desperate situation they'd put themselves in. Now he noticed anew how lovely she was, even in this shabby cabin. Her dark hair swirled about her shoulders as she worked. Her mouth, set in a determined line, had a shape that made his stomach flutter. She'd been at a fancy party in Denver before they met up. They lived in different worlds now.

She looked over at him and smiled. "How are you doing? Did you get enough to eat?"

"Yes, thanks." Jared turned to look at the older woman. "Annie, that may not have been the most elegant meal I've ever eaten, but it was the most welcome."

"Thankee." Annie stacked the dirty dishes. "We'll save these for later. I can wash dishes anytime, but those horses haven't had a drink of water all day. We'll melt snow until they've had what they need, then we'll think about wash water."

"I hate to send you out again to take it to them," Patricia said to Jared. "Maybe I could go this time."

"No." He climbed to his feet. It was too dangerous to send either of the women outside in the howling storm. "I know it's not far to the lean-to, but I can't touch the cabin wall all the way because of the woodpile. I brought my rope in off my saddle, and I'm going to tie one end of it to the door handle outside. Didn't see anything else it would hold on. And I'll fix the other end to something in the lean-to. Then I won't take a chance on missing my way."

"It's that bad?" Annie asked. "You could get turned around just from here to the shed?"

"Easy." Jared pulled on his damp boots. Good thing he'd greased them well before he set out on this adventure.

"Take these two kettles and fill them with snow," Annie said. "I hate to keep opening that door, but we'll have to melt snow all night if we want enough water for those animals and our own needs."

"It's all right, Annie," Jared said. "Just make me a place to sleep on the floor when I come in. I'm tired to the bone." He pointed to a space between the table and the stove. "There. I'll be able to keep the fire up in the night without disturbing you two any more than necessary."

"Now there's a gentleman." Annie nodded at Patricia. "You're young. You take the top bunk."

Patricia started to protest then shrugged. "Yes, ma'am. I guess that makes sense."

"You're exhausted." Annie propelled her toward the bunks against the far wall. "While Mr. Booker tends to the horses, you pile into bed. And I don't want any arguing from you."

An hour later, Jared settled down on the floor with a wool blanket under him and a tattered quilt as a covering. The two women seemed to be asleep already. There was no question about Annie; her gentle snores, with occasional louder snorts, reminded him of the night noises in the bunkhouse at home. He assumed Patricia lay beneath the mound of blankets on the top bunk, having seen no sign of her since his last foray outside for more snow to melt.

He blew out the lantern and pushed it carefully to one side on the floor. He could still see a glow of orange through the draft holes on the box stove, but the night was so dark that he couldn't tell where the two windows were. The wail of the wind keening about the little shack soon obliterated even Annie's snores.

Was this whole trip a mistake? His father had bequeathed the three-year-old stallion to Bill Logan. The copy of the will Jared carried in his inner coat pocket was indisputable. But what if Bill was still angry with his old friend and wouldn't accept his final gift? Patricia seemed friendly enough, although their perilous situation today hadn't left much opportunity for them to renew their acquaintance. He'd like to. All these years, he'd thought of her as a cheerful little pest. He'd missed her plenty and had wished he could see her again. But he'd never dreamed she'd grown into such a beautiful woman. How would she and Bill react when he revealed the purpose of his journey? Had she absorbed her uncle's resentment of Rupert's behavior?

Jared rolled over and tried to find a comfortable position on the cold board floor. Patricia's attitude was very important to him. More than anything, he wanted her to forgive his father. Unless she did that, she probably wouldn't welcome Jared back into her life. And he wanted to be in it. He'd come back to Colorado to stay. If the Logans wouldn't welcome him, life could be miserable. His last waking thought was the beginning of a garbled prayer. *Lord, let her forgive us. . .and let Bill accept Chief.*

Patricia awoke in a dim gray room. Someone was moving about. She opened her eyes and pushed the blankets aside and saw an old woman dipping hot water from a kettle on the stove into a dented blue coffeepot.

Of course. Annie, the midwife. The cabin. The storm.

It came back in a rush. She sat up and looked around the small room. Jared must be outside. She pushed back the covers and noted that the cabin had stayed toasty warm all night.

Annie glanced up at her. "Come on down and make your ablutions before that feller comes back. Did you say he's Rupert Booker's boy?"

"That's right. Jared." Patricia grasped the edge of the bunk and slid down, landing with a thump on the floor.

Annie went about preparations for breakfast while Patricia

quickly took her skirt from the bedpost and pulled it on over her petticoat.

"Still snowing, I take it." She looked out toward the nearest window, but frost coated it.

"Yup. Doesn't look like stopping now."

The wind moaned about the eaves, and the stovepipe shivered where it met the wall. The door opened, and Jared kicked his boots against the top step before entering. Even so, he brought a great deal of snow in with him. He stood a long-handled shovel up against the wall by the door and pulled off his gloves.

"Good thing they left that shovel in the lean-to. I didn't see it last night."

"How deep is the snow?" Patricia asked.

"Past my waist. About up to the window ledges, I guess. Of course, it's drifted in around the buildings. Took me awhile to make my way out to the horses, but we've got a path now, provided the wind doesn't throw all the snow I've shoveled back into it. How much water have we got, Annie?"

"Enough for one bucket full." Annie lifted one pail off the stove. "Bring me back some more, and I'll melt it for the other critter."

"How many buckets of snow does it take to make a bucket of water?" Patricia asked. The process seemed painfully slow with their few containers.

"Four or five, I reckon." Jared took the pail from Annie.

"Coffee and hot porridge will be ready in about half an hour," Annie told him.

Jared went out once more into the swirling storm.

"What can I do to help you?" Patricia asked. The old woman nodded toward the shelf on the wall above the table. "Pick out something to go with this porridge. I reckon there's a little brown sugar in that small crock, and the canned fruit doesn't seem to have frozen."

"Aunt Edna's applesauce!" Patricia reached eagerly for a pint jar on the shelf. "I helped her put this up last fall, and we sent a few jars out to each of the line shacks."

"Bless her for thinking of it." Annie plunked three tin plates on the table. "I reckon we've got food for another three or four days. A week if we go half rations."

Patricia stood still and stared at her. "Do you think we should do that?"

"No guarantee we'll be able to get out of here sooner. This storm ain't over yet, and no one knows we're out here."

"But...Aunt Edna and the baby..."

Annie patted her shoulder. "There, now. Don't think about that. It's not like she's alone. She's got your uncle Bill and a dozen cowboys."

"But Uncle Bill's never delivered a baby. Not a human baby, anyway."

"Just pray, child. It's all we can do."

Patricia recognized her wisdom and prayed silently as she finished setting the table.

After Jared had filled all their empty pails and kettles with snow and brought in several more armfuls of wood, they sat down together to eat.

"So what brings you back to Colorado after all these years?"

Annie asked Jared. "I thought your pa moved you down to Mexico."

"Southern Texas," Jared said. "Well, you see, ma'am, my father died about three weeks ago."

Patricia caught her breath. "Jared, you didn't tell me."

"I wanted to." His brown eyes filled with contrition. "It didn't seem like the right time when we were at the livery stable, and then we had all we could do to deal with the storm."

"I'm so sorry to hear about Uncle Rupert."

"Well, thanks." Jared picked up his tin cup and looked down into his steaming coffee. "It's because of his passing that I'm here."

"What do you mean?" Annie asked.

Jared looked at her and smiled grimly. "Before my father died, he wrote a will, and in it he left the stallion I've got out there in the lean-to—Chief, we call him—to Bill Logan. I'm here to deliver the bequest."

Patricia gaped at him. "But why would Rupert send a horse to Uncle Bill?"

"Weren't they friends in the old days?" Annie asked.

"Well, yes. But they had a big fight, were so angry that they split up their friendship. Uncle Rupert took Jared and left us." Patricia felt the heat rise above her collar, into her cheeks. Uncle Bill had fumed about the situation for years. He still got riled up whenever anyone mentioned Rupert. She rounded on Jared. "He and Uncle Bill had worked together twenty years. But that didn't count with your father. He tore our family apart."

"Trisha, you know we're not really related."

"You can say that if you want to. When I came to this ranch, I was all alone. Uncle Bill and you and your parents were the only family I knew. Then your father started chasing that pesky stallion. Uncle Bill told him to stop, but he wouldn't. And after he finally caught it, he packed up and took you away." Tears filled her eyes, and she turned her face away. He didn't understand at all. Apparently the rift hadn't affected Jared nearly as deeply as it had her. It was almost as if a married couple had two children and one left, taking one child, while the other kept the second child. Patricia had lost her own parents early. Losing Uncle Rupert and Jared had been a second bereavement for her. Even though she knew Uncle Bill loved her to distraction, his awkward attempts at fatherhood couldn't make up for her sorrow and the wounds of abandonment that Rupert's defection had left.

She glared at him. "If your father hadn't insisted on chasing that wild stallion and spending all his time and money on horse racing, we'd still be a family."

Jared stared at Trisha. He wanted to deny the things she said, but he couldn't. He'd felt the sting of his father's actions himself. But he'd learned to live with the situation and become accustomed to their new life. He saw the good things about it and enjoyed helping his father raise and train horses. But he could not refute her argument that his father's pursuits had put the Logan ranch in danger and made life more difficult for Trisha and Bill Logan. How many times had he asked himself what would have happened if his father had stayed out of horse racing?

"Trisha," he said gently.

She looked up at the sound of her name. Would she listen if he told her how he had suffered as well and gave her his perspective on the changes he had undergone? He cleared his throat.

"You're right about a lot of things. I know that you were hurt when we left the ranch. And I know your uncle was more than just angry. He was hurt."

"How do you know that?" Her blue eyes glinted like cold steel. "How do you know what we felt?"

Jared set down the coffee and inhaled deeply. "Because I was hurt, too. I didn't want to leave. I had no desire to go into horse racing then, but we did it. We left here with a fast stallion and a half dozen decent mares. My father built his racing stable from the ground up. I've worked for Pa these ten years. But I never liked the racing life. And I told my father that. I told him I didn't want to stay in it."

"What'd your pa say to that?" Annie stood and reached for the coffeepot and refilled her cup.

"He didn't like it. But he knew that was what began the trouble between him and Bill. Pa wanted to go into horse racing, but Bill preferred sticking with cattle ranching. Pa didn't see much future in the ranch. After twenty years, they still hadn't made good, at least not in my pa's eyes." Jared took a sip of his cooling coffee and went on. "My mother's family, the Contreras, are established in Mexican horse racing, and his brother-in-law—my uncle Manuel—tried for a long time to get Pa to go down there and get into racing."

"I never knew that." Trisha wiped her eyes with her hand and sniffed. "You mean, after your mother died in '02?"

"Yes, but before that, too. I don't think Mama wanted to do it. She liked the ranch, and she liked being with you and Uncle Bill. She felt Bill was a stable influence in my father's life. Despite her family's leanings, she had a calm nature. She saw her brothers get mixed up in a lot of devilment, and she didn't want to see Pa get into it."

Patricia seemed to mull that over while she nibbled a piece of bacon. "I recall when your father caught that wild stallion. He wanted to race him."

Jared nodded. "He took him to the fair in Denver, and he won."

Trisha nodded, her eyes wide and thoughtful. Annie ate her breakfast quietly, but Jared could tell she hadn't missed a word.

"My pa wanted to breed the stallion to some of the ranch mares, but Bill refused to let him. The horse was ugly and ornery, it was true. Your uncle said the only thing he was good for was running, and his colts wouldn't make good cow ponies."

"I didn't know all that," Trisha admitted. "I knew they fought at the last and that Rupert wanted to race, but Uncle Bill never told me the details."

"Well, I guess they realized at last that they had different dreams, so they split up. Pa took the wild stallion and moved us to Texas. Uncle Manuel lived about fifty miles away, just over the border. He encouraged Pa to race, and pretty soon we started racing the stallion and other horses at the tracks in Texas and Mexico."

"Did you win?" Annie asked.

"Sometimes. That wild stallion had speed and heart. His earnings set my father up pretty well. And Pa bred him to a lot of mares." Jared chuckled and shook his head. "The colts were all ugly, but they were fast."

"Well, that colt you're bringing Uncle Bill isn't ugly," Trisha said. "He must not be the wild one's offspring."

"But he is." Jared leaned forward and looked into her sober eyes. "He's a grandson of the wild one, Trisha. Pa bred the stallion to a beautiful Arabian mare and got a fast mare that didn't look too bad. He went another generation, breeding her to a thoroughbred stallion, and Chief was the result. Finally he got a colt without the Roman nose and stubby ears."

"Can he run?" Annie asked.

They both laughed, but Trisha's eyes still held that wary, defiant glint.

"Yeah," Jared said. "I think he can. But we haven't raced this one. Not yet."

"But why did your pa leave Chief to Uncle Bill?" Trisha asked.

"I'm not sure, exactly." Jared sat back. This was a question he had wrestled with on his trip north.

"Probably just to prove his point to Uncle Bill that he was right all along and racing paid off."

Jared's jaw clenched. "That's a pretty mean thing to say."

"Well, leaving us alone was a pretty mean thing to *do*."

"Yeah? Well, just 'cause you're still mad at Pa, doesn't mean you should yell at me."

They both shoved their chairs back and stood on opposite sides of the table.

Trisha's eyes snapped blue fire. "Who's yelling at whom?"

"You are!"

Annie whacked the table with her spoon. "Here, now! You two pups settle down and quit your barking at each other. I thought I was stuck here with two adults, but it seems I was wrong."

A wave of shame washed over Jared, immediately followed by a splattering remnant of anger. How could he have imagined that Trisha had become a refined, sweet, and gentle woman? She was as stubborn and ornery as she'd been at twelve.

Chapter 6

The next morning dawned gray and quiet. At first Patricia thought the snow had stopped, but when Jared opened the door to go to the lean-to, she realized it was still falling hard. The little cabin was nearly buried in it, and for that reason, the wind no longer buffeted the walls.

"Looks like my path has a foot or more of new snow in it," Jared observed. "It's drifted on the far end, near the lean-to. I'd best clear it before I take the water out." He reached for the shovel and went outside.

Trapped. Patricia threw a bleak glance at Annie, but the old woman calmly went about preparing their breakfast. Remorse tugged at Patricia's conscience, and she hurried to help.

When the three of them sat down together to eat it later, Annie asked a blessing.

"Lord above, You've stuck us here, and we don't know why. But You do, so that's good enough. Thank You for these vittles. Amen."

Jared and Annie picked up their spoons and plunged them

into their portions of oatmeal. Trisha noted that Annie had prepared less of the porridge than she had yesterday. Instead of opening a jar of fruit, they'd added a few raisins to the oatmeal. That and coffee was all they would eat until noon. If they could tell when it was noon. None of them had a watch, and the dim light that reached them through the windows was barely enough to get by with, but they'd agreed the night before to save the lamp oil as much as possible, and so they sat in the twilight.

Patricia cleared her throat. Annie kept eating, but Jared glanced up at her, an uneasy frown touching his mouth and eyes.

"I want to apologize for the mean things I said about your father yesterday, Jared. I mean. . .about the horse racing and. . . and his character in general. I loved you and your father. I admit I was repeating things I heard Uncle Bill say in his worst moments. I shouldn't have done that. Will you forgive me?"

Jared's dark eyes softened. He laid down his spoon. "Trisha, I believe Pa missed Bill—and you, too—after we left Colorado, and I think he hoped someday he could reconcile with Bill."

"You do?"

Jared nodded. "Pa enjoyed his life in Texas, but that fight with Bill bothered him all these years. When he became ill and suspected he would die, he talked to me about the business. I'd told him before that I didn't want to stay in horse racing, but Pa had hoped I'd change my mind. But at the end, he could see that I hadn't. After he got sick, he sold the racing stable."

"Well now," said Annie.

Patricia just stared at Jared, feeling more miserable than before.

Jared picked up his tin cup, looked at it, and set it down. "I inherited a large sum of money, because Pa had done well the last few years. I came here for two reasons. To bring Chief to your uncle and to look around for a place of my own."

"You want to stay in Colorado?" Patricia asked, a surge of hope rising in her.

He nodded. "That's my dream. A ranch of my own, near where I grew up. I've always remembered the Logan ranch, and that's where my heart is. I want to live in this area and raise cattle."

Patricia sighed. "I wish you success, Jared. And. . .welcome back."

"Thank you."

Annie leaned over and snaked her arm out to reach the coffeepot off the stove. "Seems to me you're tenacious enough to make your dream come true, boy."

Jared smiled, and Patricia's heart lifted just looking at him. There was the boyish Jared, the optimistic, confident Jared.

"I hope so, Annie. But there was one thing that's always been more important to me than where I lived or what I did for a living. That was my dream of seeing my father receive Christ."

Annie clucked in sympathy and refilled his coffee cup. "Did it happen?"

Jared glanced over at Patricia, his face somber once more. "You know your uncle Bill led me to Christ when I was a little boy."

Patricia ducked her head. "Yes. I'd almost forgotten that."

"Your uncle is a good man, Trisha. I've always been grateful. And I witnessed to my pa many times, right up to his death, but so far as I know, he never believed."

Patricia felt her heart soften and melt. How could she have been angry with Jared because of things his father did so many years ago? She had been unjust and immature in her judgment of him. Tears sprang into her eyes. She reached over and grasped his wrist gently. "I'm so very sorry, Jared. I acted despicably yesterday."

He closed his hand over hers and gave her fingers a squeeze. "Forgiven. All forgiven."

Even Annie's eyes glistened.

Patricia reluctantly pulled her hand away and fumbled in her pocket for a handkerchief. "Perhaps we could pray together this morning. For our safety, and for Aunt Edna and the baby."

"A good idea." Annie nodded. "You start, boy." She sniffed and wiped her eyes with her sleeve.

That afternoon, Jared allowed Patricia to brave his path with him to the lean-to and help him feed and water the horses. The snow was now shoulder-high to him on each side of the path, and as high as Patricia's head, so they were able to reach the horses while staying out of the fierce wind.

The blowing continued, but by evening, Jared was sure the snow had stopped falling, though the gale still flung the loose stuff on the surface all about.

On a top shelf, Annie discovered a board marked off in squares and a tin containing dark and light rounds of wood. Half were charred, half were not, and she immediately recognized the primitive checkers game. This welcome diversion helped them pass the hours in the cramped cabin, and they used some of their precious lamp oil to continue the play into the evening hours.

The next morning they awoke eager to do something—anything—to free themselves from their prison. The storm had ended, and the sun sparkled on the snow. Jared climbed on what was left of the woodpile and surveyed the range. The dips and slopes of Bill Logan's south forty kept him from seeing more than half a mile, but he knew exactly in which direction the house lay. Two miles. So close.

He wondered if they would be able to dig out. The snow had drifted deep around the shack, but perhaps out on the open rangeland, it was not so deep. The wind had surely scoured some of the accumulation away. Was it best to wait for the sun to do its work and compact the snow? He glanced toward the lean-to, where Chief and Patches were snuffling their morning ration. They had already ingested most of the hay, and the oat barrel wouldn't hold out longer than two or three more days.

He climbed down and went to the door, kicked the snow off his boots, and went inside. Annie and Patricia looked toward him expectantly.

"I think I could make it to the ranch house by riding across the range."

Patricia's jaw dropped. "Isn't the snow over my head?"

"Not in the open. It's probably still belly-deep to a horse in most places, but I think Patches could do it. Chief might panic if he got mired in a drift, but Patches is steady. I think I should try. If I can even get within sight of the house, maybe I can get their attention."

Annie's eyes glittered as he spoke. "You don't have a gun, do you?"

"No."

"Well, too bad. But you can take some tinder and a few matches and start a fire. They might see that. Then they could take that workhorse team of Bill Logan's and break trail out here to get us."

"I don't know if they'd be able to do that yet," Jared said. "But they could bring me some snowshoes, at least. We can walk out if we have snowshoes."

"Well, come on, then," Annie said. "Let's pack up your gear."

"Travel light, for Patches's sake," Patricia said. "Dress warmly, but don't carry anything you won't need."

They argued good-naturedly over what he might need and what his chances were of making it through or getting stuck somewhere between the cabin and the ranch house.

Annie insisted he take a small amount of food in his pockets, and Patricia carefully packed his fire-making supplies in a saddle-bag while he layered on his extra shirt and socks.

"Hey." Patricia's head jerked up, and she looked toward the door. "Did you hear that?"

Jared and Annie stopped what they were doing and listened. Sure enough, Jared heard what sounded like a muffled shout.

He threw the door open and dashed outside. Climbing on the woodpile, he looked out over the range and whooped.

Three cowboys from the Logan ranch wallowed through the snow a hundred yards out, riding the big draft horses Bill used to haul hay wagons in summer and logs for firewood in winter.

"Hey!" Jared waved his hat in the air. A yodeling call from one of the men answered, and another of the cowboys fired a rifle into the air.

"How many people you got?" came the faint cry.

"Three," Jared shouted. "We've got the midwife."

The three men seemed to consult and changed course, heading the big horses toward the cabin. The largest took the lead, but the snow was up to his breast, and he tired quickly. After a few yards, the next horse moved ahead and broke trail for a few yards.

Jared hopped down from the woodpile and ran inside.

"It's men from the Logan ranch. Put your woolies on, ladies! We are leaving here before you know it." He seized the shovel and ran out to carve a way out of the drifts around the buildings. By cutting into the side of his path, he hoped he could move enough powder so Chief and Patches could work their way up to the level of the draft horses and follow their messy trail home.

In no time, Patricia had her boots, coat, scarf, hood, and gloves on. She hurried outside. Jared was throwing shovelfuls of snow as fast as he could out of the recess he'd dug earlier.

"Where are they?"

He raised his head and stood on tiptoe to look. "Just up the knoll. Fifty yards now."

"What can I do to help?"

"Go throw the blankets and saddles on the horses. The bridles and saddlebags are inside. We can be ready by the time they reach us."

"Those men will want to warm up and have a cup of coffee," Patricia said. "I'll tell Annie." She ran inside and returned carrying the two bridles and Patches's saddlebags. "Annie's putting on some flapjacks. She says their horses will be exhausted and need to rest a bit."

Jared straightened and looked again. "She's right about that. It's heavy work for them. But we can give them some melted snow and a small ration of oats." He stomped the snow underfoot and realized he could walk up his enlarged pathway now. Soon he stood, from the waist up, above the higher level of the snow, looking out across the surface. The low point of the path, at the cabin's doorstep, was five feet below him. He waved to the cowboys, who were now within easy talking distance.

"Did you say you've got old Annie there?"

"Yup. She was trying to get to Miz Logan and got snowed in here."

"Hallelujah," the man shouted back. "We was headed down to her place in the holler. Miz Logan thinks today's the day!"

Jared turned and called to Patricia, who was inside the lean-to, "Did you hear that, Trish?"

"No, what?"

"These men were on their way to fetch Annie. Miz Logan says it's time for the baby."

Patricia came to the opening of the lean-to. "Oh, Jared! We've got to hurry. Annie needs to be there."

"We're working as fast as we can," he replied.

Behind him, the door opened. "I heard that," Annie said. "I've got our clothes and such all packed up."

Patricia took a few steps toward her along the snow-walled path. "Annie, what if we don't get there in time?"

"Don't worry, child. First babies take their time gettin' here. Still, we won't lollygag none."

The man on the lead horse called to Jared, "The snow's getting deeper. I don't think we should bring the horses any closer."

"No, don't," Jared told him. "It's a good five feet deep here near the cabin. Just let them rest, and I'll shovel the last few yards out to you. We've got oats and a little melted snow they can have. And Annie's got hot coffee and flapjacks inside."

"Sounds good," the man said.

Jared squinted at him. "Aren't you Joe Simmons?"

"Yup. Do I know you?"

"I'm Jared Booker."

Joe's face broke into a toothy grin. "Well now! Welcome back, sonny."

Patricia scrambled up beside Jared, floundering through the snow, and he reached out a hand to boost her.

"I knew he'd remember you," she said.

Joe's mouth opened and his eyes flared. "Is that you, Miss

Trish? What on earth are you doing here? Your uncle was sure you'd used your head and stayed in Denver with that school chum of yours."

"Well, it's a good thing he didn't know otherwise, or he'd have worried about me."

"Can't believe you've got Annie here. That'll save us a good two hours or more. We're not even halfway to Annie's place. I wasn't sure these nags could make it that far, but the boss said to try."

Another cowboy added, "We saw your smoke from the stovepipe here and figured some poor soul got caught out in the blizzard."

Patricia laughed. "Three poor souls. And we're mighty glad to see you."

Joe hopped down from his horse and staggered to his feet, waist deep in snow. "Let me come help you shovel, Jared. You must be tuckered out."

Half an hour later, they set out with the strongest draft horse in the lead. Annie went next on Patches, at Jared's insistence.

"And if we get to where the path is easygoing, Miss Annie, you just go right on ahead and ride up to the ranch house," he told her. "We'll follow as quick as we can."

The other two workhorses fell in behind Patches, with Trisha riding double behind Joe Simmons. Jared brought Chief along last, hoping the trail would not be too hard for the colt after the bigger horses had trampled it twice. The going was slow, and the horses soon dragged their feet, but they kept on with lowered muzzles.

Before long, they could see the ranch house, and shortly afterward they entered a pasture where the cattle had trampled down the snow. A herd of about a hundred head huddled together where the hired men had thrown hay for them that morning. Annie broke away from the line of horses and loped Patches across the field toward the house.

Soon they were all on better footing. Jared sighed with relief when they reached the barnyard. He jumped out of the saddle and ran his hands down each of Chief's legs in turn.

"Is he all right?"

He straightened to find Patricia standing near him.

"I think he is, praise God."

She smiled. "Let's put him in a nice, comfy loose stall and rub him and Patches down."

Jared shook his head. "You go on into the house. I know you want to see how your aunt's doing. I'll take care of these critters."

Half a dozen cowboys had come from the bunkhouse to greet them, and one of them seized Patches's trailing reins where Annie had left him ground tied and led him into the barn.

Patricia hesitated. "You gave me my wish, Jared. You got me here on time."

"Go on," Jared said with a grin. "After all we went through, you don't want to miss the big event."

She leaned toward him and placed her gloved hands on his

shoulders. Before he realized what she was doing, she'd stood on tiptoe and kissed his cold, scratchy cheek. Then she backed away from him, her blue eyes gleaming, turned, and streaked for the ranch house.

Jared led Chief into the big, airy barn. On both sides of the aisle, horses were champing hay. Because of the weather, all of the cow ponies were inside, and all the tie-up stalls were full. Chief snorted and pranced as Jared walked him farther down the row.

"Bring him on down here," a man called. "Got a spot here for your stallion."

Jared recognized the large foaling stall. He nodded at the cowboy who held the door open. "I appreciate it."

"The boss hasn't got a stud right now," the man said. "Will that one behave himself in here?"

"I think so," Jared said. "He's young, but he's fairly docile. Needs a good rubdown and a blanket. We had a rough trip up here from Texas."

He set about grooming Chief. A cowboy brought him a soft brush and a hoof pick, and another brought a bucket of water for the colt.

Jared worked methodically around from the horse's near shoulder to his rump and up the off side. He took a loaned blanket off the half door of the stall and spread it over Chief's back, pinning it at his chest, then stroked his face and glossy neck.

"There, now. Feeling better, fella?"

"Jared Booker."

Jared froze at the words and straightened slowly, turning his head toward the doorway. Bill Logan stood just outside the stall, peering in at him and Chief.

Chapter 7

Jared hesitated only an instant. He hadn't planned what he would say to Bill Logan when he met him, and it might have been easier if Patricia or one of the cowpokes had stuck around. But no, this had to be man-to-man.

"Mr. Logan."

He stepped over to the door, shifting the brush to his left hand and extended his right. Bill reached out to shake it over the top of the closed bottom stall door.

"Well now. You've grown some."

"Yes, sir."

"Patricia told me you'd brought her from town, and I figured to come out here and skin you alive. Foolhardy business, setting out in the storm like that."

Jared swallowed hard and forced himself to meet Bill's gaze. "I can't disagree, sir. At the time, it seemed like an easy ride in the lull of the storm, but looking back, I'd be the first to admit it wasn't the wisest thing I ever did. We were sure happy to run across your line shack and find it had wood and foodstuffs and rations for the horses."

Bill nodded soberly. "You'll have to give me the details later. I know Trisha's headstrong, and she claims she forced you to bring her. It's probably true."

Jared shrugged, but he couldn't help a grim smile. "I understand you're to be congratulated, sir. I'm pleased to hear you found a fine woman."

Bill nodded, but a worried frown took up residence between his eyebrows. "Edna's one of the best things that ever happened to me. I'm just praying now that things go well today. You. . . know about the baby?"

Jared nodded. "That was Trisha's trump card, if I can be so blunt. She was sure her aunt needed her, and she couldn't stay put in Colorado Springs."

"Well, I'm glad she's here, and Annie, too. When I think that she might have frozen to death out on the range. . ." He shook himself and leaned on the door. "God has been merciful to us all."

"Amen," Jared said softly.

Bill straightened and focused beyond him on the coal black colt. "That's quite a horse you've got there, Jared."

A smile started deep inside Jared and worked its way up to his lips. "Yes, sir. This is the crowning jewel in my father's string. We call him Chief. Mr. Logan, I brought him to you as a gift from my father."

Bill's face clouded. He turned away from the doorway. "I don't need any racehorses. I told Rupert that ten years ago."

Jared quickly unlatched the stall door and hurried after

him. Bill's long strides had already taken him to the other end of the barn, and he was about to open the door.

"Mr. Logan! Please, sir. I have a letter here from my father." Jared hurried toward him, reaching inside his coat for the sealed letter he had carried from Texas.

Bill stopped and turned to face him. "I don't care what your father has to say in that letter, Jared. He was always a hardheaded man, and he would never listen to me. Why should I listen to him now?"

Jared stood five feet from him with the envelope in his hand, unsure of what to say.

At that moment, the door swung open. Patricia stood silhouetted against the bright, snowy yard outside, her eyes bright and her cheeks rosy.

"Uncle Bill! Come on! Edna's asking for you."

Bill whirled toward her. "Is she all right?"

Patricia grinned. "She and your daughter are just fine."

"Praise be!" Bill sprinted for the ranch house.

Patricia laughed and shot a glance at Jared. "Uncle Bill's going to be so happy now."

"Yeah."

Jared's tone was doubtful, and she looked closer at him. "What's wrong?" She noticed then that he held an envelope.

He tapped the letter against his other hand. "He says he doesn't want Chief, and he won't read the letter Pa wrote him."

Jared looked so forlorn that Patricia stepped closer and laid her hand on his sleeve. "I'm sorry, Jared. You didn't tell me that your pa wrote him a letter before he died."

Jared stood still for a moment, his lips compressed. "You know, I don't think I told him that Pa passed on. You didn't tell him, did you?"

She shook her head. "No, I forgot to mention it in all the excitement over the baby." She threw her shoulders back and forced a smile. "Listen, everyone's distracted now, but Uncle Bill is bound to be in a more jovial mood. Let's give him time to get to know his daughter, and I'll help the cook prepare a nice dinner. After he's eaten and calmed down a little, you can talk to him again. Tell him everything."

"I don't know, Trish. He sounded like he knew his mind."

"But he doesn't know the circumstances. Look, I know Uncle Bill can be stubborn. But I also know that he loves the Lord, and once he sees things laid out plain and simple, I think he'll back down. We both know he loved your father. It was Rupert's deserting him that's kept him so bitter all these years. But now he's found Edna, and you're here with a wonderful peace offering. Surely he won't keep holding a grudge against an old friend who's died."

"Well. . ."

She could see that he wavered, so she slid her hand through the crook of his arm. "Come on in the house. You're tired. We all are. Grab your saddlebags, and I'll show you to a room where you can clean up and rest for a while."

"Oh, no, Trish. Don't do that. I'll go over to the bunkhouse."

"Nonsense. After what you did for me this week? You are an honored guest in this house."

With a little more coaxing, she persuaded Jared to collect his gear and go with her into the low ranch house. Sarah, the wife of one of the cowboys, served as the Logans' cook now, and when Patricia took Jared in through the back kitchen door, she gladly told Patricia to show Jared to the spare room where Edna and Patricia did their sewing.

"Isn't it wonderful?" Sarah asked, her eyes swimming with tears. "A new little baby in this house!"

"It's delightful," Patricia agreed. "Have you seen her yet?"

"No, but I heard the boss shouting, 'Praise God,' until Mrs. Logan hushed him. He's so happy! We'll celebrate today."

Patricia and Jared laughed.

"I intend to help you prepare for that celebration, Sarah. Excuse us while I show Mr. Booker his room, and then I'll be back to put on my apron."

As they walked through the big main room that Edna referred to as the parlor and Bill called the settin' room, all was quiet. Jared walked silently beside her into the hall.

"Jared," she said softly, "I'm sure Uncle Bill will come around. But just in case we're not clear, I want to tell you straight out, I forgive you and your pa for all the past hurts, whether real or imagined."

He gave her a little smile. "Thank you. That means a lot."

"Deep in my heart, I never was angry with you. I think I just absorbed Uncle Bill's attitude about your father, though, and that wasn't right."

444

He shrugged. "You were loyal to your uncle, and that's not all bad."

They heard Annie's practical voice coming from the master bedroom. As they walked past the open doorway, the old woman said, "There the kids are now."

Suddenly Uncle Bill filled the doorway, holding a soft white bundle in his arms. Patricia and Jared stopped, and Patricia reached out to lift the edge of the blanket, exposing the new infant's little red face.

"Oh! She's sleeping!"

Uncle Bill nodded with a smile. "Jared, Patricia," he said formally, "I would like to introduce you to my daughter."

Patricia had already seen the baby, but she could play along.

"We're charmed, sir. And what is this adorable creature's name?"

Bill's smile extended to nearly split his face in two. "We've decided, finally. May I present Hazel Dorothy Logan?"

Tears sprang into Patricia's eyes. "My mother's name," she whispered.

Bill nodded. "Jared, my lad, are you still walking with the Lord?"

Jared cleared his throat. "Yes, sir. I'm doing my best, with His help."

Bill nodded. "Would you give a prayer of thanks for this little one's safe arrival?"

Jared lowered his saddlebags gently to the floor. "I'd be happy to, sir."

After Jared's prayer of thanks, little Hazel began to fuss, and Bill hastily handed her over to Patricia. "If you wouldn't mind, Trish, could you please take her back to Edna? I think she wants her momma, and I need to speak to Jared for a minute."

"I'd love to." Patricia cuddled the baby, wrapped in a soft white blanket, against her shoulder and carried her into the bedroom.

Jared and Bill walked back to the living area together.

"Have a seat, Jared," Bill said.

Jared sat down on a leather-covered chair. His skin prickled all over, and he made himself sit still and not scratch, but he couldn't deny he was nervous.

"Boy, I want to apologize."

Relief washed over Jared, and he closed his eyes for an instant. "No need for that, Mr. Logan."

"Yes, there is. I had no call to be upset with you. Well, if the truth were known, I've no right to stay mad at your father, either, after all this time. I'll give it to you straight. I deliberately nourished bitterness in my heart for the last ten years. I was angry with Rupert. I admit it. He was wrong. Well. . .so was I." Bill looked Jared in the eye. "Can you forgive me?"

"Oh yes, sir. That's not hard at all. I've missed you and Trisha something awful, and I hoped you'd let me stop a day or two with you while I look around for some land."

"Land? You want to move back up here? What about your father?"

Jared bit his upper lip. He reached in his pocket for the envelope and leaned forward with it in his hand.

"Seems I went about this all backward, sir. The first thing I should've told you is that my pa died three or four weeks ago, down in Texas. And shortly before he passed away, he wrote this letter to you. One of the last things he did was to ask me to bring the letter and the black colt that's out in your barn. That's why I came, sir. That's how I met up with Patricia. I was on my way to deliver this letter to you, along with Chief."

Bill's hand came forward, an inch at a time, until his fingers touched the envelope. Tears shone in his eyes. "I've been a big old fool."

Jared swallowed hard and said nothing.

Bill ripped open the envelope and withdrew the paper that was inside. Jared winced as he saw the lines written in his father's shaky hand. He looked toward the window. The sun still shone outside, and it appeared the storm was truly over.

Bill let out a big sigh. "You should hear this, too, Jared. Do you mind if I read it to you?"

"No, sir."

"It says, 'Bill, if you're reading this, it means that I'm gone. Well, there are some things you need to know. When your turn comes, we'll meet again. My son has told me many, many times that I needed Jesus. I admit I was pretty mean to him about that. Told him he could believe that if he wanted, but I was doing fine on my own. Rupert Booker didn't need "saving," as you called it.'"

Jared bowed his head as he heard the words. So often he'd

tried to tell his father about Christ. Hearing again how annoying he found that made his eyes burn and his nose stuff up.

Bill went on reading, his voice choking now and then. " 'Yes, Bill, the truth is, I resented your part in getting my son to be religious. That was your doing. You told Jared when he was a boy that he needed to be saved, and Jared went along. I didn't. I guess that was the beginning of my bad feelings toward you.' "

Tears poured from Jared's eyes, and he swiped at them with the back of his hand.

" 'And then the whole thing with the wild horse herd. I wanted that stud. He was faster than anything I'd ever seen. Well, it's time to put all that behind us. You were right, Bill. About God and about a lot of things. I believe in Him now. He's forgiven me all the things I did to you and Jared and my wife and anybody else who crossed my path over the years. And I'm asking you to forgive me, too. I want you to have the black colt, Chief. He's the best colt I ever bred, and I hope you'll take him as a reminder of the friendship we did have in the past. He's black like my heart used to be. But I'll see you again one day, up in heaven. Very truly yours, Rupert Booker.' "

A huge lump in his throat prevented Jared from speaking. He stared at Bill Logan, knowing his face was streaked with tears and not caring. A slow smile spread over Bill's face as he folded the letter.

"My father believed," Jared croaked out.

"Sounds like it. I'm really glad, son."

Jared nodded and pulled in a deep breath. "I do hope you'll accept his gift, sir."

"Well now." Bill sat back, looking very pleased. "You know, Jared, this isn't a good time to buy land. Everything's under a heap of snow. Why don't you stay here with us until spring? I could use you. We do a lot of repairs and such in the winter. Get our wood for next year down out of the hills—you remember."

Jared nodded.

"Well, if you want to stay on here, I'll give you a job. And next spring, when the snow is off, I'll help you find a good place for ranching. There's a fellow over on the North Branch who was talking about selling out last summer. I don't know if he did or not, but we could find out. It's a decent spread."

Jared cleared his throat, wondering if he could trust his voice. "Thank you, sir. I'd like that a lot, but there's something else I need to tell you."

"What's that?" Bill fixed his gaze on him, and Jared sat a little straighter.

"I love Patricia, sir. I think I always have. I'd like your permission to court her."

Patricia couldn't keep a smile off her face as she watched her aunt hold the sweet baby. Dinner was over and the kitchen put to rights. Uncle Bill and Jared had drifted out to the barn, and she'd settled in for a cozy chat with Aunt Edna.

"I like your young man." Edna shifted on her snowy white pillows. "I expect I'll be up and about tomorrow, and I look forward to getting to know him better."

"You'd best take it easy for a few days." Patricia leaned

forward and touched the baby's hand with her fingertip. "She's so soft!"

Edna smiled. "I think she's sleeping now. I'm feeling a little tuckered myself."

"Let me take her. I'll put her in the cradle. Or maybe I'll just hold her and watch her sleep for a while, if that's all right." Patricia looked eagerly at her aunt. Edna did look weary.

"Go ahead. But if Bill comes in, tell him not to stay away. I want to see him even if I've dozed off."

Patricia stood and bent over her to ease the slumbering infant into her own arms. Edna sighed, adjusted the covers, and closed her eyes. "Thank you, dear."

Tiptoeing out of the bedroom, Patricia nuzzled the baby's silky hair. "You darling."

Uncle Bill and Jared were coming in from the barn. They stomped the snow from their boots and wiped their feet on the rag mat inside the door to the sitting room.

"Aunt Edna's resting, but she wants you to go in anyway, Uncle Bill," she said.

"All right, but that's my daughter you're holding, missy. You take good care of her." Bill hung up his coat.

Patricia grinned and sank gently onto the sofa. "You needn't worry about that. I'm going to cuddle her for a few minutes, and then I'll put her in the cradle for a nap."

Her uncle left the room, and Jared came hesitantly to stand beside her. He looked down at little Hazel.

"Isn't she an angel?" Patricia asked.

He smiled.

She looked up at him and tucked her skirt against her thigh. "Sit down, Jared. She's just the sweetest thing I ever saw."

"I recall you mothering a rabbit kit when you were about eight years old." He folded down onto the seat beside her, looking at the baby.

The memory brought a flash of joy. "Lulu! I loved her so much."

"She kept getting in the garden."

"Yes, we did have a time with her."

"Well, I expect you all will have a handful with this one, too." The smile still played at his lips. "Think a human kit is better than a bunny?"

She wrinkled up her face at him. "You're horrid! Of course it is. I want one of my own someday—that's for certain sure."

Suddenly she realized that he had inched closer and extended his arm along the back of the sofa.

"Trisha, if you can give me just a teeny, weeny bit of attention here, I'd like to say something."

"What is it?" She turned her head and found Jared's brown eyes, warm and tender, assessing her. She swallowed hard but didn't draw back.

"Your uncle and I had a chat earlier."

Her heart skipped a beat. "What about?"

"About us."

"You and Uncle Bill?" she asked.

"Well, that, too, but I meant you and me."

It was a moment before she could respond to that. "Was he upset with you? I told him you were a perfect gentleman, and that you saved my life. It wasn't your fault that we almost—"

He reached out and brushed back a strand of her hair, and she sat very still, looking deep into his eyes.

"That wasn't what we talked about."

"Oh." It was a mere squeak.

"Trisha, this may seem kind of sudden, but. . .well, I don't know how else to put it. I love you. I asked Bill if I could court you."

"What did he say?" she whispered.

"He said it was up to you. Said he couldn't force you to let me, but if you decided you cared for me, he wouldn't be able to stop you, either."

She smiled. "Smart man."

Hazel whimpered and stirred, and Patricia looked down at her. "There now, baby. Shh." She glanced up at Jared again. "Do you want to hold her?"

"Who? Me?" His eyes widened. "I don't think so. She'd probably cry if I did."

Patricia chuckled and nestled the baby closer, brushing her cheek against Hazel's head. "You do want children, don't you, Jared?"

"Who? Me?"

She widened her eyes at his repetition, and he had the grace to blush. "Yes, you. I'm speaking to the man who just said he wanted to court me. It's important."

"Well, sure. Someday. I mean. . ." He hesitated and then held out his arms.

Patricia leaned over and kissed his cheek, then carefully

transferred Hazel to him. Jared gulped and sat back, staring down at the baby.

"Don't be so stiff," Patricia whispered. He shifted slightly, easing Hazel's tiny head into the crook of his arm.

"She hardly weighs anything." He glanced up and shot her a tentative smile. "Pretty amazing."

"Yeah." Their gazes locked.

"Hey, you two." Uncle Bill emerged from the hallway and came to the back of the sofa. "Let me see that little dumpling."

Jared stood and passed the baby to him over the back of the sofa.

"You don't mind, do you?" Bill asked.

"No, sir. But she sure is a pretty little thing."

"Oh yes, she is."

Patricia laughed as Uncle Bill walked back toward the bedrooms, uttering baby talk all the way.

Jared sat down again, suddenly shy it seemed. His smile flickered then disappeared as he sucked in a deep breath.

"Jared, I'd be honored if you'd court me."

They both sat stock-still for an instant. His expression cleared, and everything about him seemed to soften: his eyes, his lips, the set of his shoulders. He lifted his arm behind her and slid closer. She met his kiss with exultant anticipation.

Epilogue

Thanksgiving morning, 1914

Patricia and Jared leaned together on the bottom half of the foaling stall's door.

"He's absolutely magnificent," she breathed.

Jared smiled. "Not yet, but he's got the lines to be in a couple of years." He slid his arm around Trisha and squeezed her.

"I suppose I'd better get into the house and get ready. But I had to see the new arrival first."

"I knew you'd want to see him."

"It was very considerate of Lady to drop her foal on our wedding day."

"Wasn't it?" Jared drew her into his arms and kissed her.

Patricia lingered for a moment and then pulled back. "Here now, you're not even supposed to see me before the ceremony."

"Aw, your Aunt Edna's the superstitious one. Just sneak in

the kitchen door, and don't let her know we came out here to see the foal."

"What if she's in the kitchen now?" Patricia stifled a giggle and met his next kiss with enthusiasm.

A moment later, Jared released her and turned her away from the stall, his arm about her shoulders. "All right, I suppose we have to go in."

"Yes, we do. Our guests will be arriving in less than an hour." They walked to the barn door. Jared's wagon was already loaded and sitting on the barn floor, loaded with her hope chest, assorted household goods, and the bags that held her clothing. "I'm glad we'll only be a few miles from Uncle Bill and Aunt Edna."

"Me, too. God must have had that ranch waiting for me to buy and your uncle primed to help me find it."

"We'll raise the best beef in Colorado," she said with a sigh.

"And a whole tribe of little Booker cowpokes." Hand in hand, they crossed the yard to the kitchen door of the ranch house.

SUSAN PAGE DAVIS

Susan is a horse lover and a writer of historical novels, cozy mysteries, and romantic suspense novels. She also has two novels for young people among her credits. She is a wife, mother of six, and grandmother of five. Her usual place to be snowed in is Maine. Visit her Web site at www.susanpagedavis.com.

Dressed in Scarlet

by Darlene Franklin

Dedication

To Anita Gardner, who joins me on my writing adventures. We shared an unforgettable weekend at the Brown Palace Hotel. Thanks for all your support, Mom!

A special thanks to the staff at the Brown Palace for their marvelous service and patience with my questions.

Who can find a virtuous woman? for her price is far above rubies.
. . . She is not afraid of the snow for her household:
for all her household are clothed with scarlet.
PROVERBS 31:10, 21

Chapter 1

December 1913

Fabrizio Ricci glanced around the garage at the Brown Palace, making sure everything was in order. Peerless Roadsters jostled next to Cadillac Phaetons and a single Ford Model T, a bit of an oddity for the Brown's well-heeled clientele. Big or small, fancy or plain, he loved all his charges, even the smell of motor oil that permeated the air. His job was to keep the cars running and available to hotel guests. He loved driving cars he could never otherwise afford. Whatever money he didn't give to help his family, he saved toward having his own shop.

No one would drive anywhere tonight in the storm that hit Denver yesterday. More than twenty-four hours later, the snow had not even slowed down. Anyone would be a fool to drive in weather like this. Even the trolleys that he sometimes took had stopped running. It was a good thing he kept a pair of Nordic skis in the garage. If he didn't leave soon, he would have to spend the night at the hotel, or longer, if the snow kept up. As the only son remaining at home, he knew his parents depended on his help.

Fabrizio changed his work shoes for boots and strapped on the skis. He hadn't planned for the cold, but he didn't think that would be a problem, not with the long woolen scarf knitted in green and yellow by Mama. He would dress like that character in the Christmas story. What was his name? Bob Cratchit, that was it. *A Christmas Carol* had to be one of the best stories in the English language. Not as beautiful as Italian, of course, or that's what Papa would say.

Fabrizio looked out the window at the swirling snow, wishing he had taken the time to go to the kitchen for a last cup of hot coffee before he left. Too late now. The snow danced in the air before landing gracefully on the ground. *Bella neve.* Beautiful snow.

Wrapping his scarf around his nose and throat before winding its length around his body, Fabrizio pulled his cap as far down on his head as it would reach and turned the collar of his coat up over the scarf. He hadn't brought any mittens, but his work gloves should do the job. He pulled them on and hoped the oil stains wouldn't get on his clothes. Mama complained about his soiled work clothes; four sisters created enough laundry without him adding any more.

Fabrizio opened the door and headed out into the snow. He shivered, tugging his coat closer. It wasn't usually this cold when it snowed. He looked down the street. Where he should see the Daniels & Fisher tower lit against the night sky about a mile away at the other end of downtown, he saw nothing but a curtain of snow, obscuring all but a few feet ahead. Still, following the street should not present a problem.

The ground outside the garage was packed down, trampled by horses and guests who came and went at the hotel. The snow fell rapidly, filling in even the most recent footsteps. Wind flung handfuls back into the air, redistributing them across the ground. He dug his poles into the snow and pushed forward to the front of the hotel.

"*Buona notte*," the doorman called. "Be careful tonight. See you tomorrow."

"Buona notte," Fabrizio called back. He headed west from the hotel, down Sixteenth Street toward the D&F tower, and then across the bridge to his home.

He picked up speed, getting into rhythm, feeling rather like a four-legged creature as he used the skis and poles. The push-and-pull gave way to the grace of gliding over the snow as if weightless. The exertion warmed him. He kept his eyes to the ground to avoid the sting of the snow, looking up only when warned by the jingle of a horse's harness or the crunch of car tires. He breathed deeply, his nose aching from the rush of cold air. He closed his mind against the cold and thought instead of the bowl of warm, fragrant minestrone that Mama would have waiting for him. Three miles, that was all. He had walked the distance many times. He would be home soon.

Natalie Daire looked at the bright lights inside the train s where she had dropped off her friend Patricia Logan. She debated about stopping for a cup of hot chocolate. She was very cold, in spite of the red woolies and warm scarf and the driving bonnet that cut some of the wind. Father would have forbidden her attendance at Thalia's party if he had known the snow would last so long. She knew he must be worried about her; that's why she left the party early instead of spending the night as she had planned.

Her car, the Cadillac Model 30, had proved its worth as "The Standard of the World" on the drive from Thalia's house. The train station stood halfway to her home in Westminster. She decided to drive to the Brown Palace, only a few blocks away. They must have a phone. She would call home and purchase a hot drink while she was there.

She leaned forward, breathing warm air against the front windshield, rubbing a small patch clear. She managed to move her feet in the correct clutch-release pattern to start the Cadillac moving forward again. The car slipped as she turned right toward the Brown Palace.

The tall buildings of downtown Denver provided some protection against the wind. The windshield wipers did their best, but she could only see a few feet ahead of her. Heaven and earth met and melted into a dotted wall of white in front of her. She slowed the car even further. One car passed, a silver ghost under the veil of snow. The Brown Palace couldn't be much farther.

A figure loomed in front of her, bent against the wind, gliding over the snow, and straight in her path. Natalie slammed on the brakes. Tires skidded on the slippery street.

She didn't know what happened next. One foot on the brake pedal tried to stop the car. The other on the accelerator veered away from the approaching figure. Her car spun in a circle and crashed into a wooden stall on the sidewalk. Natalie flung her head forward between her arms.

"*Signorina*, are you all right?" A deep voice penetrated the blackness behind her closed eyes.

The world stopped spinning. Natalie opened her eyes. A tall, black-haired man stood beside the car, dark eyes burning with concern. *This must be the man who caused the accident.*

"What were you doing in the middle of the street?" she demanded. "I was trying to avoid running into you."

"I am sorry. You are unhurt?" He repeated his concern.

Natalie took another look at the man. He presented an improbable sight, a pole in each hand, feet ending in long skis, his coat tugged as tightly as possible against his body, a bright scarf wound around face and neck and torso like a barber pole, only burning black eyes visible beneath the visor of his cap.

No, she wanted to say. *I'm cold and hungry, and I want to be at home with my family.* Instead, she checked herself for injuries. Her hands had not loosened their grip on the steering wheel. Her feet had slid off the pedals. She shook herself. Her head complained, but the rest of her seemed fine. Fine particles covered her coat. Snow?

That was when she noticed the shattered windshield, the wiper blade paused in midair as if trying to rid the air itself of snow.

"Oh no. My car."

"I can help." He extended a hand to assist her from the carriage, removed his skis, and took her place in the driver's seat. He turned the key, and the engine restarted. "The car, it is in good condition. Only the windshield is broken."

"But I can't drive home if I can't see," Natalie wailed.

"Come with me. I will fix it." He brushed glass and snow off the passenger seat with a dark-stained glove and invited her to sit. "Let us go to the Brown Palace. You can spend the night, and tomorrow the car will be ready to go."

"That's where I was headed," Natalie said. "I can use the hotel telephone to call my father and tell him what happened."

After the man packed his skis in the backseat, he drove the car without regard to the snow that flowed through the broken window pane.

"Thank you for helping me." She wondered where he was going when she had her accident. Away from the hotel.

"It is right to help others," he said. "I can fix your windshield tonight."

"No, no," Natalie said. "Tomorrow is soon enough." She hoped to see him again, to look at him in better light. Did his appearance match his deep, lightly accented voice?

"As you wish." He did not speak again during the short drive.

They arrived at the hotel. The man carried her luggage inside the lobby. Natalie reached for her purse to tip him.

"*Non*, it was my pleasure, signorina."

"It's Natalie. Natalie Daire."

"Signorina Daire." The man did not offer his own name. He disappeared through a back door.

Half an hour later, Natalie sipped hot tea and looked out through the window from her top floor accommodations. Snow painted the windowpanes with a puzzle of crystals. "Thank You, God, for bringing me here safely."

Tomorrow she would see her mysterious rescuer again.

Chapter 2

Fabrizio stirred, ready to start the day. He had lain awake for some time in the double bed he shared with Patrick O'Riley, the front desk clerk. More staff than usual stayed in the servants' quarters; many spent the night at the hotel rather than risk the weather. He liked the Irishman well enough, but he had grown since the last time he had shared a bed before his brother married and left home. The bed felt cramped with two of them in it. He bundled up his coat for a pillow, and the blanket didn't quite cover both of them. Cold wind pounded on the window, building up ice and creating drafts.

He welcomed the arrival of dawn. Would the hotel expect him to stay through the storm? Common sense suggested that no one would want their horseless carriages in this weather. Then again, Signorina Daire had tried driving through the snow, and look what had happened. Anyone should learn from her mistake.

No. He shook his head. It was unfair to blame the young woman for an accident that he caused by appearing out of the darkness. The good Lord had protected both of them. He would replace the windshield in Signorina Daire's car and then ask if he could go home. Mama and Papa would need his help more than ever with this snow.

He hurried through breakfast in the hotel kitchen, gobbling eggs and biscuits and drinking a cup of coffee as hot as he could stand it. *"Grazie."* He set his plate beside the sink and headed for the garage.

No new cars had arrived since the Cadillac on the previous evening. Snow covered the windows set high in the garage doors. He hoisted himself on a box and looked out. The driveway he had shoveled yesterday afternoon had already filled again. No one should drive in this weather. If the streets were cleared, snow would fill them again within minutes. He hoped the manager would allow him to leave.

First, he would repair the young signorina's windshield as promised. He had a piece of glass that was the right size. He did not worry whether she could pay for the work. She came from money; anyone who owned a fine piece of machinery like the Cadillac Model 30 did. He ran his hands over the Dewar Trophy–winning auto. Well built. Sleek. *Expensive.* In the same class as its owner. So why could he not get her soft blond curls, frozen in place by the snow, or those expressive gray eyes out of his mind? *Fabrizio, Fabrizio*, he scolded himself. *You must not let a pretty face fool you.* Someone like Signorina Daire had no place in the dreams of a poor immigrant.

If only his heart would listen. He finished replacing the windshield.

John Livingston, the hotel manager, lifted an eyebrow when

Fabrizio asked if he could go home and stay until the snow stopped. "Do you think that's wise?"

"I do not know," Fabrizio admitted. "But I must try. They will worry."

"You have my blessing. It's my guess that no one will require your services for a few days." Livingston shook his head at Fabrizio's foolishness. "But if you can't make it home, you're welcome to stay here. There'll be plenty for you to do."

Fabrizio thought of his worried parents and the cramped quarters he had shared last night. He must try to reach his family's home located in the Highlands district of Denver. Once again he wrapped his bright green and yellow scarf around his neck, strapped on the skis, and slipped his hands into his gloves. He looked over the world gone white, took a deep breath, and braced himself for the cold air.

Once outside, he could get no rhythm going. Instead of gliding over the surface, his skis sank into deep snowdrifts. Memories of the lovely Signorina Daire interfered with his concentration. Her face swam in front of his eyes, adding color to the landscape. He made it as far as the place where the accident had occurred the previous evening. Snow covered the wooden stall, obliterating any hint of what had happened only twelve hours before. The sight reminded Fabrizio of one of his favorite Bible verses. "Come now, and let us reason together, saith the LORD: though your sins be as scarlet, they shall be as white as snow; though they be red like crimson, they shall be as wool." Isaiah could have been looking down Sixteenth Street in Denver when he wrote those words.

Was Signorina Daire looking at the same scene? Did she like snow? How foolish to drive in such weather. What father would allow his daughter to drive in a blizzard? His own papa would not allow his daughters to drive at all, even if they could afford a horseless carriage. But he suspected that the spirited young woman would not accept any curtailment of her activities without a protest. She might even be one of those—what was the word?—suffragettes.

Fabrizio realized he had been staring at the stall for several minutes. Thank the good Lord that neither of them was hurt. Now he must get moving before he turned into a statue made of ice. He pushed ahead with his ski pole. It broke through the crust into a deep pocket, plunging several feet. He toppled forward and flailed his arms, catching himself on the edges of the stand before he could fall.

The street stretched before him. Tall buildings protected it; snow would drift even higher away from the center of the city. He faced the truth. He could not make it home. Mama and Papa would trust the Lord for his safety; and he must do the same for their needs.

He made a wide circle and started back for the Brown Palace. Already snow had filled in his tracks. He prayed the Lord would keep his family safe and warm. Somehow he didn't mind returning to work. He might see the enigmatic Signorina Daire again.

The clock was striking ten when Natalie stirred on Wednesday morning. It took a moment to orient herself. She snuggled under a dark green comforter. The mattress on the immense four-poster was soft but unfamiliar. She stretched and banged into the headboard. The nudge set up a complaint in her head. Natalie ran her hands over her forehead and discovered a bump.

The events of the previous night came back to her in a rush. The drive from Thalia's house. The decision to spend the night at the Brown Palace. The mysterious stranger who appeared out of the darkness and caused an accident—who then in turn rescued her and brought her safely to the Brown. Her entire body ached, her head most of all.

She rubbed her eyes and stared at the clock, not believing the hour. Surely it couldn't be that late. The light coming through the window suggested early morning. Natalie tugged her negligee about her and walked over to the window. Where she expected sunshine—after more than twenty-four hours, surely the storm had stopped—instead she saw the same wall of white, snow flying in ten directions at once. She doubted that she could leave today. Still, it wouldn't hurt to find out if that nice young man had repaired the Model 30 as promised.

Natalie rang the bell for one of the hotel maids. A brief glance in her dressing room mirror confirmed that her forehead sported a bump the size of a mothball that was coloring. She touched it gingerly. She remembered the shattered windshield and thanked God that she wasn't hurt more severely. Not a single scratch. Perhaps it was just as well that she could not return home today. Father would worry if he could see her face or the car.

She wanted hot tea and a warm breakfast; then she would search out the young man who had been both the cause and savior of last night's accident. Perhaps he was visiting the Brown from Europe. He spoke with some kind of accent. French perhaps? She didn't think it was Spanish; several of their household help came from Mexico, and she knew a little of the language. He called her "Signorina." Italian, definitely.

Sunny Italy. Given the blizzard, he might wish he had decided to stay home for the holidays. What was he doing on Sixteenth Street in the middle of a blizzard, wearing skis? Perhaps he was an angel, sent from heaven because of the accident. Natalie smiled to herself. She doubted that angels wore bright scarves or had such handsome dark looks.

She debated on whether to don the dress she had worn to Thalia's party for a second day or to wear a different gown. She thought of the handsome stranger and opted for a new outfit. Fur trim accented the tiered skirt, and the robin's egg blue of the material flattered her coloring. After the maid helped her dress, she studied her reflection in the mirror. What could be done about the bruise on her forehead? She fingered her hair and teased a few curls over it. Perhaps it would deflect attention from the multicolored hues. Satisfied at last with her toilette, she left her room and headed down the stairs in search of brunch.

Walking into the foyer of the Brown Palace always gave Natalie a thrill. She loved the sight of liveried doormen, the low hush of voices from tables, the magnificence of the stained glass overhead, even when obscured by snow as it was now. In addition to the cosmopolitan mix of guests, she could usually count on meeting acquaintances, more often than not one of Daddy's fuddy-duddy business associates. Unlike that handsome stranger. She intended to find the mysterious Italian; she could ask him about the car as an excuse for seeking him out.

She rang the bell at the front desk, and a young man whose lilting voice and bright red hair proclaimed his Irish heritage appeared. "May I help you, miss?"

"I am looking for one of the guests." Natalie felt heat rise in her cheeks. Maybe the clerk would attribute her color to the blast of warm air from the vents. "He assisted me last evening, and I wanted to thank him properly."

"What is his name?" The clerk, whose name tag read "PATRICK," smiled.

"You see, that's the problem." Natalie twisted a handkerchief in her hands. "He disappeared without introducing himself. He appeared to be Italian. Tall, dark, in his twenties." *Do I dare say* handsome? "Oh yes, and he was wearing a very distinctive scarf. Yellow and green stripes, as bright as a summer day."

The front door crashed open, and cold air blasted in. Patrick's eyes widened in recognition. "You're in luck. I believe this is the man you are looking for."

He's here? Natalie rotated on her heels. First she noticed a snow-crusted cap covering dark hair, then the bright yellow and green scarf. She suddenly was very glad that she had decided to wear her most becoming frock.

"Fabrizio! I see that you decided to return." Patrick greeted him warmly.

Fabrizio. So that was his name. The syllables rolled around in her mind. It tasted exotic, like basil and garlic and maybe a hint of sweet tomatoes. But why was he traveling in this weather? On foot?

"Miss Daire, is this the gentleman?" Patrick spoke in a low tone. She appreciated his discretion.

"Yes." God must be behind this encounter; she didn't expect to run into him so soon.

"You should know. . ."

Fabrizio approached the counter before Patrick finished his sentence.

"Fab—" Natalie stopped. They had never been properly introduced, after all. She coughed and spoke again. "I wanted to thank you for your assistance last night."

"Signorina Daire." The snow on Fabrizio's head melted in the warm lobby, and his dark hair sprang into curls. "Your car, it is ready." He paused. "But you will do well not to leave today. The snow, it is too deep."

Natalie shook off his admonition. "I intend to wait out the storm at the Brown. But thank you for seeing to my car." She took in features of Fabrizio's appearance that she had missed in the dark the previous evening. His coat was frayed around the edges. A faint oily odor clung to him. And his shoes—her father would never wear such shoddy workmanship. She looked into his beautiful brown eyes with growing suspicions.

"Miss Daire." Patrick interrupted her thoughts. "I see you have already made the acquaintance of our coachman, Fabrizio Ricci."

"You may tell Patrick when you will leave. I will bring the car for you." Fabrizio nodded respectfully and walked away.

Her mysterious rescuer was not a guest from the Continent. He was one of the hired help. Natalie stared thoughtfully at his departing back.

Chapter 3

Natalie!" A familiar voice called her name. It belonged to Eleanor Royal, one of the circle of friends she palled around with in Denver. She could be outspoken but fun, the kind of person her father expected her to associate with. Unlike her mysterious rescuer from the previous evening. Natalie cast a longing look at the door through which the coachman had disappeared and greeted her friend. They entered the dining room together and observed as a waiter floated a fresh tablecloth over a window table and laid out two place settings.

"I expect we shall be here several days." Eleanor tucked her napkin in her lap. "I love the Brown, but I fear it will become boring."

"Not at all. We shall just have to organize parlor games and other activities, as we did at school." Natalie paused. "Speaking of school, I expected to see you at Thalia's party. We had a wonderful time."

"Father refused to let me go when the snow started falling. It's just as well. Have you ever seen a storm like this?"

Natalie stared out the window. Down here on the ground level the prospect was truly frightening. Snow climbed the lower half of the window.

A querulous voice interrupted her thoughts. "Waiter!" An older woman, hair falling in precise silver waves, bellowed and jutted out her chin. A small, round man rushed to her side. "Yes, Mrs. Rushton?"

"I have two butter knives and no dinner knife. The standards at the Brown have deteriorated."

The poor man dashed away and returned with a fresh set of silverware. The cantankerous older woman didn't bother to thank him.

I hope I can avoid her at mealtimes. Natalie chastised herself for the unkind thought. No, God said to love everyone, not only pleasant people. Perhaps she could do something to cheer the older woman.

Natalie realized that she was staring. She turned her attention back to Eleanor. What would her friend think if she told her she wished she could go outside and build a snowman as they had when they were children? Eleanor had always preferred to stay inside where it was dry and warm. So instead, Natalie described her arrival at the Brown the night before.

"You mean to say that you drove in this weather? I don't want to drive those scary things. But you go bravely about in that splendid car of yours." Eleanor peered at Natalie's forehead. "Were you hurt in the accident?"

Natalie tugged at the curl covering the bruise. "Only a small bump. Really, it was nothing."

"And tell me more about the handsome stranger who rescued you. How romantic."

"How *providential*," Natalie corrected. "God sent me help when I needed it." She paused. She wasn't ready to tell her friend about her rescuer's true identity as the hotel's coachman. Nor would she admit her interest in him. She wanted to discover more about him, and she thought she knew how to make that happen. "I expect you shall see him soon enough. Now, let's see if the desk clerk will show us to a room that we can use for parlor games."

Natalie waited until Eleanor returned to her room to freshen up before she approached Patrick. "I believe the guests will become restless because of the snow." She smiled in the way that usually won her way. "I am planning some parlor games, and I would appreciate the help of someone on the hotel staff."

The redheaded clerk smiled back, a coconspirator. "And did you have someone particular in mind, Miss Daire?"

"I thought perhaps some of the staff cannot perform their normal duties because of the snow. Someone like—Mr. Ricci?" She blushed as she said his name.

"Certainly. No one will require his services in the garage today. Did you have a room in mind for the party?"

"I was thinking of the Ladies' Ordinary." Natalie mentioned the facility used for ladies' club activities. "Only for this occasion we will welcome male guests and children." Patrick confirmed the availability of the room and completed arrangements for a high tea service.

Later in the day, Natalie made her way to the room by

herself. She was envisioning the arrangement of chairs when she heard the door open. Eleanor swept in, followed by Fabrizio. He looked as handsome as ever, if a bit uncertain. "Mr. Ricci. I'm so glad you could join us." She walked toward him, hands outstretched.

He bowed low over her hands, a lovely Continental gesture. "I am glad to be of service."

"And have you met my friend, Eleanor Royal?"

"Signorina Royal." Fabrizio acknowledged the introduction.

Natalie loved the way "signorina" rolled off his tongue. She would have to study Italian.

"Oh, do let's dispense with formalities." Eleanor insisted in her usual blunt style. "We are planning a party, after all. We must be on a first-name basis. As you know, I'm Eleanor, and Miss Daire's given name is Natalie."

"As in *Buon Natale*."

For a brief moment, Natalie thought that Fabrizio was calling her pretty, and she felt heat creep into her cheeks.

"In Italian, *Natale* means *Christmas*." Fabrizio's explanation deflected some of the heat.

"Why, that's the same thing Natalie means in English. Her birthday is the day before Christmas, you know," Eleanor gushed.

"Which is still a few weeks away." Natalie wanted to get the attention off herself. She did not want to mention her coming-of-age party, and the inheritance that came with it, in front of Fabrizio. She suspected that the quiet coachman would retreat even further into himself if Eleanor revealed that. "While today we are holding a party for people stranded here at the hotel. What do you think? Shall we arrange the chairs in small circles or in a large grouping?"

"I understand that Molly Brown seats everyone in a large U-shape." Eleanor giggled. "So her guests can meet new people."

Molly Brown did not set Denver's society standards, but Natalie liked the plainspoken, kindhearted matron. "Then that's what we shall do. We may be spending several days together, and it would be good to become better acquainted at the outset. Let's get started."

Natalie's hopes to learn more about Fabrizio seemed doomed to failure. Never speaking unless spoken to, he moved with quick, precise movements, never a step out of place. She remembered how easily he moved over the snow on the skis. Every now and then a smile passed across his face. Perhaps he was thinking about his sweetheart. He could even be married. Why did the possibility leave her with a pang in her heart?

They finished arranging the room with time to spare. Eleanor wrote the names of people, places, and things from the Christmas story for a get-acquainted game. Fabrizio clasped his hands together and trained his eyes on the floor when he spoke to her. "May I do anything else to help you, signorina?"

She wished he would say "Natalie" again. It warmed her heart like the glow of Christmas candles and a cup of hot, spiced cider. But he wouldn't; Eleanor's suggestion to use first names probably made him uncomfortable. Guilt hit her. The poor man had arisen hours before she had, repaired her windshield, braved the weather, and then spent the afternoon helping them set up for the party.

"I hope you will join us for the tea—as our guest." She made it an invitation, not an order.

"That would not be wise." Fabrizio seemed determined to respect the social boundaries that separated them.

Natalie racked her brain for an excuse to see him again. The perfect answer came, one that would address two problems. "There is one thing you could do for me."

"Anything, signorina."

"Please invite Mrs. Rushton to join us for tea. And escort her if she needs help." Natalie suppressed a giggle at the surprise that flitted through his eyes.

"*Fino ad allora.* Until then, Signorina Daire." He sketched a bow and left the room.

Fabrizio's feet whispered along the plush carpet to Mrs. Rushton's room. He could have left word of Natalie's invitation at the front desk. He should have left it there. Everyone in the hotel avoided the old lady if possible. Her temper was legendary, and she expected perfect service, regardless of the circumstances. She would not welcome his intrusion.

But Fabrizio could not bring himself to disappoint Natalie. In his private thoughts, he savored the sound of her name. It suited her, with her golden hair shining like an angel's halo around her head, her richness of spirit, as well as purse, that spoke in everything she did. Her dress probably cost more than his entire family spent on clothing in a year's time. But away from her, he allowed his thoughts to linger on how the blue fabric brought out the color in her eyes. He scolded himself. The likes of Natalie Daire were not for the likes of Fabrizio Ricci.

He hesitated at the door to Mrs. Rushton's room then knocked. He expected a maid to answer, but instead Mrs. Rushton herself cracked the door open. "Yes?" Dressed in a robe and shoulder wrap, she looked elderly and frail, not at all like the terror of the entire hotel staff.

Fabrizio cleared his throat. "Signorina Natalie Daire invites you to tea in the Ladies' Ordinary this afternoon." He handed her an ivory envelope.

"Nonsense. I always have tea in my room."

"The signorina asks for you especially." Fabrizio didn't know why he made the extra effort. The guests would enjoy the party more without the presence of the grumbling older woman. Still, Natalie asked for Mrs. Rushton in particular. "She thinks the guests, they will be bored in all this snow." He paused and added a final word. "She asks me to escort you to the tea."

Mrs. Rushton's face lined in a frown, but she did not speak.

"I will come for you in an hour." Fabrizio left before Mrs. Rushton could refuse. He had done as Natalie wanted. Maybe now he could get the lovely heiress out of his mind. Hotel gossip buzzed about the fortune she would inherit from her grandfather on her next birthday. Fabrizio smiled. He also received a legacy from his grandfather—his name. If he could be the man his grandfather was, as brave in coming to a new country and as dedicated to his family, he would consider himself rich.

Fabrizio went to the kitchen for a bite of lunch. Conversation centered on the news from St. Clara's Orphanage.

"Those poor *Kinder*, freezing in this terrible snow. They say the place has run out of coal." Braum, the heavyset German cook, stirred soup at the stove.

Fabrizio winced. St. Clara's housed a multitude of orphans, many of them from Denver's Italian community. They would indeed suffer without coal to heat the home.

"The *Denver Post* has offered to send wagonloads of coal," a maid mentioned. "But I don't see how they'll get through the snowdrifts."

Fabrizio's thoughts flew to his own family. Did they have enough coal? He looked at the able-bodied men sitting around the staff table. How he wished he could have made it home. His parents counted on him to help with the heavy work. His only brother, the eldest child, had married and lived with his new wife and their little ones. His four younger sisters could only do so much. If only he could find a way home. Maybe he could hitch a ride with one of the *Post*'s wagons. The road to the orphanage passed near his house. Perhaps, if his manager would release him from work...

An hour sped by, and he returned to the fourth floor to escort Mrs. Rushton to the tea. He determined not to let Natalie cajole him into staying. Staff did not dine with guests. A smile tugged at his mouth. Not only that, but he did not want to be the only gentleman present. Since the Ladies' Ordinary was the hotel's clubroom for women, men might hesitate to brave the gathering.

A transformed Mrs. Rushton answered his knock. Her beaded dress shimmered with Christmas splendor. A hint of a smile suggested her pleasure at Natalie's invitation.

"*Signora* Rushton, you are lovely."

The smile vanished. Had he spoken aloud? Fabrizio could not believe his folly. Mrs. Rushton might accuse him of familiarity to the manager. But aside from a little color in her powdered cheeks, she did not respond. "Shall we take the elevator, Signora Rushton?" He feared the steps to the eighth floor, where the tea was located, would prove too much for the older woman.

"I am not an invalid, young man." That was classic Mrs. Rushton.

"Signorina Daire asked me to escort you."

"Daire's daughter? She's a sweet young thing." The compliment surprised Fabrizio, and he almost missed the fact that she handed him a small mesh bag. "Since Natalie insists, you may carry my reticule."

Mrs. Rushton paused on the eighth-floor landing to catch her breath. Natalie must have spotted their approach, because she dashed forward to greet them. "Mrs. Rushton! I am so glad that you decided to join us." Natalie took her arm and led her to the open door. She looked over her shoulder and mouthed "thank you" to Fabrizio. At that moment, he felt as though he would do anything she asked. He followed close behind.

Loud voices laced with laughter leapt through the door. Eleanor greeted Mrs. Rushton and pinned a piece of paper to the back of her dress. INNKEEPER'S WIFE. Fabrizio wondered if the appellation was intentional; he could imagine Mrs. Rushton turning away a young couple, even if the wife was pregnant. Through the open doorway, he could see a few men and several children mingling with female guests. Natalie led Mrs. Rushton to the seat of honor.

Fabrizio hovered near the door, watching the gaiety, remembering happy gatherings at home. He was preparing to leave when Natalie returned. "You will join us for tea, won't you?" Steady gray eyes pleaded with him.

A few minutes ago, Fabrizio had felt ready to do anything this beautiful woman asked of him.

He would do anything, that is, except to cross the social barriers that stood between them, as thick as the Great Wall of China.

Chapter 4

Natalie watched Fabrizio's departing back. He looked good in his uniform, so broad shouldered, so quietly strong. If only he would have agreed to stay. Not a single man at the tea captured her interest as he did. How had he managed to convince Mrs. Rushton to attend the party? Natalie had sent the invitation but had not expected the woman to accept. She surprised her by showing up, dressed to the nines, and a kind word for "that nice young man who carried my reticule." A brave young girl hovered near her, giving her clues about the name pinned to her back.

Natalie lingered a moment, until Fabrizio disappeared around a corner, and then wandered to the window. Snow swirled in the air. She doubted that anyone would leave the hotel tomorrow either, whether staff or guest. Patrick had assured her that the hotel generated its own electricity and drew water from an artesian well. They did not have to fear the loss of power.

The afternoon tea achieved a moderate success. Too late,

Natalie realized that she had not invited the staff, and none attended. They must be as bored and stressed as the guests. Social distinctions paled in the face of their shared experience, snowbound by the weather. People already referred to the storm as "Denver's big snow." It was certainly the worst that she had ever seen. She decided that she would plan a mixed activity for staff and guests together, perhaps a carol sing. Everyone sang the same songs of the season. Even better, she knew the right man to help her set up the music room. She invited her guests to return that evening for another event.

After the tea ended, Natalie sought out Patrick. She reserved the Ladies' Ordinary for the following day. "Tonight I'd like to hold a carol sing and invite the staff to join in. What time is most convenient for them to attend?"

The clerk murmured a protest, but Natalie insisted. He agreed that most of the kitchen staff as well as the maids would be finished by half-past nine. She beamed. "Please be sure to let everyone know that they are invited."

"And would you be needing Mr. Ricci to help you set up for the party?" Patrick suggested.

"Please." Natalie knew her cheeks must look nearly as red as the Irishman's hair.

The carol service dominated conversation during the staff supper. Fabrizio had not decided whether to join the celebration.

Braum stirred a bubbling pan. "I am making hot cocoa to bring." He hummed a few phrases in German.

What was that tune? "Oh, Christmas Tree," that was it.

Most of the hotel staff intended to go. Fabrizio was torn. He loved music. His family probably whiled away hours of snowbound tedium singing around the fireplace. The thought tugged at his heart. Did he dare spend more time in Signorina Daire's presence? She already occupied more of his thoughts than she should; she crept in at all hours of the day. That afternoon, he had helped her move the piano and chairs. When she sat down to play, the chords flew like an arrow from the keys to his heart and lodged there.

After the music started, he could not stay away. He found a chair next to Patrick in the back row. Natalie had changed into an emerald green dress, and lights from the chandeliers danced on her golden hair. She announced each selection in her clear soprano voice. Fabrizio lost himself in the songs, humming through unfamiliar verses, adding a bass line to others. Patrick sang tenor. When Fabrizio closed his eyes, he could almost imagine he was at home with his family, singing in four-part harmony.

When they started "Silent Night," Natalie changed her routine. "I've heard a story about this carol. I'm not sure if it's true or not. The organ at St. Nicholas Church in Oberndorf, Austria, broke down on Christmas Eve. So the assistant pastor, Joseph Mohr, wrote a song that he could accompany with his guitar. It would be lovely to hear the song in the original language. Surely someone here speaks German?"

"Ja, I do." The chef, Braum, raised his hand.

"Splendid." Natalie smiled. "Would you be willing to sing it for us in German? We would all enjoy it so much."

The rotund man stood. Still dressed in uniform, he hesitated. Someone—Natalie's friend Eleanor, perhaps?—clapped, encouraging him forward. Red flooded his face more than when he stood over a hot stove. He sucked in a deep breath and nodded at Natalie. In a pleasant baritone, he began singing. *"Stille Nacht! Heil'ge Nacht!"*

A hush descended. Fabrizio closed his eyes and repeated the words in Italian, envisioning the holy family in the stable that first Christmas night. *Thank You, God, for sending* Cristo il Salvatore *to us.*

When Braum finished, the group sang the same carol in English. Natalie made another suggestion. "Next, let's sing 'Angels We Have Heard on High.' I've heard some lovely harmony from the group. Mrs. Rushton—"

Fabrizio had not anticipated the older woman's presence at the caroling. He looked around the gathering and saw her seated near the heater vent. She looked startled.

"I heard your lovely alto voice. Please come sing with me."

Pink colored Mrs. Rushton's high cheekbones as she made her way to the piano. Natalie twisted on the bench and sought Fabrizio in the crowd. "Mr. Ricci? Mr. O'Riley? We would welcome four-part harmony."

Patrick jumped to his feet. The Irishman loved to put on a show. Fabrizio took more time. When he stood, Natalie's eyes sparkled as if the very stars of heaven shone in them. She arranged the quartet so that Fabrizio stood next to her. He felt her nearness, the warmth of her shoulder. It confused him so that he missed the introduction and joined on the second note. Once he started, he lost his self-consciousness in the music, imagining the wonder of the angel choir on that first Christmas night. "Gloria in excelsis Deo." Glory to God in the highest. His voice deepened and slid down to low bass notes, while Natalie's soared into the highest.

A worshipful silence greeted the end of the song. Then Natalie thanked the quartet and invited them to sit down. Eyes shining as bright as a silver coin, she swiveled on the bench. "The singing has been wonderful. Let's end our party by sharing Christmas memories."

Fabrizio tensed. Would she talk of the elaborate gifts she must have received? Of fancy holiday parties her family had hosted?

"My birthday is on Christmas Eve." Natalie glanced at the floor, as if embarrassed to share a personal detail. "My grandfather tells me that I am blessed to share my birthday with the Savior of the world. Somehow I've always known that my cake and candles were also for that other Christmas baby, Jesus. On my twelfth birthday, I realized that God had given me the best present I could ever hope for: His Son. So Christmas is my birthday twice over: I was born the first time; then I was born again as God's child." Joy that only came from the Holy Spirit shone in her eyes. "Would anyone else like to share?"

Fabrizio's heart danced. Natalie believed in his Lord. They both belonged to the family that truly mattered, with God as their Father and Jesus as their brother. A few others mentioned special memories. Braum described the German Christmas tree tradition.

Food filled Fabrizio's memories of Christmas. Rather than the turkey and ham that Americans enjoyed, they ate *baccala*, salted codfish. His mother competed with his grandmother over homemade pasta and melt-in-your mouth molasses cookies. But those memories, though pleasant, would not lift up the Savior whose birthday they celebrated.

"That's so interesting, Mr. Braum. Thank you for sharing. I love learning about Christmas traditions in other countries." Natalie scanned the rows of carolers. Her gaze drew Fabrizio to his feet like a puppet on a string.

"My family, we came to Denver from a small village outside of Potenza, in Italia. Three weeks before Christmas, we bring a *presepio* into our home. The presepio is a manger such as the one the baby Jesus slept in. Every time we help someone, we add hay to the presepio. We want it to be as soft as possible for the Christ child." He ran out of words and sat down.

"What a wonderful tradition! Let's practice the same thoughtfulness ourselves. Instead of complaining about the snow, we can think of what we can do for others." Natalie beamed as if Fabrizio had given her the perfect conclusion to the evening. "I hope all of you will join us upstairs in the Ladies' Ordinary for more games tomorrow afternoon. We have something planned for your children in the morning. Feel free to come and go as your duties allow."

From the look Natalie sent in his direction, Fabrizio suspected she would require his assistance again. Somehow, after the memories they had shared, it no longer seemed like such an impossible idea. What would the alluring signorina decide to do next?

Chapter 5

Fabrizio had predicted Natalie's intentions correctly. Patrick contacted him early in the morning. "Miss Daire would like to see you in the music room. After breakfast, to be sure. She was mentioning that baby Jesus crib you described last night."

Fabrizio forced himself to sit down for a cup of coffee and a cinnamon roll first. Music bubbled inside him, echoes of last night's carols, Natalie's lovely soprano soaring above them all. What plans had she made for the day? A scant fifteen minutes later, he joined her.

"Fabrizio! I'm so glad to see you. The boys will be here any second."

Wood sat in a neat pile in the center of the room, as well as a bale of hay in one corner. A variety of tools were spread across a table.

She explained. "I had planned for the children to draw some Christmas decorations. But the crib you described would be so much more fun for the boys." She hesitated. "You do know how to *make* the crib, don't you? I figured with your talent for fixing cars. . ."

Fabrizio nodded his head. He had learned how to build a crib at his grandfather's side.

"That's good. Do we have everything we need?"

"There is plenty, signorina."

"Oh, good. Patrick gathered wood for us. After the boys finish the—what did you call it? presepio?—we can get everyone involved in filling it with hay. I love the idea of preparing for the baby Jesus." She paused. "I hope you will join the adult party later this afternoon. Patrick said he was certain several of the morning staff would join us. Please say you will."

"I do not know, signorina." The *Denver Post* might attempt to deliver coal to St. Clara's today. If they did, he intended to go with the wagons. He looked into her eyes, bright in their eagerness, and lost all reservations. If he was still in the hotel, he would come.

Natalie hung the homemade Christmas cards around the Ladies' Ordinary. They added a homey, festive atmosphere. She almost wished the room used candlelight, instead of the electric fixtures, bell-like lamps hanging from a chandelier. Who would come today? Her maid had promised to attend with some friends. Perhaps games could break down the awkwardness between staff and guests. Denver's big snow could become a magical memory for those staying at the Brown.

Why did that thought bring the tall, dark Italian to her

mind? But would the one person she most wanted to see join them? Her mind darted to his deep voice booming in celebration of the coming of the Christ child. To the memories he shared. To his patience with the boys while they built the crib. He was good with children. He would make a good father someday. The thought shocked her. She had no business thinking about such things.

At the appointed hour, the room quickly filled. Most of yesterday's guests returned, even Mrs. Rushton. The gentlemen must have convinced more of their friends to join them. Her maid came with a handful of friends. They sat at one end of the circle, as far as possible from the guests. Nearly every seat was filled when at last Fabrizio made his entrance. He nodded at her, and her heart soared.

Natalie looked at the seating arrangement—guests to the right, staff to the left—and knew she had to do something to encourage the people to mingle. She already had decided on the game.

"I will be 'it.' I will ask one of you, 'Do you love your neighbor?' If you say 'no,' you must change places with one of the people on either side of you. I will try to take your seat." Natalie smiled as she said this. "And I warn you that I am fast. Or. . ." She shook her finger around the circle. "You can say, 'I love all my neighbors except for everyone wearing blue, or with brown hair,' or whatever you like. Then everybody who is wearing blue has to change seats. If you say, 'I love everyone,' all of you have to change seats."

The people nodded in recognition of this variation on a familiar game.

The men removed the few extra chairs while Natalie debated who to approach first. Eleanor, who else? Her friend would jump into the spirit of the game. She stood in front of her friend and asked, "Do you love your neighbor?"

Eleanor glanced around the circle. Mischief danced in her blue eyes. "I love everyone except people who are younger than ten years old." Giggles erupted from the children. They jumped to their feet, shrieked, and ran in every direction. Natalie slipped into the chair Eleanor vacated. The game picked up pace. The children delighted in saying, "I love everyone," and making the whole group run around. Natalie passed Fabrizio a few times. He kept quiet, reserving his brilliant smiles for the youngest children, who loved to tease him.

Natalie called a halt to the game before the older guests could tire. "Let's enjoy some of the marvelous refreshments before we start our next game."

Servers had arranged platters of the Brown's famous macaroons and carafes of beverages. Natalie stood guard to discourage children from grabbing more than a couple of the meringue-light coconut cookies at a time. She poured a cup of tea for herself and turned face-to-face with Fabrizio. His hand hovered over the sweets as if he didn't dare to take one.

She handed two of them to him on a napkin. "Please eat these. I don't want the children eating too much sugar."

"The *bambini*, yes." He smiled at a pair of young girls giggling in the corner. "The girls, they remind me of my sisters." He looked sad.

"Do you come from a large family?" Some families among

the Italian community burgeoned with as many as ten children. She could not imagine it herself.

"One older brother and four younger sisters. I worry about them in the storm." He bit into a macaroon then looked guilty, as if regretting his pleasure when his family suffered elsewhere.

"God will watch out for them. As He looked over the Christ child in the presepio." She smiled. "I checked the crib after lunch. People have already added a thin layer of hay. Thank you for sharing your tradition with us."

"I am glad to learn we both believe in the Christ child." Fabrizio's dark eyes lifted long enough to gaze into hers. Then he took another bite of macaroon.

Natalie sensed that he wanted to convey more than their common faith. "We all kneel before the same manger, whether we are shepherds or wise men from far away. He is the King of us all."

"*Sì.* Yes, He is the Lord of lords, and He even made the snow." He gestured to the window where they could see white swirls in the air.

"Maybe He sent the snow so that we could become friends?" *Or more than friends?* Why did that thought even cross her mind?

Thanks to the storm, they shared a magical experience outside the normal social boundaries. But as soon as Denver dug out from the big snow, they would return to their normal roles. The thought sent a shadow across her heart, dimming her joy.

"*Sì.* Maybe He did," Fabrizio whispered.

The shadow fled in the light of his smile. For a brief moment they stood in a silent circle of delight, oblivious to everything around them. Then Eleanor's voice interrupted them.

"The macaroons are almost gone. Perhaps we should start again?"

Fabrizio nodded at the two women and walked back to his seat. Natalie clapped her hands to gain everyone's attention. The guests rejoined the circle, and Natalie explained the next game, You're Never Fully Dressed without a Smile.

Natalie took the first turn as "it." She made comical faces while everyone else tried to keep their faces solemn. As she expected, Eleanor was the first to smile in return. "Now you're 'it.'"

Eleanor coaxed grins and outright laughter from a number of guests. One "it" after another told jokes and made faces. Laughter echoed throughout the room. Fabrizio won by keeping a straight face the longest. This time his silence did not bother Natalie. He had joined in the fun of the marvelous afternoon.

"I saved a couple of macaroons for the winner—Fabrizio Ricci!" He bowed over her extended hand and for a moment she wondered if he would kiss it. She hoped he would. Instead he straightened and said a simple "grazie." He left when the party ended a few minutes later.

She couldn't wait until tomorrow. Surely Fabrizio would return.

Fabrizio rose before dawn. This morning, the *Denver Post* would deliver coal to St. Clara's orphanage. He had determined to accompany the coal wagon in an effort to reach his family. He slipped a couple of rolls from the previous evening's dinner into his coat pocket, wrapped his scarf around his neck, and strapped on his skis. He arrived at the *Post* building as the wagons pulled out. Stalwart horses lowered their heads and began their slow progress through downtown and across the river.

Fabrizio ate one roll in slow mouthfuls. In addition to the rolls, he carried the macaroons he had won during yesterday's festivities. The smiles that he had suppressed during the game escaped. Natalie made playing games as much fun for the adults as for the children, for the staff as for the guests.

In fact, Fabrizio almost had not gone with the coal wagons today. For the first time in his life, he longed to remain in the company of a young woman rather than take care of his sisters. He wished that he could remain at the Brown until the snow melted and the magical interlude ended. But in the end he did his duty. Snow still blanketed the sky, whether from fresh powder or the wind whipping the accumulation into a frozen batter. Even with the wagons traveling in front of him, he could barely ski over the ground. In a few more blocks, he would need to leave the safety of the horses' trail for home.

The wagons' slow progress stalled as they approached West Twenty-Sixth Street. Away from the center of town, the snow drifted deeper, and the horses could no longer move.

Fabrizio ate his second roll while the wagon drivers talked together. What could they do? He sent up a prayer that God would make a way. Noise pierced the air, a sound foreign on the snowy day—the trumpet of elephants. Could it be? Barnum and Bailey's circus spent the winters in Denver.

The mammoth animals rounded the corner, towering over the snow, complaining with loud voices about their forced departure from their warm barns. Wrapping their trunks around the rear axles, they lifted the wagons off the ground and began to push. Terrified that they would be run over by their own wagons, the horses reared and plunged into the snow. Once again they moved forward. Fabrizio wondered if anyone would believe the story.

With the snow now packed by horses' hooves, wagon wheels, and elephant feet, Fabrizio skied effortlessly over the ground. Two blocks later, he came to the intersection where he had to turn to his parents' home. The wagons continued in the direction of the orphanage, the elephants' trumpets announcing their progress.

How could he reach his home? Snow drifted as high as his shoulders in some places. He searched the walls for a break, where he could clamber to the top, but found none. If he could remove the skis, perhaps he could climb a tree and search the horizon. But if he removed the skis, he could not traverse the ground. He found a spot low enough to look across the blanketed city. Although his family's home lay only half a mile away, he could not see it. Even the smoke from the hearth fires blended into the white sky. He could not possibly make his way through the snow.

Behind him snow lined the trampled-down path. He shivered, tightened the scarf around his neck and under his arms, and headed back to the light and warmth of the Brown Palace.

To the place where Natalie waited.

Chapter 6

Disappointment nettled Natalie when she failed to catch a glimpse of Fabrizio during the morning. *He's probably working somewhere else*, she told herself. *The hotel needs his services.* When he didn't appear at the afternoon gathering, disappointment deepened into a disturbing sense of loss. After tea, Natalie approached Patrick. "Is Mr. Ricci working elsewhere today?" She hoped she did not sound overly eager.

The Irishman shook his head. "No, miss. He followed the coal wagons headed to the orphanage, trying to reach his family. He's been mightily worried about them."

"He went out? In the storm?" Natalie remembered Fabrizio's mention of younger sisters, and for the first time she considered his family, snowbound without his strong back. "Then I shall say a prayer for his safety." The evening hours dragged by. When had Fabrizio's presence come to mean so much to her? She examined the shelves of books thoughtfully provided in her room, only to discover that most of the titles were in other languages. She recognized several of the romance languages—French, Spanish, Italian—and others that appeared to be in Swedish. At last she found a book in English, American short stories and essays, and whiled away an hour reading an excerpt from *The Autocrat of the Breakfast-Table*.

When Sunday morning dawned, Natalie checked outside. The storm had slowed; only a few flakes drifted lazily through the air. She said another prayer for Fabrizio and slipped into her green gown, freshly laundered by the hotel staff.

One of the guests, a visiting minister, had offered to lead a worship service in the Grand Salon. It should be a lovely spot, if any sunlight could come through the stained-glass windows. She ate breakfast in her room before descending to the second floor.

To her surprise, she saw a dark head and broad shoulders seated toward the back of the room. *Fabrizio.* She felt her cheeks flush, and she held her Bible close to her chest like a shield. He caught sight of her and moved over a seat. She took that as an invitation and joined him on the hard-backed chairs.

The congregants sang a few hymns. Fabrizio's bass voice vibrated through the book that they shared and up her arm. She thanked God for his safe return. What had happened to his trip home? Surely the Brown had not required him to return to work the following day. She forced herself to concentrate on the sermon.

After the final amen, Natalie turned to her companion. Aside from windburn on his cheeks, he looked as handsome as ever.

"I prayed for you yesterday. Patrick told me you tried to go home?"

Regret flickered in Fabrizio's dark eyes. "I followed the wagons as far as I could. From there, I could not break through the snow. So I returned."

The breath caught in Natalie's throat. Was it so terribly wrong of her to take pleasure in his forced return? She pointed to the window. "Sunshine is starting to break through the clouds. Soon the snow will stop falling and begin to melt." *And you will be able to leave, and so will I.* The thought saddened her.

Fabrizio nodded. "We will shovel tomorrow."

Natalie stilled. Their time together would end as surely as the snow would melt.

"*Fino a domani*, Natalie. Until tomorrow. I must return to work." For a moment, he bowed his dark head as if in prayer and then strode out of the temporary chapel.

Natalie. He called her *Natalie*. So why did she feel so downcast?

On Monday morning, Fabrizio joined the male staff at the front door of the Brown. As Natalie had predicted, the snow had stopped falling. Today they must begin the process of clearing the areas around the hotel. They all dressed as warmly as they could, but few had adequate protection. Still, he expected exercise would keep them warm. He wrapped his scarf around his angular body and considered his gloves. If he didn't wear them, cold would bite and then numb his fingers. If he did wear them, he might ruin the soft leather that he prized for working on cars. He sighed. If only he had a pair of Mama's knitted mittens, as darned and patched as they were.

An outburst of giggles drew his attention to Natalie and the children gathered around her. She waved at him, and warmth spread through Fabrizio's body even as someone opened the door and cold air struck him breathless. He plunged into the narrow space under the awning, which had not collapsed under the weight of the snow. The slight protection kept the drifts to under a foot deep. A glance down the intersecting streets in front of the Brown told the real story. Snow tapered to knee height in a few places and surged past shoulder height at others, a nature-made miniature of the Rocky Mountains that dominated Denver's western horizon. Not that they could see the mountains today. The men divided into teams and worked east, north, and south from the front entrance.

Fabrizio's group worked past the music room, where Natalie entertained the children. He waved at a boy who pasted his face against the glass, the longing to frolic outside instead of spending yet another day indoors written on his face. The child waved back, and Natalie joined him at the window. Sunlight glinted on a length of scarlet fabric dangled over her arm. She smiled widely when she saw Fabrizio. He returned the gesture, wishing he could stay basking in the warmth of her presence. The men around him moved ahead. He tipped his cap and bent back into the job of snow removal.

The men worked in shifts, wanting to persevere as long as the sun remained high in the sky. In the distance, other voices rang out, suggesting that people were digging out from the snow across Denver. When the sky paled behind the mounds of snow, the manager called a halt for the day. They had made good progress; another hour in the morning would see a path cleared all the way around the hotel. The weary men stumbled into the lobby, grateful for the reprieve.

Once inside, an aroma of hot chocolate greeted them, bowls of the warm liquid sparkling on white-linen-covered tables. Eleanor ladled the steaming drink into cups. But where was Natalie? Fabrizio found her at the opposite end of the table, tying together paper-wrapped bundles. She waved him over.

"Fabrizio! I have something to give you."

How he loved the sound of his name on her tongue, the American pronunciation softening the *r* sound. He shook off the snow that caked his hair and unwound his long scarf in the heat of the lobby.

"Natalie?" He could get lost in the depth of her eyes, blue streaks darting through calm gray.

She gestured at the table. "I saw you outside with the others today. You all looked so cold and miserable. Oh, I didn't give you a chance to get a cup of hot chocolate. I'm sorry." She dashed over to Eleanor and returned with a cup and saucer.

"Grazie." Fabrizio sipped the rich drink. Its warmth fought against the cold and sent shivers to his extremities. "It is good. It will give warmth."

Behind the table, Natalie bounced on her feet. "But you need more when you're outside. I wondered if there was something I could do, and I came up with an idea." She pointed to the packages on the table. "When the ladies learned what I was doing, they all supplied some material and helped me cut and sew a few things. It's not much, but I hope it helps. Will you help me distribute them?" She handed the last one she had wrapped to him. "Open it and see."

The paper crackled and flexed in his hands, suggesting something soft within. Fabrizio wiggled his still-cold fingers and untied the ribbon. A hat, mittens, and scarf set, sewn in bright scarlet wool, nestled against the plain wrapping. It reminded him of. . . He blushed. The ladies had offered their unmentionables, what they wore to bed at night. He fingered the material and imagined its warmth in the biting cold. They were perfect.

"They're clean. My maid, Annette, helped me launder the material before we used it." Natalie sounded apologetic.

"They are wonderful." The admiration Fabrizio felt for Natalie colored his voice.

She is not afraid of the snow for her household: for all her household are clothed with scarlet. Fabrizio remembered King Lemuel's words, repeated in the book of Proverbs in the Bible.

He had found the virtuous woman he wanted to treasure above precious jewels: Natalie Daire. He turned away before she could see the tears in his eyes. He had fallen in love with a woman who could never be his.

"The mittens, I will tell the others." He trained his eyes on the floor and made his escape. Back to the garage where he belonged.

Chapter 7

What did I do to offend Fabrizio? Natalie wondered when he disappeared so quickly. She fingered the red wool. Did the source of the material embarrass him? She hadn't worried about that when she hatched her plan. She only knew how cold the men looked and how light-headed she felt when she thought of a way to provide them with warm clothing. No one should catch cold and get sick because of digging out from this storm. Least of all the handsome Italian man who occupied so much of her thoughts.

She followed Fabrizio's progress through the crowded lobby. The workers made their way to her. She thanked each of them for his hard work and for making the guests' snowbound experience almost magical.

But the person she most wanted to thank did not return. Fabrizio had done so much more than shovel snow that morning. From the night he had returned to the Brown with her car instead of going home, he had helped her in every way. She thought about the way he pitched in with the daily activities, even joining in the games, although they made him uncomfortable. The night of the carol sing, his bass voice added so much to the music. He had shown the boys how to make a presipio such as the one his family had at home.

Her eyes drifted in the direction of the music room, where she knew hay filled more than half of the manger. Wistfulness washed over her. Would anyone bother to fill the manger once the snowbound guests left and no one else knew the story? She hoped so. The staff at least could continue the tradition. She had observed so many small deeds of kindness, perhaps inspired by Fabrizio's story. He epitomized the spirit of cooperation. And more. Her self-made grandfather would approve of the coachman.

Natalie's heart cried after him. She did not want their friendship to end. She wanted it to grow into something more. For the first time in her life, she felt the weight of her father's money dragging her down. It stood like the snow that flanked the hotel, cold and impenetrable. She would simply have to find a way to melt it.

On Tuesday morning, the workmen finished clearing a path around the hotel. The sky shone brilliant blue, and the sun had begun melting the ice crystals on her window. However, aside from lanes carved through the drifts here and there, snow still stretched as far as Natalie could see. The street level had risen several feet, transforming windows into doors. She could not drive her Cadillac on the street today. Even horses would have trouble wading through the drifts. At least one more day remained to enjoy their snowbound family.

For today, she could still join the excitement downstairs. Perhaps she could organize a few outdoor games for the children, who began misbehaving out of boredom. After braiding her hair, she donned her warmest dress—a jacketed outfit with fur trim that added layers. She arranged with Patrick to invite children to a snowman-making contest in the early afternoon. Fabrizio did not appear in the lobby.

"Mr. Ricci is by way of going back to the garage." Patrick must have noticed her searching gaze. "The guests will be needin' their cars soon."

The news drained some of the warmth out of the sunlight that streamed through the stained glass overhead. Then she heard excited chattering behind her. A couple of boys had seen the notice about the snowman contest and cheered the idea. Natalie pushed Fabrizio to the back of her mind. She looked forward to experiencing the wonder of four feet of snow with the children.

Shortly after dinner, the children assembled with Natalie in the lobby. She assigned five captains and let them choose teams. Their astonished gasps when they walked into the wintry playground made her decision worthwhile. Even though the melting snow was starting to compact, it was still piled higher than anything she had ever seen. Soon the children packed handfuls of snow and rolled them along the edge of the shoveled path. The balls fell apart easily.

Wind stirred snow from the top of the drift and scattered it on the children's heads. A little girl looked up, confused.

"Is it snowing again?"

Natalie rushed over and brushed away the powder. "No. It's only the wind. See? The sun is shining." She wondered if she should have asked more adults to supervise the contest.

At that moment, she spotted a bright green and yellow scarf over the top of a snowdrift. *Fabrizio*. God had heard her unspoken prayers and sent the help she most wanted.

"The day, it is beautiful." The scarf wrapped around his throat and mouth muffled the deep voice. Delight filled Natalie when she saw bright red mittens on his hands and a red hat on his head. Fabrizio continued speaking. "No one has called for their cars. I thought, maybe Natalie needs my help. And so here I am."

A snowball one of the older boys had tossed hit Fabrizio in the chest. "You want a snowball fight, eh?" He scooped snow, bright white against the red mitten, and patted it together. "This snow, it is not good for snowball fights." He whispered. "It is like—soap powder." His dark eyes asked permission to initiate a game. She nodded. He smiled, teeth almost as white as the snow that surrounded them, and tossed a handful at her. She laughed and joined in the fun.

Soon white powder covered everyone, melting and seeping through their clothes, and a few children shivered. Natalie's nose started dripping. She called a halt even though none of the teams had finished their snowmen. The snowball fight substituted for the snowmen, and she did not think the children minded the change of plans. A healthy color spread over their cheeks, and they gave one last yell before returning to the quiet of the lobby.

She paused for a moment at the main entrance while the

children dashed inside. Fabrizio waited beside her. *I don't want this to end.* Had she spoken aloud?

Fabrizio removed his mittens and reached for her face. *Is he going to kiss me? I want him to kiss me.* She closed her eyes and felt his fingers tuck a curl behind her ear. A whisper of a touch, which disappeared almost as if she had only imagined it.

"They are waiting for us." Did his voice reflect the same regret that she felt?

When she opened her eyes, Fabrizio had opened the door for her. He would not meet her eyes.

Natalie did not see Fabrizio again that day or the next. She thought about him, though, longing for another opportunity to spend time with him. A bad case of the sniffles kept her confined to her room. From her window she observed people out clearing the streets. She wasn't surprised when Patrick called her room on Thursday to announce that her father had sent the Daire family driver, Bob Cochran, to take her home by sleigh.

At the news, she arose from bed and called Annette to help her dress. How tired she was of the three dresses she had taken to Thalia's party. She laughed at how extravagant she had felt, packing two additional outfits for a one-day trip. Now she would gladly give them all away. Didn't Fabrizio have four sisters? Would he take offense if she offered them? Men liked to provide for women and not the other way around. She probably shouldn't make the suggestion. How silly to worry about something she could do so easily.

Fabrizio. She couldn't go without saying good-bye. She

wouldn't leave him still stranded at the hotel. He was desperate to return to his family. As soon as she descended to the lobby, she asked Patrick to ring for him.

During the time she had spent sequestered in her room, she wondered if she had exaggerated the dark splendor of his eyes, the curls that sprang on his head, the broad cut of his shoulders. When he entered the lobby, dressed as usual in his uniform, she knew that, if anything, she had forgotten how marvelously handsome he was.

"Signorina, you asked for me?"

Signorina. The return to formality disappointed Natalie. She rushed into her explanation. "My father has sent a driver to bring me home." She gestured toward Cochran, dressed in a uniform almost identical to the one Fabrizio wore. "I know how anxious you are to reach your family. We can take you there on the way to Westminster. Are you free to leave?"

Chapter 8

Fabrizio had managed to push Natalie to the back of his mind during the time she had spent in her room. Her reappearance made his heart sing, informing him his longing for her had only been hiding. He could not, must not, allow it to continue fermenting. He backed away, shaking his head. "Signorina, I cannot ride with you."

"Of course you can." Natalie said the words with such fervor that she coughed. "Do you have permission to leave?"

Fabrizio looked to Patrick for help, but he shrugged. "I suggest you accept Miss Daire's offer. I'll tell the manager you've gone." A hint of a smirk played with the clerk's lips.

"So it's settled then." Natalie looked relieved.

Fabrizio couldn't say no to those pleading eyes. "I will come with you."

"We'll wait for you while you collect your things."

Fabrizio dashed down to the basement and gathered his skis and scarf, as well as the red hat and mittens that Natalie had made. He had filled the empty hours of her absence polishing every inch of every car. No duties kept him at the Brown. Heart racing with excitement and exertion, he ran back up the stairs, eager to leave. Any excuse to spend another few minutes with Natalie.

She had donned a lovely navy coat with matching hat, mittens, and scarf made out of some of kind of soft wool. Gray eyes peeked over the scarf and sought him out. He hurried to her side.

"Cochran—that's the driver—is waiting with the sleigh out front." Her eyes sent a different message. *Do I have to leave?*

Fabrizio opened the front door and held on to Natalie's elbow to steady her. For one breathless second, he allowed himself to imagine entering the Brown as a paying guest, with the lovely young woman on his arm. The illusion played itself out as he lifted her onto the sleigh and joined her on the seat, tucking a blanket around their legs and another around their shoulders. She appeared to be cold, her cheeks as bright red and cheerful as Christmas morning.

Sunshine threw white-encrusted roofs into sharp contrast against the blue sky. The horses trotted down the quiet street, rising and falling as the snow had melted more in some places, less in others. They turned onto Sixteenth Street, where Fabrizio could make out the black hands on the D&F clock tower in the distance. Snow still coated most of the tower. Here a plow had cleared the street, and the sleigh made better progress.

"It's so beautiful." Natalie sighed. "It's like a Currier and Ives lithograph come to life." Her voice sounded lower than her usual lilting soprano, roughened by a cold.

The sleigh followed the same route the coal wagon had taken

a few days earlier. After they made their way across Cherry Creek, Natalie asked, "How do we get to your home from here?"

She sounded wistful. Did she feel the same sadness that he did to see their time together end? *Let her go.* It was time to say good-bye, *arrivederci,* and not until tomorrow, fino a domani, as it had been during the days the storm kept them housebound together. The boundary between her world and his was as clear as the horizon that marked the white snow and the blue sky. He straightened his back, increasing the space between them.

"Leave me when we get to Tejon Street. I will tell you when." He gestured to his cross-country skis. "Now that the snow has stopped, I can ski home."

Natalie shook her head. "We will take you to your door. I insist." Her blue hat fell off, and a few strands of blond hair lay loose around her shoulders. Overly bright eyes looked at him. "Are you so eager to say good-bye?"

No! Fabrizio's heart shouted. "There is no need to trouble yourself, signorina." *Natalie.*

After that, silence reigned between them, broken only by distant cries of children at play and the jingle of the horse's harness. Beside him Natalie started humming. "Dashing through the snow. . ."

He joined in. "Oh, what fun it is to the ride in a one-horse open sleigh!"

Natalie broke into a paroxysm of coughing after the last note and fell over in a heap.

Natalie! Without thinking, Fabrizio picked her up and carried her toward his house.

Natalie struggled to wakefulness. Where was she? Not at the Brown. Not at home. Half dream, half memories flitted through her mind. She recalled strong arms bearing her across the snow as though she were as light as a snowflake, lips brushing her forehead. Had that actually happened? The mere possibility made her blush. *I'm at Fabrizio's house.*

"The signorina is awake." An older woman, hair flecked here and there with gray, bent over the bed. She poured water from a pitcher.

"You must be Mrs. Ricci." *Fabrizio's mother.* She could see the resemblance in their lively brown eyes, their well-formed ears.

"Call me Rosa."

"What happened?"

"You passed out from the fever. The doctor told us to keep you here until you were better. Now you are awake again." Rosa fiddled with a packet and took out two pills. "The doctor said for you to take these."

Natalie swallowed them with the glass of water.

"Now I will fix you a bowl of soup. Sofia, come here! I promised Fabrizio that we would not leave you alone," Rosa explained. "He is outside helping his papa with firewood."

Not one, but four young women ranging in age from maybe ten to eighteen, crowded around the doorway. *Fabrizio's sisters.*

"We heard voices." The smallest girl scooted forward under her older sisters' arms. "And we're all anxious to meet the signorina." She took a step toward the bed and curtsied. "Pleased to meet you, Miss Daire. I'm Isabella. The youngest."

Mrs. Ricci disappeared while the others came forward. Natalie made mental notes. Sofia, the eldest, lived at home while waiting for her upcoming wedding in the spring. Angela, the next oldest, wore an apron and refilled Natalie's water glass. Studious Maria wore glasses perched on top of her nose, a book of poetry in her hand. After brief introductions, Sofia shooed the rest of the family away. Soon Natalie fell back asleep.

When she woke again, Natalie sat up in the bed and looked around the room. The presence of a framed wedding picture and a man's pipe on the nightstand suggested it was the Riccis' room. Her maid at home had larger quarters. She felt embarrassed. *I kicked them out of their own room.*

"Can I get you something, signorina?" The studious girl appeared in front of Natalie. *What was her name?* Maria, that was it. The girl straightened the glasses on her nose.

Before Natalie could answer, she heard a brisk knock at the door, and a stranger entered, followed by Fabrizio.

"I see our patient is awake. This is good." The doctor put a thermometer into Natalie's mouth and placed his stethoscope against her chest. "Much better. The Riccis have taken good care of you."

"I am well enough to leave?" The warmth of the loving family invited her to stay, but she couldn't. She shouldn't inconvenience them any longer than necessary.

"Not yet. You need to rest and regain your strength. You may get up for a short time today if you feel up to it. I will return tomorrow, and we will see."

Mrs. Ricci chased the girls out of the room after the doctor, leaving Natalie alone with Fabrizio.

With a start, Natalie realized that she had never before seen Fabrizio dressed in everyday clothes. He looked every bit as handsome as he did in his uniform. But the same dark curls sprang from his head, and the same impressive muscles rippled underneath a plain white cotton shirt. He settled into the rocking chair beside the bed and dangled his hands between his legs. Before Natalie could speak, he began. "Natalie. I was so worried. You should not have left the Brown so soon."

Speaking of the Brown, why wasn't Fabrizio at work? Did he stay at home for her sake? Natalie waved aside his apologies. "I can't thank you and your family enough for everything they've done. This is your parents' room, isn't it?"

Fabrizio nodded. "Papa joined me in the attic room, and Mama is sleeping with Sofia." He smiled. "It is a good thing that *Nonno* Fabrizio is staying with my older brother."

"Nonno Fabrizio? Who is that? Are you named for him?"

"*Certamente.* My brother, Giacomo, is named for Papa's father, and I am named for Mama's father. It is the custom among Italians. I would like for you to meet my nonno. You would like him."

I will, if he's half as wonderful as you are. "I hope I will, someday." *Will his family become my family?* At that moment, Natalie realized how much she wished it could happen. *Did he kiss me?* Heat rushed to her cheeks.

Concerned, Fabrizio jumped out of the chair. "We have

tired you out."

"No, I'm fine." Natalie protested. But she slipped down on the pillow and allowed him to tuck the corners of the quilt around her shoulders. She relished the strength of his hands, his nearness, and wished he would kiss her again. If he had indeed kissed her and it wasn't just a dream.

"Fino ad allora, *cara* Natalie. Rest well." He closed the curtains against the sunshine and left as Mrs. Ricci returned.

When Fabrizio had passed beyond earshot, Natalie asked Rosa, "What does 'cara' mean?"

The woman smiled secretively. "It means *beloved*."

Natalie tingled from head to toe. "Cara Fabrizio," she whispered under her breath.

Chapter 9

Fabrizio paced the tiny attic loft that he shared with his father. Today was the last day Natalie would spend in his house. The doctor had called the Daire home when she had improved enough to travel. And it was time, past time, for him to return to his job at the Brown Palace. He had used the phone at a nearby cheese factory and called the manager, pleading a family emergency.

"Take as long as you need," came the reply.

Fabrizio examined his memories of the past few days. Who ever would have imagined that the rich young heiress who ran her Cadillac into a vegetable stand would bring so much joy into his life? He had glimpsed her warm nature at the Brown, in the way she included Mrs. Rushton in the parties, in the activities she planned for the children, in the hats and mittens she fashioned out of scarlet wool.

These last few days had shown him a new side of his beloved. She listened to Maria read poetry; she ate every dish his mother served without question—with relish, even. She discussed wedding plans with Sofia as if she were a member of the bridal party. She acted as though she *belonged* in their household, unselfconscious and unpretentious. When he came across Sofia and Angela exclaiming over two lovely dresses, he knew that the ever-generous Natalie had even given away her clothing. He loved her more than ever.

And today he could lose her. Cochran, the driver, would return and escort her back to the world that awaited her. Could she care for him? Mama told him that Natalie had repeated his words, calling him "Cara Fabrizio." But first he must speak with her father, and that prospect frightened him almost more than the big snow.

"Are you coming down?" Little Isabella peeked around the door. "You must say good-bye."

"I am coming." Fabrizio turned away from the window and followed his sister, who skipped down the stairs. He made the final sharp turn in the narrow stairs that climbed from the basement pantry to the attic and came upon Natalie in the front room. She was wearing his favorite blue dress, one that floated about her like angels' wings. She must have sensed his presence, for she turned and smiled at him. For one unguarded moment, he let his feelings camp on his features, all the longing and impossible love he felt for her. Then he reined in his emotions. "Natalie." The effort spent on restraining himself made her lovely name come out curt, sharp.

"Fabrizio." In contrast, her voice softened, almost capturing the exact accent on the *r*. She gestured to his mother. "I was just telling your mother that you and Sofia must come to my birthday party on the twenty-fourth. I would be most pleased."

Natalie's birthday. Hotel gossip said that on the day she turned twenty-one, she would inherit a fortune. *She will forget about me.* He paused on the last step.

Her gray eyes locked with his, sending a silent plea. *I want you there. You are special to me.*

The soft sound of a horse's nicker interrupted their silent communication. Out the window, Fabrizio could see the fancy Daire sleigh. The driver, Cochran, had returned, bringing a stranger with him. A well-dressed, imposing man who could only be Natalie's father approached the house. Cochran remained in the driver's seat. A lump the size of a snowball formed in Fabrizio's throat.

Sweet Isabella dashed forward and flung open the door. *"Benvenuto, Signore!* You must be Natalie's father. Welcome to our home."

Daire did not reply right away. His bulk filled the doorway while his gaze surveyed the small quarters, crowded today with the entire Ricci family eager to welcome him. With his hair expertly barbered and his coat tailored to an exact fit, he looked as out of place as a flower blooming on Christmas Eve. His gaze settled on Natalie, and the solemn expression on his face eased.

Hesitant, almost shy, Natalie approached and kissed her father on the cheek. Although the quiet greetings didn't match the exuberant welcome his father received every evening, Fabrizio could not deny the affection in their reunion. Daire held his daughter at arm's length. "We were so worried."

"There was no need. The Riccis have taken good care of

me. Let me introduce you."

Natalie introduced each member of the family with a brief biography. Again, she amazed Fabrizio with how much she had learned about them in such a short time, in spite of her illness. Last of all, she introduced the two men.

"Father, this is Fabrizio Ricci. The man who rescued me during the storm and who brought me into his house when I fell ill. We—we spent a lot of time together at the Brown."

Although Natalie didn't mention the fact, her father must know that he worked at the hotel.

"So you're the one who let my daughter travel when she was already sick."

Fabrizio gulped. "I did not realize. . ."

A twinkle appeared in Daire's eyes, and the snowball in Fabrizio's throat began melting. "If I know my daughter, she did not leave you much choice." He greeted each family member by name. At last he asked Mama, "Is there a place where I may speak privately with your son?"

The melting snowball re-formed in Fabrizio's throat. Mama led them to the kitchen. Neither man spoke while she made a fresh pot of coffee. While it brewed, she sliced some cream cake and laid it on her best china. After she poured the coffee, she left the room and shut the door on the waiting family.

Fabrizio sipped the coffee, hoping its warmth would ease the tension freezing his muscles. It did not.

"I understand that you work as a coachman at the Brown Palace." Daire broke the silence.

"Yes, sir." Something compelled Fabrizio to share a dream

he had told few people. "Although some day I hope to open my own garage. I am good with the engines."

"Hmm." Daire's fingers drummed the polished surface of the table that had seen so many family dinners. He looked out the kitchen windows without appearing to see. "Did your family pay for the doctor? Medicine?" He reached into his pocket.

"Non, I mean, yes, we paid, but it was our privilege. We do not need your money." *Now I sound like an ungrateful child. How can I ask this stranger for permission to court his daughter?* Fabrizio sent a prayer heavenward and opened his mouth to speak.

But what Daire said next stopped Fabrizio from speaking. "Ricci, I have the impression that you care for my daughter."

Is it so obvious? "*Molto*, very much." Fabrizio set the cup on the saucer and looked straight at Daire. Natalie's eyes looked at him out of her father's face. "I would like permission to court your daughter."

Daire met his gaze. "I, too, was once young and in love and ambitious. In fact, I was brash enough to ask the richest man in Denver for permission to court his beloved child."

Fabrizio held his breath.

"That was so long ago. I've forgotten what it was like." Daire spoke more to himself than to Fabrizio. "But seeing your family here reminds me of my own beginnings." Daire took a bite of the cream cake. "This is delicious. I'll have to applaud your mother." He didn't speak again while he finished the food.

Fabrizio couldn't eat, even though he loved Mama's cream cake. He watched Daire's mouth opening and closing around his fork and imagined all the terrible things he would say.

Daire drank the last of his coffee. His lips curved in the same way Natalie's did when she felt mischievous. "Yes, you have my permission to court my Natalie."

What is going on in the kitchen? Natalie wished she could have remained in the front room with her ear pressed to the kitchen door. Instead, she had retired to the second floor bedroom that Angela shared with Maria. All the girls waited with her.

"Perhaps Fabrizio is asking for your hand in marriage." Isabella spoke the words that Natalie dreamed. "Would you like to be our *sorella*, sister, Natalie?"

"Hush, bambina." Mama Rosa quieted her youngest. But her eyes asked the same question.

"I. . ." Natalie was saved from answering by the sound of Father's shout from below.

"Natalie?"

"Coming, Father." Natalie hugged each of the Ricci women in turn. They followed her down the steps, forming a human staircase. Fabrizio waited at the bottom. The uneasiness she had sensed in him earlier had disappeared, his shoulders straightened as if relieved of a heavy weight.

Father's face betrayed no emotion. "Go ahead, my dear. I will join you in a moment." Perhaps he intended to pay Mrs. Ricci for her care.

"I will walk you to the sleigh." Fabrizio had slipped the familiar green and yellow scarf around his neck. He held her coat for her to put on. Once outside, he slipped her hand into his. "Your father, he has given me permission to court you. I think that you will not mind."

Natalie felt light-headed, as if her illness threatened a relapse. "Oh, Fabrizio, I was so afraid. . ."

"You were afraid of me?" Fabrizio's teasing voice somehow stilled the tempest in her heart.

"Of course not. I was afraid that you would let. . .things. . . come between us." The light-headedness persisted, and she grabbed his hands to steady her. "I have loved being with your family, in your home. I am not afraid of what the future holds. As long as it is with you."

"That is good." Fabrizio brushed his lips over the small portion of her cheek exposed to the elements. "I will see you again. Soon."

Two weeks later, Natalie held on to the memory of Fabrizio's kiss while she dressed for her birthday party. Choosing the right outfit with the seamstress had proven harder than she expected. She wanted to look her best, but she did not want to look, well, *expensive*. She did not want Fabrizio to think she expected fine clothes and the latest fashions.

When she first left the Ricci home, she felt certain that she was living out her own fairy story, a God-ordained match made in heaven. The days since then had blurred her initial joy. She and Fabrizio had spoken twice by phone. The conversations left her unsettled, neither of them able to express their true feelings, knowing that others could listen in. She could not see those beautiful dark eyes that gave away his feelings when his words did not, or the hands that moved so surely over anything he touched. Even the hoped-for visit when he had returned her Cadillac did not occur. He left before she finished with the dressmaker.

She had told a few friends about her own private big snow miracle. "How romantic," they all chimed; but she knew they made fun of her behind her back. Tonight she would show them differently. She would walk through the door to her party on the arm of Fabrizio, and they would see his sterling quality for themselves. The only ones who seemed to understand were the same group of friends who attended Thalia Bloom's party. In fact, she had learned that the early Christmas snow had brought romance to all four of them.

She looked forward to seeing her friends again this evening. They understood how ambivalent she felt about receiving control of her inheritance today. She had plans for the money, plans she had not even told her father. Plans that would make sure the money would do good and not come between her and Fabrizio.

Natalie fidgeted while her maid adjusted the stiff collar of her dress around her neck. She hoped Fabrizio liked her outfit, a pretty claret-colored linen with an ecru bib. Next, Annette dressed her hair in her favorite Grecian style. Natalie tugged a few tendrils to curl around her face. Fabrizio seemed to like it that way.

Deep voices drifted up the stairs, and Natalie sprang to her feet. "Is that. . ."

"I'll look." Annette tiptoed to the top of the stairs and ran back. "Mr. Ricci is here." She sounded as excited as Natalie felt, her stomach happy and bubbling like hot cider. She checked the mirror one last time and descended the stairs slowly, the way a lady should.

Fabrizio—her Fabrizio—waited at the foot of the stairs. Dressed in a new suit that showed off his broad shoulders; hair cut to a perfect curl above the collar; tall, dark, and handsome as ever—he took her breath away. He had braved her world to come to her party. He bowed low, as courtly as an Italian count, and presented her with a single red rose. "Many happy returns of your birthday, Natalie. A rose to dress you in scarlet." Did she imagine it, or did a faint blush tinge his dark cheeks?

Natalie fingered the rose, lifted it to her nose, and inhaled the scent. The color red would forever symbolize their love.

"I will put the rose in a vase, miss." Annette took the flower from her hands. "In your room."

"Perfect. I can fall asleep looking at it." And Fabrizio would not feel embarrassed comparing his single perfect rose with the abundant bouquets lining the ballroom.

Natalie accepted Fabrizio's arm and walked toward the waiting guests.

Chapter 10

Dressed in his first-ever new suit, Fabrizio felt almost worthy of Natalie. He drank in the warmth shining in her eyes, her exclamations over the rose he had found for her. But the splendor of the Daire mansion dazzled him. The initial feelings of goodwill evaporated when they entered the ballroom.

What am I doing here? Fabrizio wondered. This one room alone was almost as big as the first floor of his house. A dozen vases filled with hothouse flowers decorated various tables. His new clothes suffered in comparison to the well-tailored men and women who thronged Natalie.

Natalie introduced him without apology and even with pride to one and all. Her special school friends welcomed him eagerly. Those names he remembered: Thalia Bloom, Maximilian New-bolt, Rose Fletcher, Dr. Thomas Stanton, Patricia Logan, and Jared Booker.

"Natalie tells us that you were the one who rescued her during the big snow."

"I would never drive a car like that. She was blessed that you were there."

"She says you have a wonderful voice. Promise you'll sing for us tonight?"

No wonder Natalie had formed a lasting friendship with these women. They were as kind as she was. Fabrizio relaxed a tiny bit.

Everyone else treated him with distant civility. Behind gloved hands and polite glances, Fabrizio heard the whispers start. "Who is that man? Look at his clothes. Where did Natalie find him?"

At last Fabrizio saw a familiar face, Eleanor Royal, the young woman who had helped Natalie with the activities at the Brown. He allowed a smile on his face and bowed in her direction. "Signorina Royal. It is good to see you again."

Eleanor raised an eyebrow and took Natalie aside. "What is *he* doing here?" She whispered in her friend's ear.

Humiliated, Fabrizio stumbled back. Eleanor had treated him well at the Brown. He thought—well, no matter *what* he thought. Her reaction to his arrival proved that he did not belong in Natalie's world. He never would. He grabbed a cup of hot cider from the table and looked for a corner to hide in.

A hand clapped down on his shoulder and a deep voice drawled, "Some women don't know when to keep their traps shut." It was Jared Booker, Patricia's escort. "Let's get some air." The two men walked out of the ballroom into the courtyard.

Jared looked as uncomfortable in his suit as Fabrizio felt. "I hope Patricia doesn't expect me to attend many of these affairs. Give me the open range any day."

"Signorina Logan seems to be a lovely young woman. You are blessed."

"And so are you, if I'm reading the signals right. Don't let the whispers bother you."

Fabrizio looked through the doors, where he could see Natalie arguing with her father. He shook his head. Daire must regret his decision to give Fabrizio permission to court his daughter. His spirits sank even lower. Everyone at the party could see what a mistake it was.

Patricia Logan appeared at the door. "There you are, Jared! I wondered where you had gone."

"Duty calls. I'll take it like a man." Jared moved toward her with an easy grace. "Remember what I said."

Jared's departure left Fabrizio alone in the nippy air of the courtyard. He would rather endure the cold than face the party. The starlit sky taunted him, teasing him with his dreams of a life with Natalie. The sky under which he hoped to profess his love for her now suffocated him.

"Fabrizio?"

The gentle sound of Natalie's voice froze him in place more effectively than the chill air. He calmed his features and turned to face her.

"Signorina."

"You call me Natalie." Tears glittered in her eyes.

"It is best that I call you signorina." Why did he still want to dry the tears from her eyes?

"You heard what Eleanor said." She made it a statement, not a question.

"She is right. I do not belong. . .here." He made a sweeping gesture meant to indicate the house, the gaiety—her.

"Father said you might feel like that. He told me I should come after you." Natalie tugged his arm. "Let's go for a walk. The paths are cleared."

Fabrizio agreed. After he made his apologies, he could return to his own place.

They walked among the trees, blue spruce intermingled with denuded oaks and aspens. Natalie shivered, and Fabrizio reprimanded himself. She should not be out in the cold after she had been so ill. He gave her his jacket and slipped his arm around her shoulders.

Natalie stopped underneath a spreading elm tree, moonlight gilding its bare branches. "Father told me you felt uncomfortable with the guests tonight. What Eleanor said was inexcusable."

So that is what they were arguing about. "She only said what others were thinking. Me, I should not have come."

Natalie shook her head. "You're wrong. Oh, I won't pretend people weren't thinking mean things. But they're not important. They only came to my party because my father is rich, and now that I'm of age, I have money of my own. But you—I think you see the real me." She took a deep breath. "You know that today I received my inheritance. What you don't know—what I haven't even told my father yet—is how I plan to use the money. I want to help support that orphanage that needed coal during the storm, St. Clara's. And I want to invest it in new businesses—businesses opened by young men with the same drive that made my grandfather's and father's fortunes—maybe even a garage run by an excellent mechanic?"

She was offering his dream to him on a plate. Words froze in Fabrizio's throat. When at last he could speak, he said, "Do you know why I brought you a *red* rose?"

Natalie shook her head. "It's a beautiful flower, but you meant something more?"

"You dressed the staff at the Brown in scarlet. You gave of your own bounty to keep us warm. King Lemuel, in Proverbs, he said that describes a virtuous woman. 'She is not afraid of the snow for her household: for all her household are clothed with scarlet.' You are that virtuous woman. The king said a man should treasure her like a precious jewel. I love you, Signorina Natalie. I want to treasure you above all others. But I am a poor man. I am unworthy of your love."

Natalie swiveled in his arms, facing him, starlight streaming across her face. Fabrizio allowed all the love and longing that he felt for her to show. She ran a gloved finger across his chin. "It is I who am unworthy of *you*, Fabrizio. You have been my champion, protector, my hero, since we first met." She lifted her face to gaze at him.

Fabrizio met her lips in a kiss. In this place, on this night, he knew that one day they would become man and wife before the good Lord who had made them both.

Epilogue

December 24, 1914

A year had come and gone since Denver's big snow. Such momentous news filled the intervening months that the six-day blizzard began to fade into memory. A great war had engulfed Europe after the assassination of Archduke Ferdinand in Sarajevo. So far, Fabrizio's beloved Italy maintained a neutral stance.

But the big snow of 1913 would always remain the fulcrum of Natalie's life. That's when she met the man who today had become her husband.

Natalie changed out of her wedding dress into a red woolen afternoon suit and white linen blouse that coordinated well with the roses woven into her hair. She passed through the kitchen of their second floor apartment, decorated with much affection by Mama Rosa.

"Signora Ricci!" Her husband called to her from the street,

where he waited by the Cadillac Model 30 that had brought them together during the storm. Friends who had attended their small wedding ceremony had tied a banner reading HAPPILY MARRIED to their bumper.

"I'll be right down!" she called. They planned to spend their wedding night in nearby Colorado Springs. They wanted to return to Denver in time for Thalia and Maximilian's wedding on New Year's Eve. Rose had married her doctor early in the year, and Patricia and Jared had wed at Thanksgiving. Love had fallen on all four of the school chums during Denver's "big snow."

Natalie heard feet on the stairs, and a door flung open. "I can't wait any longer." Fabrizio twirled her in a circle and kissed her soundly. "We must go soon, or I will not want to leave."

Natalie allowed Fabrizio to lead her down the stairs. She paused on the steps, looking out over the showroom. New cars gleamed, and a faint smell of oil suggested motor repair in progress. Ricci Motors, a dream come true.

Fabrizio followed the direction of her gaze. "Cara Natalie," he murmured as he covered her lips with kisses. "Today God has given me a good wife worth more than all the silver in the mountains."

"And I will strive to deserve your trust, to always clothe you in scarlet."

Hand in hand, Mr. and Mrs. Fabrizio Ricci stepped forward into the future together.

DARLENE FRANKLIN

Award-winning author and speaker Darlene Franklin resides in the Colorado foothills with her mother and her lynx point Siamese cat, Talia. She is the mother of two children. Her daughter has gone ahead of her to glory; her son lives in Oklahoma with his family. She loves music, reading, and writing. She has published two books previously, as well as numerous devotions, magazine articles, and children's curriculum. Visit her blog at http://darlenefranklinwrites.blogspot.com.

A Letter to Our Readers

Dear Readers:

In order that we might better contribute to your reading enjoyment, we would appreciate your taking a few minutes to respond to the following questions. When completed, please return to the following: Fiction Editor, Barbour Publishing, Inc., P.O. Box 719, Uhrichsville, OH 44683.

1. Did you enjoy reading *Snowbound Colorado Christmas*?
   ❑ Very much—I would like to see more books like this.
   ❑ Moderately—I would have enjoyed it more if _____
   _____
   _____

2. What influenced your decision to purchase this book?
   (Check those that apply.)
   ❑ Cover   ❑ Back cover copy   ❑ Title   ❑ Price
   ❑ Friends   ❑ Publicity   ❑ Other

3. Which story was your favorite?
   ❑ *Fires of Love*   ❑ *Almost Home*
   ❑ *The Best Medicine*   ❑ *Dressed in Scarlet*

4. Please check your age range:
   ❑ Under 18   ❑ 18–24   ❑ 25–34
   ❑ 35–45   ❑ 46–55   ❑ Over 55

5. How many hours per week do you read? _____

Name _____

Occupation _____

Address _____

City_____ State _____ Zip _____

E-mail_____

If you enjoyed

SNOWBOUND *Colorado* CHRISTMAS

then read

A BRIDE BY *Christmas*

**FOUR STORIES OF EXPEDIENT MARRIAGE
ON THE GREAT PLAINS**

An Irish Bride for Christmas, by Vickie McDonough
Little Dutch Bride, by Kelly Eileen Hake
An English Bride Goes West, by Therese Stenzel
The Cossack Bride, by Linda Goodnight

If you enjoyed

SNOWBOUND
Colorado
CHRISTMAS

then read

Wyoming
CHRISTMAS
HEROES

LOVE COMES TO THE RESCUE
IN FOUR SEASONAL NOVELLAS

Doctor St. Nick, by Jeanie Smith Cash
Rescuing Christmas, by Linda Lyle
Jolly Holiday, by Jeri Odell
Jack Santa, by Tammy Shuttlesworth

If you enjoyed

SNOWBOUND
Colorado
CHRISTMAS

then read

A CONNECTICUT
CHRISTMAS

Four Modern Romances Develop at a Christmas Collectibles Shop

Santa's Prayer, by Diane Ashley
The Cookie Jar, by Janet Lee Barton
Stuck on You, by Rhonda Gibson
Snowbound for Christmas, by Gail Sattler

Available wherever books are sold.
Or order from:
Barbour Publishing, Inc.
P.O. Box 721
Uhrichsville, Ohio 44683
www.barbourbooks.com

You may order by mail for $7.97 and add $3.00 to your order for shipping.
Prices subject to change without notice.
If outside the U.S. please call 740-922-7280 for shipping charges.